Praise for *Exile*

"*Exile* hinges on a brave and clever conceit: What if an advocacy group rescued the wrong dissident? … There are a number of ironies author Ann Ireland could have overworked in this novel, and few would have complained, given the strength of dialogue, pacing and description. Instead she spaces her moments of revelation and insight, her writing an exemplar of restraint and confidence."

— *Toronto Star*

"Ireland's writing has remarkable humour, and gentle but unshying insight into character. As a past president of PEN, no doubt she's heard tales to make one shudder…. The consequent unravelling of his [Carlos's] Canadian experience makes for an unusual and often delightful portrait of an artist-in-exile who's a kind of literary Homer Simpson."

— *Globe and Mail*

"*Exile* is a tour de force. I haven't been so amused and appalled by a fictional character since reading Vladimir Nabokov's *Pnin*…. To see ourselves as others see us is a gift indeed."

— *Hamilton Spectator*

Praise for *The Instructor*

"Scrupulous, vivid detailing of emotion, compulsion, struggle — bloody awful old love.... It's chilling, the way you feel the artist in her, not just the women, going under. The huge disparity between what one lover is ready to give and the other is able to take — when you realize what her role in his life is and his in hers — that's to me the real discovery. And that's when the story transcends this story, these particular people. It doesn't say, 'Good thing she got away from that asshole, about time she figured him out' in the standard, boring feminist style. It says something like, 'Look — this is how we are, this is how we live.'"

— *Alice Munro*

"... a brilliant study of power and obsession in a relationship."

— *Quill & Quire*

Praise for *A Certain Mr. Takahashi*

"On a surface level, this is a fine and entertaining piece of work. *A Certain Mr. Takahashi* is humorous and compassionate, funny and sad. Beneath the surface, this is a serious book, presenting an inventive perspective on fantasy and obsession as an entry to the world. Winner of the 1985 Seal First Novel Award, Ann Ireland has made an exciting and accomplished debut with this book."

— *San Francisco Chronicle*

"... this is a work of the highest literary merit, simply and cleanly written, yet complex in its implications."

— *Calgary Herald*

The BLUE GUITAR

ANN IRELAND

DUNDURN
TORONTO

Editor: Michael Carroll
Design: Jesse Hooper
Printer: Webcom

Library and Archives Canada Cataloguing in Publication

Ireland, Ann
      The blue guitar / Ann Ireland.

Issued also in electronic formats.
ISBN 978-1-4597-0586-9

      I. Title.

PS8567.R43B58 2013   C813'.54   C2012-903864-4

1   2   3   4   5   17   16   15   14   13

We acknowledge the support of the **Canada Council for the Arts** and the **Ontario Arts Council** for our publishing program. We also acknowledge the financial support of the **Government of Canada** through the **Canada Book Fund** and **Livres Canada Books**, and the **Government of Ontario** through the **Ontario Book Publishing Tax Credit** and the **Ontario Media Development Corporation**.

Care has been taken to trace the ownership of copyright material used in this book. The author and the publisher welcome any information enabling them to rectify any references or credits in subsequent editions.

J. Kirk Howard, President

VISIT US AT
Dundurn.com | Definingcanada.ca | @dundurnpress | Facebook.com/dundurnpress

Dundurn
3 Church Street, Suite 500
Toronto, Ontario, Canada
M5E 1M2

Gazelle Book Services Limited
White Cross Mills
High Town, Lancaster, England
LA1 4XS

Dundurn
2250 Military Road
Tonawanda, NY
U.S.A. 14150

To dear Berkeley friends

Acknowledgements

I interviewed several eminent classical guitarists during my research for this novel. Big thanks to Denis Azabagić, Peter McCutcheon, Lily Afshar, Anna Graham, and especially Steve Thachuk, who is a patient and inspiring teacher, top-notch guitarist, and pretty funny, too. These musicians are in no way responsible for what I did with their stories and information.

I am grateful to the Canada Council of the Arts and the Ontario Arts Council for financial help.

Thank you Jenny Munro and Tim Deverell for your close readings and helpful feedback along the way.

They said, "You have a blue guitar,
You do not play things as they are."

The man replied, "Things as they are
Are changed upon the blue guitar."

— WALLACE STEVENS, "THE MAN WITH THE BLUE GUITAR"

PROLOGUE

ELEVEN YEARS AGO TOBY HAUSNER WAS THE ONE TO BEAT. IF you'd seen him stride onstage, shaking those blond dreadlocks, guitar tucked under one arm like a surfboard, you would have felt the confidence blow off him, scary yet tantalizing. The spotlight held his form as he made his way to centre stage to the simple bench waiting there and the custom footstool. The old hall smelled like socks and mould after a solid week of rain.

He plunked himself down after a quick bow, then swung the guitar onto his lap and tuned while staring, eyes shut, into the spotlight. Not a hint of impatience stirred the audience. Hadn't everyone been talking about this kid all week, noting his intense focus mixed with a joy of performing, unusual in one so young? Much was made of his rolled-up trousers and bare feet. Toby claimed that his body was a vibratory presence and must connect directly, flesh to floorboards, to create an acoustic chamber.

Whispers crested through the auditorium as he wiped each palm on his trousered knees. Huddled at the back of the hall were his colleagues, musicians from around the world who had been eliminated from earlier rounds of the competition. They sat forward on their seats, knowledge and nerves burning off them.

Near to the front was the row of judges, clipboards in hand. This was what they'd been waiting for all week: one final chance to be dazzled and moved. If this barefoot kid played the way he did in the semis, he'd walk off with the grand prize and an international career would be launched.

Toby's elegant hands wrapped around the instrument, and as he raised his fingers over the sound hole, he let out an audible exhalation of air. When a person dies, they may sigh deeply at the end. So it went for Toby.

He began to play but it soon became clear that something was wrong. The judges squinted at their programs in the dark: allegedly the boy was playing Scarlatti, but this was not what they were hearing. Something more full-throttle and dissonant coasted through the hall, something improvisatory, no known composer, light-years from Baroque mode. Toby's upper body bobbed up and down, and his mouth moved with each twinge of phrase. He was certainly enjoying himself up there, ripping through weird chord sequences and arpeggios, and despite their horror, no one stopped listening or watching, any more than you'd take your eyes off a kid tumbling from an open window.

This happened in Paris — some stage for a meltdown.

ONE

PAMELA FROWNS OVER HER BIFOCALS AND MAKES THAT SCRATCHY noise in her throat that drives Toby nuts. Very slim and brittle, she glares at the manuscript page on her music stand as if the notes were in a foreign language. Toby taps his baton on the side of his own stand.

"Let's jump in at bar twelve, kids," he says. "Right after the key change."

This reference to "kids" is a joke, given that the members of Guitar Choir are all at least a dozen years older than Toby and a couple are pushing sixty.

"Twelve?" Pamela repeats, eyes widening. "Twelve?" she says again, sounding mystified by the request.

Toby wonders if she's growing deaf, something that happens to people as they get on in life. He feels a spurt of impatience but fends it off, and instead starts to sing her part, tapping out the beat. At the same time he glances at the wall clock — nearly 4:00 p.m. Soon the after-school crowd will blow in, snapping basketballs in the upstairs gym. This church is multi-use, and Guitar Choir shares space with AA and a Montessori preschool.

The amateur musicians scramble through the passage and onto the next. Their instruments sound a bit like balalaikas, plinking away. Finally, Bill, a retired fireman, cries in recognition, "It's a Beatles medley!"

Indeed it is — eight songs sewn into a cunning five-minute package by Toby.

"Don't forget the Parkdale Community Centre concert in two weeks," Toby reminds them, and they yelp with excitement before coming to a ragged halt.

Then Pamela repeats, "Two weeks?" and lifts her glasses, indicating this is news to her.

Toby tugs his jeans over his narrow hips and inhales deeply. Last night was ball hockey, and he feels it in his upper arms and left shin, where someone nailed him with a stick blade. Then there were the half-dozen post-game beers, and didn't they end up at The Duke singing Broadway tunes?

"That's right," he says brightly. 'Where were we? Bar forty-something."

"Forty-three," Bill supplies.

Toby runs a hand through what's left of his hair and gives Pamela a meaningful look. "Note that second guitars enter a bar later."

She actually smiles, that strained face pleased to be recognized.

The choir chugs on, tight with concentration while Toby keeps the beat and cues entrances. Tom, who rarely gets the rhythm right, is lagging on "Norwegian Wood" while the others trot into "The Long and Winding Road." Toby sings his part, coaxing him back into the fold. For a few lines everything goes smoothly. It is one of those moments where effort turns into music, and they feel it, hardly dare to hope it will continue.

It is Matthew, the lawyer, who breaks the spell.

"Someone's out of step!" he protests, and the group staggers to a halt again.

"Don't quit!" Toby pleads. He continues to wave his baton, but it's no use. They sit in silence, a dozen grizzled faces staring at him, waiting for guidance.

"Quitting might be the advisable position," Matthew says, leaning back in his chair and cradling his instrument.

"What's that supposed to mean?" Pamela asks.

Matthew doesn't answer right away. Instead he tilts his head and looks into the distance before answering, "The Beatles. Is this what we want to play?"

Here goes. About twice a year Matthew likes to cause trouble.

Last time it was over seating arrangements; another time he got the idea they should all use the same kind of strings, the most expensive ones available.

"I'm not fond of what happens when classical players get hold of pop music," Matthew adds.

Toby secretly agrees with this, but still feels a flare of irritation. He'd been so sure they would love playing the songs of their youth.

There is a short, tense silence, then Toby jumps in, tapping the stand with his baton. "Where do we pick it up?" he asks cheerily.

"Sixty-four," someone says.

"Sixty-seven," another disagrees. "Didn't we begin 'Strawberry Fields?'"

Matthew is mumbling something about copyright issues. Do they even have the right to sample these tunes?

Finally, the group settles back into playing and makes it to the next transition, an upbeat version of "A Day in the Life" where again they falter.

Pamela says in a tragic tone, "This arrangement is blisteringly hard." She's been a member of Guitar Choir since day one and organizes the annual fundraiser. As she looks around, anticipating agreement, her seatmate, Bert, ventures, "Not so hard if you count carefully."

Pamela snaps back, "Perhaps if you quit tapping your foot on the offbeat —"

Matthew says in a tone of laboured patience, "Counting is not the only issue here."

"Well, genius boy?" Pamela says, looking back at Toby. This term has begun to sound sardonic over the years. "We could perform the trusty Albéniz instead," she adds, waiting for the others to support this idea.

They squirm in their chairs; everyone is a little scared of Pamela. The Albéniz features her seven-bar solo, which she plays meticulously and without a shred of musical expression.

"I'm with Matthew," Tristan pipes up from the back row. He's pastor of some weird church in the city's east end. "Let's get back to real music."

Toby collapses his arms to his sides. "I thought you'd get a kick out of playing these songs." His lower back is killing him; Jasper promised to hire a Korean girl to walk up and down his spine.

"We do," Pamela says, sensing Toby's mood. "It's always like this. We flounder, we work, and we eventually succeed."

"Do you think we're getting noticeably better?" Tristan asks plaintively.

"Of course," Toby says, but hears his voice sounding less than convinced. It's a good question: are they better? They seem to have plateaued. Guitar Choir began nine years ago, beginning as a sort of therapy for him after the Paris incident.

"Because this is the high point of my week," Tristan says.

Everyone chimes agreement.

Toby feels something melt inside him.

"If we continue another nine years, we'll have to rename ourselves the Choir of the Ancients," Matthew says, waiting for the titter of laughter.

"You'll never leave us, will you?" Bert asks.

They all stare at Toby, waiting for his answer. But he's not speaking. Instead he's feeling one of those strange episodes where his sense of smell turns aggressive, wave upon wave of odours, Play-Doh and cleanser, vinyl mats rolled up in the corner, and something else that he can't pin down. It seems to radiate from his own body, acidic and nasty.

"Toby? You okay?"

It's Denise, the pretty one, younger than the rest. She tips her guitar against her chair and darts up, sliding a hand over his wrist as he stands there, swaying from side to side. He must have dropped his baton. He heard it fall, a clatter of fibreglass against tile.

"Can I get you a glass of water?"

His lips are suddenly parched. "Please," he croaks, lowering himself onto the stool, legs dangling. The women scurry about as he unzips his leather jacket and loosens his collar. He hasn't felt this claustro in years. Is that his heart ping-ponging inside his chest? Tiny points of light hit his retina, and he shakes his head. Whoa, bad idea: the room swims by.

Denise presses a glass of water into his hands, and he sips gratefully. Whiff of chlorine and fluoride.

"Know something, gang," he says after a minute. "I may have to call it quits today."

"Of course," Denise agrees, squeezing his shoulder.

"How will you get home?" someone asks. They know he doesn't drive.

"I'll run him back," Denise offers.

"No, let me," Pamela says, popping her guitar in her case. "Don't you have to pick up your kids?"

Should have eaten a proper lunch, Toby thinks crossly. No more hot dogs grabbed off a street vendor: sunk by fat and carbs. He drains the water glass, and gradually the room rights itself. His jacket, now gathered on his lap, smells like a stable. They all stare at him, faces pinched with concern. He manages a smile. "I'm feeling better." It's true. The heightened senses have begun to settle down.

They aren't convinced but soon chatter as if it were a normal break period. Tristan offers to go out and fetch coffee; someone else shows off a new digital tuner. Toby feels heat evaporate off his skin.

Matthew approaches, speaking in his plummy trial lawyer's voice: "You were quite correct in insisting that we finish playing the piece before making any decision. I suggest holding off our vote." He leans over. "On a different topic, I understand there's an international guitar competition coming up in Montreal."

"Right you are," Toby says.

The room falls nearly silent.

"Any thoughts of entering?"

Toby lets out a jittery laugh. "Last time didn't go so well for me."

They all know the story: breakdown, drawn-out recovery, and no public performances since.

"Don't pressure him," Denise warns.

"I don't mind," Toby says. "In fact, I'm flattered."

"You are one hell of a musician," Pamela says.

They have gathered in a semicircle.

"You don't walk into these things after a decade off performing," he reminds them.

"You play for us all the time," Pamela points out.

That's true. He always rips off a piece or two for them at the end of each session. And when they perform at the old folks' home or community centre, he's liable to turn a short solo somewhere in the program.

Tristan re-enters the room, carrying a tray of coffee and a box of assorted Timbits, which he lays on the table.

Eyeing these, Toby says, "A new generation's come up since me."

"One needn't win these things," Matthew says, "in order to make an impact."

What they don't know is that Toby checked the competition website last month and brushed up on the compulsory pieces, two of which he'd played in recital years ago. He studies the group for a moment, noting their eager faces, understanding that they see him as a kind of secret weapon they've been holding on to all these years. Maybe he sees himself the same way.

Toby pulls his guitar onto his lap and tunes while Guitar Choir members grab coffees and find their seats. He waits, as he's taught them to do, for the room to quiet down. Anticipation creates the silent beats before music begins.

"You're not going home?" Pamela asks, puzzled by the change in plan.

Toby nods "no" while others shush her.

Hands hovering over the strings, he lowers his eyes, then unrolls the opening arpeggio, launching into a neo-classical sonata, pure juicy pleasure, each phrase ducking into the next, the rise and fall of breath twinned to the cadence of sound. The piece is in his hands, has been since he was a teenager. A relief to send it into the world again.

Hardly pausing, he wipes his palms and starts the second piece of the compulsory program, this one a lush Spanish waltz, direct from Andalusia. He ignores the snap of basketballs over-head as the teenagers arrive. Not too fast, for a waltz is graceful, lifting off the third beat.

"Well done," Matthew booms, but he's too soon, for Toby isn't finished yet.

Their parking meters have expired, kids need to be picked up from school, and someone has a dental appointment, but no one leaves, no one dares.

The third piece is a tricky tour de force he learned at age seventeen. It's sewn into his mind; he could play its stampeding runs in his sleep — and has. He holds it now as a living creature, both tame and wild.

The last note rings a full four beats, then fades to a dot on the horizon. Toby lifts his head and exhales, thrusting his shoulders back. Glance at the clock; he's been playing for twenty-five minutes.

No one applauds at first, then an amazing thing happens: each member of Guitar Choir rises and claps.

Toby feels his whole body vibrate, the residue of performance clinging to his skin.

Jasper and Toby live at the end of a lane downtown in the lee of a factory that once produced soap and is now waiting for a loft conversion. Half a dozen Victorian-era houses press cheek to jowl opposite a squat cinder-block building that contains a walk-in clinic. This clinic is an eyesore but buffers traffic noise and makes the lane invisible to passersby on King Street West.

Toby digs out his key, but it isn't necessary; Jasper has left the door open. A thoughtful touch, but faintly irksome: are Toby's habits so predictable? It didn't used to be like this. Once upon a time he was about as dependable as a puppy. He kicks off his sneakers and moves through the front room of the flat with its off-white walls and Ikea furniture, past the jumbo-sized chair that until recently belonged to Klaus. Klaus is Toby's father, now a resident for unknown reasons at Lakeview Terrace. It's not as if he wasn't fending well at home. Toby sniffs the air: leek and potato soup, one of Jasper's specialties.

"You look different," Jasper says, glancing up as Toby enters the kitchen area. He carefully places the spoon across the rim of the pot.

Toby slides his guitar case into the corner and drops his jacket on a chair. "I feel different."

The two men approach each other, for this is their ritual, to pause before the welcoming kiss, no silly bear hug, just lips and tongue, bodies held a whisper apart. Jasper, being shorter, has to tilt his head.

When they pull back, Jasper says, "Cough up. Tell Jazz what's new."

Toby peels off his shirt, which doesn't smell exactly floral, and shoots it in the general direction of the laundry hamper. Jasper frowns as he watches the garment flop to the floor.

"I had a sort of attack at Guitar Choir," Toby says.

"Attack?" Jasper jumps on the word. "How so?"

"Like what used to happen. Only less severe."

"Did you pass out?"

"No, nothing like that."

Jasper visibly relaxes, pressing his lower back into the counter, then reaches to turn down the burner under the soup. A fresh baguette sits on a cutting board, the heel torn off and demolished.

Toby goes over to the sink and pours a glass of water, aware, as always, of Jasper's gaze. He moves his hips a bit more than needed and peers out the window onto the concrete patch where buses idle before heading north toward the subway station. Since they live on the ground floor of the townhouse, views aren't exactly optimal.

"I don't like the sound of it," Jasper says. Neatly dressed in chinos and trim cotton shirt, he has a small head, his features tidy and undramatic. He hates the swell of his stomach, a recent development.

"I ate a crap lunch," Toby says. "It was probably a blood-sugar dive."

"Maybe."

"I recovered quickly." Toby rinses out his glass and dumps it in the sink. He's bored with the topic, even though he brought it up. He knows it's mean to seek concern, then slough it off. Leaking a cautious smile, he says, "Big competition coming up in Montreal."

"What kind of competition?"

"One of those guitar things."

Jasper isn't fooled by his breezy tone. "And?"

"I may toss my hat in the ring."

"Really?" Jasper knows better than to make a fuss.

Toby prowls the flat, past Klaus's hulking chair, past the Matisse numbered print — Jasper's pride and joy — and the shelf of Toby's house league hockey trophies. He's never been the sort of musician to baby his hands.

"Chances are I wouldn't make it to the semifinal," Toby says, returning to the kitchen. "Hell, I may not make it past the first cull."

"When did this idea occur to you?" Jasper asks, his voice a little sharp.

"Not long ago. I forget."

Jasper nods, pretending to believe this. "I would never hold you back from attempting —"

"You can't," Toby points out.

"Quite so. But let me remind you that all did not turn out well last time."

"Eleven years ago."

"The consequences were fairly dire."

"Eleven years ago."

Jasper clears his throat, a picture of calm, as if dealing with one of his clients at work. "Do you really want to subject yourself to that kind of pressure?"

A reasonable question. Toby looks at his partner, feeling his cockiness bleed away.

TWO

THE LAST CLIENT OF THE DAY HAS LEFT, AND JASPER IS BUSY tidying his desk at the institute, hiding files from his nosy colleagues and renaming computer documents in the event a certain party decides to sneak in after hours and meddle. In other words — Luke, chairman of the board of the institute and currently at war with Jasper. For this reason Jasper likes to be the last one in the office, the person who turns off lights and printers and copy machines, then lowers the blinds in anticipation of morning sun. It's the most peaceful time of day, agenda swept clear and the smell of burned coffee hanging heavy in the air. There was a time when he loved his job, and that time was not so long ago. Luke was elected chair at the last AGM, and it seemed like a grand thing. Jasper dared to believe the two men shared a vision.

Toby will be getting peckish back home, he decides. Sometimes he feels Toby's hunger before the boy feels it himself; they've been together that long. His lover — a term Jasper favours over the sexually neutral "partner" — makes forays to the fridge, tears off lettuce leaves for a salad, and stirs a bay leaf into the stew pot.

Or doesn't.

Since Toby got this daft idea of entering the Montreal International Classical Guitar Competition, he doesn't always get around to cooking dinner on weekdays. Jasper can't help feeling peeved by this; after all, he's the one with a complex full-time job while all Toby needs to do is teach Guitar Choir once a week. Just for a moment he wonders what it would be like if Toby didn't exist, how much simpler his life would become — and how empty.

There are days when Jasper craves such emptiness.

The screensaver floats into view: beads of dew gleaming off iguana hide, so unlike this dry, frightened city in summer where the virus has chased citizens into their homes. The institute's walls are painted sea-green, a hue chosen by a former chairman after she read that green invoked tranquility, a mood much prized in these parts. That bare patch next to the window used to contain a Frida Kahlo print, a creepy self-portrait with mini-Diego peering out of her forehead. Jasper tore it down, for his clients crave the ordinary, not an artist's mad leap of imagination.

The elevator slides down to bustling University Avenue, crisp dusk of early autumn. As always, Jasper pauses before exiting the building to wave to the security guard, nice kid, inching his way through college a credit at a time.

Mail is trapped in the slot, though it must have arrived hours ago. Jasper pushes open the door to the flat and frowns. He can hear the stomping of feet inside. They always remove their shoes before entering — why track city filth inside? Clues rain down. Yet he's not exactly worried. It is a too-quiet room with no response that he dreads. Feeling the old jet of excitement, intact after all these years, he calls out Toby's name.

The pacing stops.

Jasper takes his time loosening his laces, kicking off his shoes, then sets his cap on the hook. He spots Toby in the middle room, dressed only in a pair of plaid boxers.

"Everything okay?" Jasper asks in a voice carefully shorn of concern.

Toby slams a bookcase with his open hand, and Jasper's collection of European history texts rattles.

"Don't touch me," Toby whispers as his lover reaches for his arm.

The kid was his merry self this morning, but evidently this morning was a different universe. He loses contact with his own skin, gets so he can't stand the lightest caress. His guitar is propped against the chair, but the metal stand has capsized and lies skeletal on the rug.

"What's happening, baby?" Jasper asks.

"I don't know," Toby says. His face is flushed. "You tell me."

"Is the practising not going well?"

"Blame music," snaps Toby. "Blame the guitar competition."

"I'm not blaming anything. I just want to find out what's wrong."

"You can't help."

"Then I won't try." This is something Jasper has learned — not to get pulled in where he's not welcome. Besides, he has things to do, especially since it's clear nothing has been done about supper, and he should call his sister out in Victoria who is turning forty today.

Toby tags along as Jasper moves into the kitchen, and then the story emerges, as Jasper knew it would.

"Who the hell do I think I am, going back to competition after all this time? Someone will be there who saw me nosedive in Paris. I couldn't stand that, Jazz."

Jasper peers in the fridge, finds the pot of soup nearly a week old, and sets it on the stove to heat up. He feels the boy press in and reaches back to clasp one of his hands, those pebbly, callused fingertips. Touch never fails; it's what Toby needs to be reminded of.

"Are you afraid?" Jasper asks.

"Of course."

"Because you don't have to do it."

"I sent in my application."

"Un-send it. No shame in a change of mind." Jasper hears the encouragement in his voice.

"Put my engine in reverse? Is that what you're suggesting?"

The men face each other, and pretty soon Toby's hands are sliding all over him, popping open Jasper's shirt, burrowing between his legs, and they collapse to the ground in a slow-motion dance. The carpet that tattoos their knees is a fake kilim, courtesy of Klaus. If the old man could see them now.

They untangle to the sound of a kettle whistling in the apartment above. Jill calls, "All set," and Miranda's feet clatter across the floor. There is a long sigh of water pouring into a teapot. That rhythmic thump is the dog's tail hitting the wall.

Jasper eyes his lover, who now lies on his back, naked and breathing evenly. Though he is nearly thirty, Toby has a face as unlined as a child's and shaves no more than twice a week. Jasper rubs his own bristly chin: night and day.

Toby's eyes flicker open, and he asks lazily, "Don't you get tired of looking at me?"

"Never."

Toby smiles and lifts himself to his feet all in one move, no creaking joints. Fourteen years younger; it makes a difference. Then he tosses his head, a gesture going back to a time when he wore dreadlocks. Upstairs, cutlery clinks against china and someone turns on the stereo: Edith Piaf, the little sparrow.

"Your soup is burning," Toby says, stretching his arms so his fingertips tickle the low ceiling.

"Shit!" Jasper rises carefully, mindful of his lower back, and heads for the stove.

"I haven't decided on my free choice," Toby says, watching the soup rescue.

"What free choice?"

"After playing the required program, we get to choose a piece from our repertoire," Toby says. "The kids go for flashy. I might be different."

Jasper stirs thoughtfully. He understands that sex has changed nothing. "Tell me why you want to do this."

Toby plucks a T-shirt and a pair of jeans from the dresser. "It's an experiment, dropping baking powder into a glass of vinegar to see what happens."

"I can tell you what happens, Toby."

"But I need to see for myself." Tugging his shirt over his lean torso, Toby says, "You understand that, Jazz." There is a plea in his voice.

In those early days Toby played a Karl Honderich instrument, such a jewel, he'll claim, but left somewhere on the Paris Metro during that explosive week. The luthier's dead now, Toby likes to remind him, and many of the old boys are gone for good; Segovia's ancient history and Bream's too old to play in public.

Toby still can't believe it might be over for him, too.

Jasper tastes the soup, a trifle charred. He grabs his own clothes off the floor and dresses, minus underwear. Upstairs the women croon along to "La Vie en rose" as if they were in some Left Bank dive — picture the bearded poet in the corner, cranked on absinthe.

"We haven't had this conversation in years," Jasper says. "I thought we were out of the woods."

Toby bristles. "I'm getting old."

Now Jasper laughs. "You're twenty-nine." And I'm forty-three, he might add, but doesn't. "I saw this coming."

Toby blinks. "Saw what coming?"

"Your need to prove yourself."

"Really?" Toby likes to discuss his motivations.

"Remember how you felt after cleaning out Klaus's house?" Toby's face freezes, and Jasper understands that he's onto something. "His carefully contained life scared hell out of you."

Klaus recently moved himself to Lakeview Terrace. He may be a senior citizen with a touch of Parkinson's plus the diabetes, but he's managing well. The move is a great mystery to his son and Jasper.

"It sure as hell depressed me," Toby says.

"Perhaps by entering the competition you're proving you aren't Klaus, or anything like him."

"That's a theory."

Encouraged, Jasper continues. "You'd be up against some of the best musicians in the world."

Toby offers a smile. "Perhaps I'm one of the best in the world."

It is so tempting to offer the damning word *were*. You were among the best, Toby, as we all were something else.

After supper Toby flees outside for a smoke, though last week he claimed he'd quit for good. Jasper lifts the blind and sees the boy perching on the top step at the same time as one of the medics pops open the clinic's rear door, heading for her own break. Pushing down her mask, she searches in her pocket for a light, cigarette already dangling from her lips. Where Jasper works, all guests and clients who enter the building must don masks and latex gloves, but once upstairs and cleared of obvious symptoms, they remove the paraphernalia — the risk of infection is still low. Tourists are keeping a wide berth of the city, and who can blame them, given media hysterics? The latest Andrew Lloyd Webber musical is packing up, and Wagner's Ring Cycle played to half-empty houses. Yet the casualty list is still under thirty.

Jasper catches a glimpse of Toby's jaw grinding molars to dental dust. The medic is speaking with animated gestures and sucks at her cigarette, then holds out her pack to Toby. Can he use another?

You bet.

Her scrubs, Jasper is sure, reek of high-power disinfectant.

Yesterday Toby said it wouldn't be a bad idea to put all the quarantined people together, maybe in the old TB hospital in the west end of the city. He got all worked up about it, a man of vision. They would be well fed and given interesting things to do during the two-week period, learning crafts like pottery and carving canoe paddles — a sort of camp. Doctors could try new antivirals and other experimental treatments. Then he stopped speaking, for in that second he'd felt the virus hover, waiting opportunistically for an opening.

Evening fog draws off the lake, and Toby shivers. Inside, Jasper shivers, too.

THREE

TOBY KNOCKED ON THE DOOR OF HIS FATHER'S HOUSE IN THE Beach and waited for the slow clump of footsteps. It was always the same: Klaus would swing open the door, gaze at his son for a moment, then say, "I'd just about given up on you," because Toby was a measly ten minutes late. Six o'clock was six o'clock in Klaus's books.

He knocked again; maybe his dad was in the bathroom. Old guys can have trouble in there. And so he waited, spinning on the concrete step and looking across the street toward the rickety clapboard bungalow belonging to their neighbours. Not many original cottages left in the Beach.

Another knock and still no answer. This was weird, for Klaus was a man of habit, an apostle of routine, and it was Wednesday evening, Toby's designated visiting hour. The car was parked in the driveway and the hall light was on. Fending off a spritz of alarm, Toby let himself in with his key. He stood in the foyer and waited to hear something, that characteristic clearing of throat, footsteps, anything.

"Papa?" he called out. His voice echoed in the hallway, bouncing off the shiny floor and walls.

"Papa!"

Zilch. No sound of toilet flushing, no clicking of shoes on tile. Now Toby was getting officially alarmed. His father never walked anywhere, didn't see the point when he owned a car and paid insurance on it. The place emitted an overwhelming pong of furniture polish and floor wax.

It might happen like this, Toby thought. A day like any other except his father will have collapsed somewhere in the neat two-storey house and it will be his task to find him.

He sucked in a breath and marched down the hallway, switching on lights and calling out, "Papa? *Wo bist du?*"

The only response was a thrum from the ancient refrigerator. Everything looked to be in order, spic and span. Toby entered the kitchen with its spongy vinyl chairs and freshly mopped floor — and that was when he spotted the note propped against the toaster: "Gone to live in Lakeview. Please dispose of household contents. K.H."

Man of few words.

Why on earth would Klaus move himself to that cheerless institution?

Holding the note, fountain pen written on the back of a recipe card — waste not, want not — Toby felt only dismay. Klaus had no need to set foot in Lakeview again, not after his wife died. You'd think he'd be grateful to be clear of the place and its antiseptic smells.

Toby began the job right away. The overhanging roof made the rooms darker than they needed to be, and he turned on lights as he prowled from room to room. When his mother was up and running, she'd fling open the windows in the spring, but she'd had no say in years. Karen had been resident in Lakeview Terrace longer than anyone, starting at age forty-seven when, the story goes, her moments of peculiarity turned into lapses of judgment and an urge to set fires. She died in neurological chaos, a slight woman with frizzy hair whom Toby didn't visit often enough. In the early days he used to take his guitar to Lakeview to play for some of the old ladies; they made a fuss over him, child among the ancients. But Klaus never missed a day during those long years, striding into C Wing to feed his wife supper because without his loving hand she refused to swallow. Not a word of complaint ever passed his lips. Say what you might of Klaus as a father, he was one hell of a husband.

Swoosh went prefolded napkins and a chipped butter dish into the garbage bag. This was the original stove, circa 1969, and ditto for the fridge, both softly aerodynamic and kept rigorously clean and in working trim. The burner coils were sausage-like, style of the day. The set of etched juice glasses were fished out of detergent boxes. No way brother Felix would be interested in any of this subpar loot, living in Powell River with snooty Leah and their kids.

As Toby tossed things into cartons and plastic bags, he felt himself move from sadness into an inchoate anger: why did the old man deliberately deprive himself? Cereal bowls were filled with those toggles that held bread together; jars that once held peanut butter were packed with elastic bands. So ostentatiously frugal, as if to buy something new or to toss something old was a moral failing. Lucky thing Jasper wasn't on hand to witness this. He had a sore spot about what he called "The German Thing" and would find all this neatness and thrift creepy.

Toby knew what was coming next when he swung open the closet door. First, he unhooked the straw broom made by the blind and set it in the corner of the kitchen. When the boys were still at home, they had regular chores and a monthly calendar indicating who did what and when. Taped to the inside of the door now was a sheet of paper ruled into columns that itemized duties from washing shutters to floor waxing and laundry. Along the top were printed dates, and tick marks noted job accomplished. A bustle of vacuuming occurred two days before Klaus entered Lakeview with his plaid suitcase. Last Thursday he'd flipped the mattress, the same mattress that Toby would soon drag down to the curb.

He roamed the house, plastic bag in tow, swinging open cupboards he'd never dare open in the presence of his secretive father. His gut clenched with each potential revelation: surely somewhere he'd discover inklings of the old man's real life, the one he'd left behind — the German life.

Instead of crispy air mail envelopes he found bundled socks in a drawer, and tucked next to them a list: "5 pair black, 2 pair white, 4 pair dress."

No yellowed letters from Klaus's own father, a Luftwaffe pilot turned owner of a popular seaside resort — just a dried-up avocado pit set into a jar on the dresser, toothpick running through its midsection.

Toby stood at the entrance to his and Felix's bedroom at the rear of the house. This was the only room that had noticeably changed: bunk beds replaced with a sofa bed and next to it the cabinet hi-fi that used to be downstairs. The meagre stash of LPs dated back to the early 1970s — Strauss waltzes, Beethoven's Fifth, and Klaus's favourite, Yma Sumac, the Inca Princess, whose soaring voice filled the house during weekend breakfasts.

The old Yamaha guitar stood in its cardboard case against the wall. Toby sat on the sofa, unsnapped the case, and pulled out the instrument, noting a hairline crack near the bridge. Dry winter days had taken their toll. He had to wrench the plastic pegs to get them to turn on the headstock. The strings felt stiff and dead, untouched for years. Tuning the best he could, he started in on that old chestnut, "Spanish Romance," the first real piece he'd learned. This room was his safe haven, and he'd practise here for hours, often beginning when he heard Klaus's car swing into the driveway. By the time Toby made it downstairs, Klaus would be cooking dinner and news from the visit to "your dear Mama" would have been forgotten.

Toby won that guitar-shaped clock hanging on the wall at some dopey talent contest when he was in junior high. They were always so proud of him, Mama and Papa.

The day she died, last December 25, Toby was basting the turkey when he got the call, Jasper hovering, fussing over internal fowl temperature.

Karen wasn't always off her rocker. For years she'd been a

real mother. That's what Jasper forgets when he calls her existence "tragic."

What was that smell? Toby hesitated at the entrance to the bathroom, though he knew without looking what it was: medicinal aroma of old country shampoo imported by specialty shops. Not that Klaus had much hair left to work with. Toby imagined Jasper snickering, "The man keeps a well-scrubbed scalp."

Does Klaus ever complain of loneliness?

Never. He likes to say that he expects little from life, so he is never disappointed.

FOUR

LUKE IS UP IN ARMS, BARRELLING THROUGH THE OFFICE LIKE a banana republic generalissimo. He's convinced that the board of directors is staging a mutiny, which is partially true, if Jasper has his way. The man's nattering on about "strategic information" that should be in his hands by now. Jasper hides a smile. At this point the best ammunition is secrecy. As Luke dances through the office, lifting file folders willy-nilly, Jasper keeps his focus on his work, while Rachel, an intern from a community college, fixes her gaze on her monitor and taps randomly at computer keys.

Luke plants himself in front of Jasper's desk. "I demand full accountability." Thin blond hair is glued to his scalp, and his suit looks a size too small, the current fashion.

Jasper glances up. "If you can't get hold of yourself, then I must ask you to leave."

Rachel's mouth drops open.

"What?" Luke hisses.

"I'm asking you to leave. Now."

No one says this to Luke, chairman of the board, and it catches the man off guard. His face pinkens several degrees, then suddenly he is gone, shiny loafers clacking down the hall.

Rachel tells Jasper he is God.

Possibly, but Jasper is shaking so hard he can't speak.

The church smells of melted candles and damp boots. A pigeon roosts high in the rafters, and with luck it won't wake up once the concert gets underway. Is it true that pigeons can't shit midair? The small audience files in, buying tickets at a table set up at the entrance, presided over by Tess, vice-chair of the Toronto Guitar Society. She doesn't recognize Toby — it's been too long. It was Tess who arranged his first recital in this same church when he was a pipsqueak carrying a borrowed concert-grade guitar.

Squinting into the rows of pews, light filtered through stained glass, Toby wonders which of the more grizzled audience members were present then. He'd ripped through Villa-Lobos, Bach, and Albéniz, not a groundbreaking program, but he was barely eleven years old. When he finished the recital, grinning his head off, he saw his parents and Felix in the front row clapping like maniacs, yet it was Tess who led the standing ovation, tears streaming down her face. In those days her skin was pale, her hair red and bushy.

Toby hesitates at the door of the church, reluctant to stride into his own storied past. Yet this evening it is not Toby who will step onto the liturgical stage, and this audience is scarcely two dozen, given the viral scare. He buys his ticket, and Tess barely lifts her eyes as she slides it across the table. This is a relief and at the same time a disappointment. He finds a seat at the end of a pew close to the front. Its shelf is crammed with prayer books and hymnals, a reminder that music is only the building's hobby. He flips open the program and reads off the list of composers — all Italian and he's only heard of half of them. Most were born in the 1970s or later.

It's been years since he's made his way to a guitar concert. He used to go to everything and they'd often wave him in for free, understanding that such a talent needed to be exposed to a range of performance styles. He'd pretend to ignore the nods and whispers, the discreet finger pointings. Not many like Toby popped up in a generation. He'd angle a spot near the front of the hall, aware of being watched, and this watching never seemed strange or intrusive. He knew from the beginning that he would be good, very good.

Tonight he might as well be invisible. A new crop of students files into the front pew where they'll get an unobstructed view of the artist's hands and face. These hands belong to Antonio Conti who, just a year older than Toby, saunters onto the chancel, guitar tucked under one arm while enthusiastic applause erupts from the small crowd. Without fuss Conti sits on the low chair, tunes, pushes back his cuffs, and begins.

He plays with a scrumptious tone, a Mediterranean bel canto full of glissandos and arpeggios that lift the man half out of his seat. Toby feels his own shoulders relax, his breathing grow deep. Conti manages to be romantic as hell, hovering on the high notes, unrolling rubatos that make Toby smile at their succulent corniness, yet there is also perfect control, no buzzes, no unruly snaps.

This is my drug, he thinks, the opposite of grim Teutonic passion. He may be his father's son, but he's never going to list the socks in his drawer, never going to stack tuna fish cans for recycling. The sound fills him with a depth charge of emotion, and he's startled to find himself close to weeping. Conti's mouth drops open, then squeezes shut as the phrase lifts and falls. Toby's program drifts to the ground. He knows now he will perform at Conti's master class the following day, that this man must hear what he can do. At the same moment he decides he will not tell Jasper.

During intermission, Tess barely glances at him as he slides another twenty bucks across the table in return for a copy of Conti's latest CD. Sprung from silence, the small audience is boisterous, pressing open the heavy church doors for smokes and a hit of unconsecrated air.

"Put me down for the master class," Toby says.

"We're full up," Tess replies, slipping the bill into a cigar box. "You may attend as observer but not to perform."

Toby rolls his shoulders back; it is these young men shooting past in their skinny jeans who are the cause of this fullness. "Can you make room?"

"No, I cannot." Annoyed, she finally looks at him, thinking, he's familiar, some crank she's had to deal with in the past.

Toby waits for her to put it together: he'd stayed with Tess's family for two weeks while his mother made the transition to Lakeview. They gave him a hook on the back of a door for his clothes and the hide-a-bed to sleep on. Tess's daughter used to practise trumpet while the son smoked pot in the cellar and offered Toby his first hit of Ecstasy, the drug that is. Their freezer was stocked with ice-cream bars and Hungry Man Dinners.

"I know you," she says, brow furrowing.

He smiles. "Toby." Waits a beat. "Hausner."

Her reaction is instant: she bounds to her feet, leaving the cash box unattended, and grabs his ears. "Toby Hausner! Look at you!"

He flushes with pleasure, then steels himself for the flurry of questions — where have you been all these years? what have you been doing? — but she just keeps looking at him with a broad grin and yanks his ears until he fears they'll snap off.

"Of course you'll play for us tomorrow," she announces. She's been around musicians so long that her speech is oddly cadenced, filtered through a dozen mimicked accents. Tonight it is faintly Italianate.

"Un-believable!" she says, stretching out the word. Toby beams under the warmth of her gaze. Her lean face has weathered well. "It is the Second Coming," she adds with a fresh burst of enthusiasm, then scrambles for a pen to add his name to the list.

"Hardly that," Toby says, but he smiles. Something is returning, his old world, and he doesn't know whether to flee or celebrate.

"Where is my dear Angus?" She looks around the dark church and finally beckons to a burly man who huddles in the corner talking to a pair of older audience members.

Angus is her husband, the founder of the Society, and ex-officio everything, having taken a turn as president, secretary, videographer, and fundraiser. Seeing her wave, he lumbers over, and Toby notes there is considerably more grey in his beard now.

Fixing his eyes on Toby, he says in a booming voice, "Is this who I think it is?"

Toby races home before intermission is over, too revved up to hang around for the second half of the program. He can manage a couple of hours of intense practice before Jasper returns from his board meeting.

Jasper rolled out of bed this morning, ranting before his feet hit the floor: "The board orders me to balance the budget while they spend months labouring over mission statements and strategic plans. They're supposed to fundraise, a fact they conveniently forget." Moments later, in the middle of shaving, he poked his head out of the bathroom and announced, "It's Luke or me, something they must understand."

When Toby dared to ask, "Is the man really so bad?" Jazz glared at him as if he was nuts. Had he not been listening these past months? Did he not understand the concept of the Gathering Storm?

Returning to the empty flat, Toby decides he'll work on a bravura Paganini sonata for tomorrow's performance: why not charge fearlessly into Conti's home territory — *la bella Italia*? No one accuses Paganini of being a great composer, but he's a riot to play. Stepping off the streetcar and veering into the familiar lane, Toby sees that the clinic is dark except for a single light that blinks to life as he passes. One of the iron street lamps is dead, its bulb shattered by a rock. An angry patient has been turned away: no OxyContin for your headache, Jack.

Jasper's switched on the porch light so that Toby might easily fit key into lock: Jasper the Anticipator.

Play the same passage many times, changing tiny elements. Accent the second beat, then the first, diminuendo just before pickup to the new phrase. Dampen the bass note. Do it all backward.

Eat me, the mushroom demands, placid little fungus.

But I'm only practising, Toby insists, keeping an eye on the clock and the hour of Jasper's return — hardly entering some cyclone that will require rescue.

To memorize is not a mysterious process: stuff a sock in the sound hole so the strings make dull clinks. Don't depend on notation, the visualized map of marks on a page. He pencils in fingerings so the score becomes even more of a hatch work. He played this same piece in master class a dozen years ago, dazzling the guest artist who'd flown up from Savannah. Gabrielle Someone, a young woman with huge hands. The episode is shaky in his mind: didn't they snort a line in her hotel room afterward, view of the CN Tower lit up at night?

Upstairs, Polly the bull terrier thwacks her tail against a wall. She's apt to take a bite out of somebody one day and slurp gratitude the next. Jasper says the girls need to bear in mind that Polly is animal, not human, and must set limits, advice they happily ignore.

Toby left the window open a crack so he'll have warning when Jasper comes waltzing up the path, giddy with post-meeting wine.

Grab an apple and a Sprite for fortification. The fridge stinks from something hidden under a layer of foil. Toby's taste buds function; the nose hasn't gone AWOL.

Right-hand fingers sink into the strings: place, pressure, release.

Jasper and his crew are drinking wine and eating tapas at the usual place near the institute. The joint is otherwise empty, so the solo waitress hovers, swabbing down menus with Vim and a damp cloth. Hygiene is very big these days. She clears her throat, then stops, mortified, as Jasper's administrative assistant drops a napkin over her salad, anticipating particulate matter. An early indicator of the virus is a neck flush. Victims display it when they're feeling fine, then note, appalled, as it spreads from pulse point to pulse point: wrists, temples, the crease behind the knees. Easy to dismiss: who wants to believe that a blush is prelude to neurological chaos? Jasper gets patients after they've been sprung from hospital and the first stint of rehab, which means they are the lucky survivors. Time to get their brains up and running, add memory where it has been scoured clean.

Toby sets his instrument down when he hears the four quick steps up the stairs to the front door. He snaps off the light and dashes into the bathroom. The bed is carefully mussed, as if he'd just left it to take a whiz. He's punched a dent in the pillow, head size.

FIVE

FASHION MASKS ARE THE LATEST THINGS. GIRLS GLUE PLASTIC
butterflies and dollar store insects onto theirs; boys add super-
hero stickers. Toby left his at home, wrapped over the gooseneck
lamp: forget breathing through gauze. The epidemic has spiked:
orange alert due to a rogue infector who jaunted about asymp-
tomatic but is now known to be sixteen years old, female. She
swept through the transit system coating handrails with viral
sweat and is now quarantined at East General, surrounded by
medics decked out in chemical suit regalia, busy draining fluid
off her brain. It's a horror, Jasper says, but we must keep things
in perspective. This is nothing compared to the polio outbreaks
of the 1950s.

Toby shows up at the Conservatory for his master class, striding
past a warning sign posted on the front door (DO NOT ENTER
IF YOU SUFFER FROM ANY OF THE FOLLOWING SYMPTOMS …),
marches down the corridor feeling a prickly dryness in his eyes.
It's a massive Victorian building, solid but creaky with age. A
second poster curled at the edges diagrams the progress of fund-
raising for the reno — stuck, it seems, at two and a half million.
An open door reveals a class of students working at electronic
keyboards with headphones clamped to their ears. Everyone
seems better dressed than they used to be in the old days.

Toby used to practically live in this place and knew all the
office staff by name. He speeds past the glass doors, not in a mood
to be recognized. Retaining focus before a performance is crucial;
what used to come so naturally now takes a studied effort.

Master class runs in room 108, and he spots Tess hovering at its entrance, directing traffic and checking names off the list. Her glasses are set low over her nose, and she waves at Toby. "You're up third," she tells him. "Make it snappy. We're ready to roll."

She's always been bossy, and he slips by her, ignoring the pump of disinfectant lotion sitting on a table. Last thing he needs is to slime up his hands and watch them pucker dry; playing requires a degree of moisture. He sits to one side of the room, guitar case tucked between his knees. Did Tess look at him with just a hint of concern? For all she knows, Toby might be out on a day pass, about to start speaking in tongues or to noodle through some incoherent improv.

He has done these things in public, or so he has been told.

Musicians make their way into the studio, nodding at each other in muted recognition. Several cast a glance at Toby, wondering who he might be.

Toby stares back with his blank game face. He spoke not a word to Jasper about this performance; he's headed for a makeup class with Guitar Choir, story goes. A small lie to prevent a familiar anxious look from crowding his lover's face.

He reaches to touch the crease at the side of his nose, dabbing enough sweat to moisten his fingertips. Nerves turn skin to parchment. This jittery anticipation is so familiar, something he's missed and even craved without realizing it. He feels fully alive on this hard chair, coiled energy, all he can do not to bob his knees up and down.

A couple of dozen folding chairs contain participants and observers. Up front is a music stand plus a footstool and two more chairs — one for Conti, the other for the performer. Most, if not all the other musicians, will be senior students from the Glenn Gould Professional School or the University of Toronto's Faculty of Music. Behind, a Steinway baby grand perches like a raven, wings aloft. Overhead ventilation ducts create a distracting racket, but if you switch them off, airs turns to gravy.

Conti isn't immediately recognizable as he strides in, guitar case plastered with airline stickers. He seems smaller than last night and rounder, his features less distinctive. Conti hasn't bothered to shave, which gives him a sleepy look. He removes his leather jacket and tosses it onto the piano lid, zipper skidding across its buffed surface. Tess grimaces, knowing there will be complaints, for the guitar isn't seen as a serious instrument by certain members of the Conservatory faculty — too troubadour or folksy, hint of the coffee house or plantation. Conti makes a joke that no one understands, though they titter nervously, two dozen young men and a couple of women. Tess strolls over to confer about the program, and after a moment Conti glances up. His eyes find Toby's and he nods.

Has he been warned, and if so — how? Others turn to look: Toby must be somebody, but who?

Focus. Don't let them unsettle you.

Setup for a master class is simple: the student's name is called and he performs a piece of his choosing. This is followed by a half-hour public class where the guest artist offers critique and suggestions, and, with luck, praise. Toby's performed in many such classes. He understands that it is possible to temporarily fool the body, and that to appear outwardly calm is to invoke inner calm. He sits very still in his chair with no nervous throat clearings, no last-minute sandpapering of nails.

First up is a skinny kid wearing a shirt buttoned to the neck. He passes Conti a score, then jumps into a piece by a modern Brazilian composer without waiting for the audience to settle down. Conti perches on the edge of his chair, feet planted firmly on the floor, watching the boy's hands intently.

There is a smattering of applause when the kid finishes, then Conti launches in, first by acknowledging the student's phrasing and dynamic range. "But left hand is so tight, like a claw. You must be strong, yet one hundred percent flexible, like the octopus."

He demonstrates a relaxation exercise, first clutching a ball, then letting it drop without changing position of the hand.

The next performer is built like a football player, muscles popping under his shirt. He lowers himself stiffly onto the chair as if still smarting from last night's workout and announces that he will perform Conti's own transcription of a Granados piano work.

The maestro smiles, enjoying this display of flattery.

The youth plays with his sausage fingers, mouth twisting into tortured expressions as he moves through the tricky piece, his body at odds with the delicate, even nuanced sounds that rise from his instrument.

Pretty damn good, Toby thinks, but not scary good. What he is — what they all are — is very young.

Conti says, "You must isolate the difficult sections."

The performer nods his shaved head; he's heard this advice a thousand times.

Conti gets the boy to try the opening section over and over, focusing on the syncopated rhythm while Conti taps out the beat. When the kid fouls up, the teacher reaches over and raps his muscled thigh. "Feel it in your body!"

The boy reddens, loses track of where he is, his old way of playing not yet subsumed to the new. Conti drags his chair even closer so that the two men brush knees, and then, on the seventh or eighth try, the kid nails it.

Relieved applause. Any one of them could be up there.

"Toby Hausner, you're next," Tess announces, peering at him over the top of her glasses.

He picks up his guitar and makes his way to the front of the room.

I don't have to do this, he reminds himself. He could blow them all off and head for the pub across the street, afternoon jazz and a banquet burger. When he was a teenager, he didn't understand this. He didn't know there was a choice.

Conti clasps hands over head and yawns loudly. "What will you play for us?"

"Paganini." Toby passes over the weathered score, an accordion fold-out, six pages long. He will play by memory, as is the custom.

The maestro smiles, lowering his arms. There are deep shadows under his eyes after a sleepless night in an unfamiliar hotel room. "I perform this on my new CD. It is all about touch, yes?" He turns to the audience, making a lesson of the remark. "Your fingers must go like the wind, maybe good wind, maybe bad."

A sprinkle of nervous laughter greets this witticism; if a person plays exceptionally well here, he might be invited to the guitar festival in Milan where Conti presides as artistic director.

Conti flutters his fingers poetically and adds, "Paganini composes this as a challenge to perform at an important concert. You know he was fantastic guitarist besides fiddle player, and a wild man."

Toby chooses his moment and takes charge of the stage, waiting for the rustles and throat clearings to subside. Time slows, divides into cells. Toby maps out the first dozen bars in his head, hearing each note ring with precision before he sets hand to fretboard.

Silence.

Now.

No, not yet. Someone is whispering, then a pencil drops and rolls across the floor.

He places his hands over the frets and sound hole, when someone screeches a chair leg.

Toby lowers his hands, flexes, takes another breath, hears nothing but the purr of ventilation, then begins to play.

The piece paws open and it's alive or dead from the first note. Pure sensation — think of uncircumcised skin or newborn rabbits. Toby snorts at such images. He sneers at any image whatsoever; there can be nothing besides the movement of sound through space and time. Soft and velvety turns brittle with a tilt of the wrist; command of tone has always been his forte. Coming up is the presto section, which must go as fast as humanly possible: hold on to your hat. Paganini was a born show-off. Toby stays inside the silky legato until the last possible moment, then lifts his right hand, making the audience wait until he is good and ready. Pause, then fingers snap across the fretboard, nailing chords and runs. Clear sailing from here to the end of the section, then retrace back to the opening theme.

Except he falters.

His fingers speed on, working via muscle memory, but they have a mind of their own. His actual mind scrambles as it chases his darting hands. Cheekbones tighten, sweat strokes his brow: maestro have pity.

Breathe.

Finally, Conti starts to sing and conduct with one hand, working Toby back into the piece, and within a few seconds he's found his way and presses on to the end.

But focus lifted for a microsecond, floated overhead, untethered, mind searching for the recognizable world.

Conti asks, "Your name is Hausner?"

"Yes."

"So hard for German people to achieve true bel canto."

Toby's head jerks up. "Is that all you have to tell me?"

The man smiles evenly. He is used to a certain deference. "No," he says, then adds, "I believe you are really an artist, but —" He holds up a hand. "You are not a hundred percent prepared today."

Tess chirps from her front row seat. "You should have heard him play when he was a kid."

Conti studies Toby. "But you are not such a kid now."

Pry open the lid of his coffee cup and let out a yelp: slashed finger from the ragged edge of plastic. Toby watches with dismay as a sizz of blood appears on the tip of his index finger where skin squeezes frets. Race to the bathroom of Tim Hortons and run cold water over the injured finger for a full ten minutes, the ganglia of nerve endings tying off, retreating. Blood colours the water crimson, then pink, then less pink, until finally it runs clear.

Conti said, "You must over-prepare, then set the piece aside for a week or two." But who has the luxury of time?

At home Jasper presses the wounded finger to his lips. "Will you still be able to play?"

"Sure," Toby says.

"Things are moving very quickly with you."

Toby tugs his finger away. "After years of slow."

Pained look. "Is that what you call our lives together, Toby? Slow?"

To a romantic there might be something ecstatic in the idea of a breakdown. Toby knows that his shipwreck caused only pain, though he'll point out that he never heard voices that were not his own, nothing borrowed from radio waves. It was a function of overwork, ecstasy minus key proteins and water.

After the Paris episode, where he was rescued by his worried father, Klaus, and taken home, Toby landed in the halfway house where a man called Jasper worked. Every Monday, Jasper corralled Toby to fill out his PAS, personalized activity schedule, the chart that broke down each day into segments: brush teeth, dress, make bed, attend day program. Toby would grumble at the tedium of it all, yet it was reassuring to tick off tasks of normalcy. The schedule saved him, he will admit on certain days, for it turned out that life skills were just what he was missing. It was the lack of such skills that had landed him in hot water, forgetting to eat, wash, take a crap. He'd fallen into abstraction.

SIX

JASPER'S THURSDAY NIGHT GROUP IS A TOUGH CREW: PASSIVE-aggressive types who nod along in agreement, then ignore every aspect of the document they create together. Sometimes he's fooled, thinking he's getting through as he watches them dutifully take notes, but they have no intention of compliance. One is Ashok, survivor from the virus in its first round, an Emergency Room physician who's become Mister Genial, bobbing his head in agreement to every suggestion, born to please. Hard to believe he was once sewing up the entrails of trauma victims, a finger pressed to some essential artery. He's almost mended physically, just a little residual swelling in the brain that will take months to heal.

"First we devise —" Jasper scribbles on the white board "— a set of modules for personal hygiene. Who will start us off?"

A voice ventures, "Brush teeth?"

Jasper writes this down, marker squeaking in the institute's activity room.

"Next?" he prompts, staring encouragingly at the physician, a handsome man whose salt-and-pepper beard is impeccably groomed. "There is the business of getting dressed, yes? Making sure tops and bottoms follow in logical sequence — no wacky plaid and floral combos."

This always gets a titter.

Jasper waits, but there are no more volunteers. "We break each task down into its components," he says, and waits a beat for someone to pitch in.

At last a voice pipes up: "Underwear."

"Socks," says another.

"Pantyhose," says Amy, a cop suffering from a terrible concussion.

"Excellent," says Jasper, scribbling these suggestions on the board. "How about trousers, skirt, shirt, or blouse ..." The list is dauntingly long. Everyone here suffers short-term memory loss.

When Toby takes on one of the Bach partitas, he breaks the piece down into its smallest sequences, learns each in turn, then pulls it together. He says he'll start with a single note, even less — sometimes the silence before the note begins.

"Brush your nose," Ashok calls out. "Blow your nails! We will assemble all clothing into a pile and burn it!" He flops back in his chair, out of breath.

Jasper stiffens. Sometimes this happens, a fizz of resistance to the labour of reconstructing what was once second nature. The man is angry at himself, at the disease, at what he's lost.

Jasper stays calm and reassuring, making sure the session doesn't get derailed by the outburst. "Humour is a tool against fear," he tells them.

Everyone has turned to stare at Ashok whose large brown eyes blink. "First we brush our nose, then we direct attention to footwear," he calls out again, though this time with less fervour. "Feet are alive, amphibious." His face darkens. Mr. Genial is taking a break. "This class is folly," he adds, touching his throat as if coaxing the words out of his larynx. Then Ashok jumps to his feet where, struck by a wave of vertigo, he sways and grabs the back of his neighbour's chair. Everyone is alarmed now, waiting for Jasper to take charge.

Approaching the doctor, Jasper gently lifts the man's elbow and guides him out of the room, down the hall to an empty office.

"Sit down, please," he says, and doesn't let go until Ashok is safely seated. Then he pours water into a paper cup and places it in the doctor's shaking hand. Crouching so that their faces are level, he asks, "May I leave you here for a short time?"

Ashok nods bleakly and drinks. Water dribbles down his chin. Poor man isn't ready for any of this, the class and the unfamiliar surroundings. He should be back in the residential rehab facility. Jasper will write this in his report.

He leaves his client and returns to the activity room, shutting the door behind him. Everyone is sitting exactly as he'd left them, notebooks on laps, and Jasper gets the idea that no one has uttered a word in his absence. The teenager squirms, moving his sneak-ered feet in circles on the polished floor. He's J.J., ex-gang member whose memory loss is a result of a bullet raging through his pre-frontal cortex. He's lucky to be alive but will dispute this.

Jasper forces a sprightly tone. "We'll pick it up from where we left off."

The rest of the session won't go well. This group can't learn in fragmented segments. Concepts must be blended together in a single uninterrupted time period.

"Righto," says Jasper. "We've gotten dressed, brushed our teeth. What next?"

"I don't want to be here," rises a lament from the other side of the door. This is followed by muffled conversation, a sharp protest, then the door pops open and Luke enters with Ashok trailing behind.

Everyone in the activity room sits up straight. Finally, some-thing interesting is happening.

"Can you tell me why this man has been ejected from your session?" Luke demands.

Jasper takes a deep breath. "Ashok hasn't been ejected. He appeared to be upset, so I suggested he take time out."

Luke forms a tight, unconvincing smile. "Is this normal protocol?"

Jasper won't stoop to arguing in front of clients. "I did what seemed appropriate under the circumstances."

A dozen pairs of eyes follow him, then Luke.

"I would suggest it's the business of this group to engage each client according to his or her needs," Luke says, seizing Ashok's arm. "Why don't you take your seat, Doctor?"

Ashok seems uncertain, so Luke adds, "I'm sure you have a great deal to contribute." Sharp glance toward Jasper. "Dr. Mishra is head of ER at York Central." Accent on "is."

Jasper returns his gaze. "As I'm well aware."

"Dr. Mishra worked on the front lines."

This is true. Jasper read the referral.

"He's one of our city's heroes," Luke adds, performing an actual little bow toward Ashok, who looks baffled by the gesture.

Jasper cuts in. "Let's continue our review of morning tasks." His marker hovers over the board as Ashok shuffles to his chair and sits down. "Shall we turn our attention to breakfast?"

Luke reluctantly leaves, but Jasper knows he hasn't heard the last of it.

One of the early symptoms of Toby's mother's illness was her odd way of repeating phrases. "I read an interesting article about knitting with dog hair," Karen would say, then immediately add, "I read an interesting article about knitting with dog hair." She started to wear double layers of clothing and even sported false eyelashes times two.

"I am a foil to your father," she stated. "A foil. To your father."

No one would argue with this. The more rigid Klaus proved himself to be the more dramatic her response. Karen was the one who taught Toby to stand on his head. This was during the period when he was cutting classes and sneaking out to get high.

"Open your heart," she commanded, hiking him up by the ankles.

He complied, hoping to save her by strict obedience.

"Pop goes the weasel!" she said, laughing when he tumbled to the floor during that first effort. He laughed, too, relieved that she'd said it only once.

The more vague their mother grew the more organized Klaus became. He took over her old jobs, shopping, cooking, signing the boys' report cards, and meeting with their teachers. They resented him for all this. The way they saw things Klaus had tucked their sweet mother into a cradle of fragility.

"Don't say anything that will cause her to worry," Klaus would warn, as if she were a teacup full to the brim and the slightest movement might cause a spill.

Klaus would hover while the boys brushed their teeth, satisfied only when they spat blood into the sink. "Not hard enough" was his mantra. He'd fix his eyes on Karen as she glided aimlessly from room to room, and when she stayed in the bathroom too long, he'd knock on the door and ask: "Everything okay in there?"

She began to leave oracular messages written in lipstick on her mirror, an idea picked up from movies.

> *Fools' names and fools' faces*
> *Always appear in public places.*

Worry crackled through their days like summer lightning. Sometimes Klaus left the house and the boys were put in charge of their mother, who usually stayed upstairs watching sitcoms while shelling ballpark peanuts, leaving termite hills of debris. Toby can still hum along to the theme songs of the decade. His mother had a true, sweet voice, and until she got sick she joined the singalong *Messiah* with the symphony every Christmas. She had the ears of a bat and could hear a spoon tap a glass clear across the room, then tell you the note hit was C sharp.

Toby was well into his punk phase, plaid pants tucked into combat boots, when their lives changed forever. He and Felix came home from school that Monday afternoon, and their father was already waiting in the kitchen. That was unusual. As a science teacher, he usually stayed late to give his students extra help.

"Your mother isn't here," Klaus said.

Felix idly picked a plum off the plate and began to eat it.

"She's moved to a facility where she'll be well taken care of." Klaus waited for them to say something, and when the boys just stared, he continued, "We're lucky to find such a wonderful place." He kept nodding, as if he was trying to convince himself that what he was saying was true.

The brothers pounced. Whose idea was this? Did Mama really want to leave them?

Klaus raised his hands, palms up. "What did you expect me to do?"

Felix sped off to his karate class, while Toby fled to his room, to his guitar. That was the year Felix got suspended for taking a knife to school.

It took Toby a full week to screw up the courage to visit his mother at Lakeview Terrace. What was she doing with all these old people using walkers and wheelchairs? She sat on the edge of her bed, wearing her beautiful black-and-red silk kimono, looking as if she wasn't sure what she was going to do next. When she saw him, her face lit up. She felt tiny in his embrace, and he shuddered, feeling her rib cage press against his. He'd rescue her, spirit her off, he thought, but after a moment she pushed him away.

"Don't worry, old bean," she said. "I'll soon get used to it here."

Then it came. "Soon get used to it here," she repeated in the same sunny tone.

Don't do that, he wanted to plead. He was certain it was repetition that had landed her here, and if she could just quit, the whole business would settle down.

She tousled his spiky hair. "You'll come and see me often, won't you?"

"Of course, Mama." And he meant to.

The old lady in the next bed turned over and farted.

"That's Mrs. Creeley," his mother said. "Used to teach piano. You must talk to her one day, being a fellow musician."

Toby stared in horror at the hump under bedclothes, the tufts of white hair.

"A fellow musician," his mother added dreamily, patting him on the knee.

She was the only one who liked his punk getups, being partial to costumes herself, hence the silk kimono.

SEVEN

THE VIRUS HAS GONE INTO HIDING. NO NEW CASES SINCE LAST week. The city unfolds in sections like an origami crane, and the restaurants and concert halls fill with cautious, then celebratory patrons.

Competition departure day looms, and Toby is restless as a cat. He imagines himself stepping onto the Montreal stage an hour before showtime for an acoustic check. He hears himself run through sections of his program, listening to notes bounce off empty seats and bare walls, then imagines how it will sound later, with an audience soaking up the music. Ears funnel in sound and dampen it, dermal upholstery.

Guitar Choir is in a tizzy of excitement. Toby has just broken the news that he will miss next week's session due to the competition. Pamela bombards him with questions: "What will you play? Are you nervous? Will you come back to us?" She looks cranky; she doesn't like being the last to know things.

The prospect of slinking back here without having made even the semifinals is so appalling that Toby tells himself that no matter what happens, he will not, cannot, return to his old life. He can hardly bear to look at them, feeling he's already betrayed their loyalty.

Denise says, "We're rooting for you," and Toby catches the pensive look on her face. Maybe she's guessed what he's thinking.

Matthew, polishing his instrument with a special chamois, says wistfully, "Will it be folly or will it be grace?"

Is he quoting someone, or just himself?

Tristan offers, in his circumspect way, "To pray, if you think it will help."

As they flock to the door and watch him head down the street, Toby understands that he is entering a world they can only dream of.

A day later Toby wheels his suitcase down the front steps of the townhouse, swinging his guitar over one shoulder, then pauses to look back at Jasper who stands in the doorway in his dressing gown. The streetlights are still burning off morning fog, and a feral cat mooches through the garbage.

Toby stares at the rumpled face of his lover who is making a big effort not to appear worried. Jasper seems almost old in this light, skin beginning to slacken at the chin despite a rigorous diet and exercise routine. This is the man who saved him, sorted him out.

"Got your toothbrush?" asks Jasper. It's a joke. He's mocking his own fussy nature.

Toby sets his luggage down and moves back to the stoop where he captures Jasper in a hug. As their bodies mesh, he feels the tick-tock of heart against heart, impossible to tell whose is whose.

"I'll be thinking of you," Jasper whispers in his ear.

"Of course you will."

But will Toby be thinking of Jasper? If luck holds — no, for it is crucial that he maintain focus on performance. With perfect timing the cab draws up, thanks to Jasper's reminder call placed fifteen minutes ago.

As Toby picks up his luggage and climbs into the taxi, Jasper can't help saying, "I've got to level with you. I don't think this adventure is wise."

Toby pretends not to hear. They've been through this a dozen times.

Jasper tiptoes up to the open window. "You're really staying in a dormitory?"

"Sure, why not?"

"Because you're an adult and adults don't stay in dormitories. You require a decent mattress, peace and quiet, good linen — all amenities lacking in such premises."

"What *you* require," Toby points out.

Jasper isn't in a mood to be corrected. He passes through the open window a boxed lunch he'd prepared the night before. "Healthier than the dreck they serve in trains."

As the vehicle pulls away, Jasper shrinks from sight in the rearview mirror. Not that Toby notices, for his eyes are already set on the road ahead. It is Jasper who watches himself disappear, a clenched figure in a blue dressing gown, waving.

EIGHT

ANOTHER DAMN LEAK IN THE PLUMBING. NOTHING WORKS in this godforsaken house. Manuel Juerta, a semi-patriot until three months ago, curses the decaying faucet, then the entire crumbling country that it is his misfortune to live in. He's been jettisoned by his wife from their perfectly serviceable house — to this piece of shit with no view of the Malecón He twists the ancient faucet, and a dribble of water appears at last — *un milagro!* — indoor plumbing, the latest invention. He splashes his furry face, brushes his teeth, then waits with cruel patience until his glass fills with water, then embarks on the morning gargling routine, making plenty of noise, since Lucia isn't here to object. It's still early, judging by the sharp light latticing through the blind. He can hear the usual cacophony of vendors selling their wares, bicycles grinding past on the pavement, and the occasional diesel-spewing *camella*, the so-called camel bus that takes state workers to their jobs.

The steady rhythmic thump on the other side of the apartment wall is Señora Pineda, pumping her treadle sewing machine for her off-the-books tailoring business that she operates when she isn't teaching English.

Manuel Juerta is not always in such a foul mood. He's generally thought to be an ebullient fellow, one of the lucky ones, which he was until recently. He spits into the corroded sink. The air reeks of mould in this cramped bachelor's box on the edge of downtown.

Visa trouble.

Sometimes a man's whole existence comes down to two miserable words, one gut-churning phrase. His current difficulty is apparently due to a quartet of nationally trained gymnasts on tour in western Canada who hopped off their trapeze into the waiting arms of the local do-gooders: welcome to the land of opportunity and bottomless stew pots. Manuel grabs his briefcase, courtesy gift from that stint as guitar competition judge in Caracas. Such a generous professor couple hosting his stay, room with attached bathroom, a local woman cooking mounds of food, much of which would get tossed to the dog at the end of the evening. He'd even played for them, a short solo recital, Ponce and then Rodrigo, the great blind composer from Valencia.

Best of both worlds is what Manuel inhabited until three months ago. He'd return home, when he was still permitted to live in his real home, after recitals or teaching and judging duties, with his pockets crammed full of dollars, ready to convert them into the national CULs, and a suitcase bursting with clothes, toiletries, electronic gizmos, which Lucia and her avaricious sisters would dive into the moment he entered the house. Within an hour the black market lines would be humming.

All this appears to be in the past tense. Manuel blames the gymnasts for the immediate difficulty, but as he tears through the flat, packing sheet music into his briefcase, he knows there's more to it, this visa denial. He pours the last of the raisin bran into a bowl and eats quickly. Even his modest addiction to this breakfast cereal won't continue. And he's out of milk, an irritating situation, given the fact that Lucia's fridge will be stuffed with dairy products and will remain icy cold, since she keeps the appliance plugged in day or night with no heed to energy conservation — thank her resort-working nephew Eric for this — and it doesn't hurt that her parents are inner circle, and that Gabi, their youngest daughter, is now receptionist at the city's swankiest hotel. They don't check her pockets when she leaves work — not a daughter of Lucia and Manuel Juerta.

The *conservatorio* is his second home — maybe his first home now. It's located at the north end of Avenida Simón Bolívar in a once-stunning colonial building, now propped with wooden beams at significant junctures so it won't collapse and kill them all. Today he arrives, ducking cyclists on the road outside, waving a beleaguered hi to Teresa, who stands guard against nothing every day, grabs a bun from Leticia, the girl with the red apron, nods at the gang in the office who labour over an ancient computer, then strides through the still-elegant courtyard surrounded by classrooms from which the usual sound salad emits: fiddles and horns and strings and the rat-a-tat of drums. He loved all this when he could leave at will to embark on his international adventures, then return bestowing gifts of strings and metronomes to his grateful students. They would soak up his stories of the world outside their island, his hobnobbing with the greats.

Lucia, never God's gift to men, has decided that Manuel is evil incarnate, and she seeks to destroy him. This is not hyperbole.

He kicks open the door of room 117 at the back of the building. His office is bright and relatively well furnished with a desk and chair, floor-to-ceiling bookcases full of imported sheet music and texts, along with multiple copies of his own opus, *Guitarra clásica: un método completo*, which still seeks an English translator.

The first student of the day knocks cautiously on the door, and Manuel roars "Enter" in English. He was brushing up on the language last night when he received the catastrophic news that he was not only denied entrance into Canada but would not be allowed to leave his own country.

Alberto steps in, a slight fellow with a long nose, aristocratic brow, and excellent teeth. Manuel thinks a lot about teeth these days, since his right cuspid was pulled a month ago and his dentist informed him there were no false teeth to be found until some vague date in the future. He might as well get used to a gap-toothed smile. Better not to smile at all.

His student clears his throat. "Mama tells me I should switch to clarinet so I can play in the National Touring Orchestra."

Sensible boy.

He feels heat flood his face. "Our separation has nothing to do with my profession."

She shrugs. "Perhaps it's easier now for you to leave us."

"Is that what you think?"

She says nothing.

"Have you been putting ideas in the heads of certain employees of the state?" he asks.

"Why should they listen to me?"

She always does this, answers a question with another question.

"I have no life without my connection to the musical world," he says, staring into a face so familiar that he could map out each crease and freckle by heart. She's changed in twenty-two years, become leaner, and those violet-flecked eyes seem duller. Life wears them all down, even the privileged few.

"My parents are coming over soon," she says.

Manuel takes a step backward and nearly falls down the stone staircase. Lucia smiles, and he can't help himself. He smiles, too. It's no secret that her parents believe he's Lucia's big mistake. She even reaches out a hand to rescue him, and they touch, her skin still soft after all these years.

No, that's a lie. Her skin is rough and dry, like his.

A baby giggles in the arms of a passing girl. The street is lively this time of the evening, last of the workers coming home, some toting packages, many with nothing. A few old-timers hang out on the sea wall drinking rum from bottles in paper bags. There is music, of course, but not the kind tourists crave, no picturesque ancients singing *son* or strumming homemade guitars: this is Mexican pop music blasting from someone's radio. Señora Castilla, who lives in the flat next door, comes out with her watering can to freshen up her window boxes. Seeing Manuel and Lucia, she waters quickly and hurriedly withdraws. She is a sensitive woman, a teacher of post-colonial studies at the university.

Lucia lets go of his hand, then steps out onto the porch with him. Her expression has changed. She looks afraid, and when she speaks, it is in a whisper.

"Eric is in trouble."

This is the helpful nephew, a brilliant boy who already manages kitchen operations at one of the sprawling beach resorts.

"How?" Manuel asks. He sees the vein in her neck pulse. She is wearing a cotton sweater and jeans rolled up mid-calf. The tiny stud earrings were a present he brought back from Italy.

He touches her thin shoulder. This is like old times, when he would comfort her through her nervous episodes.

"He's been apprehended," she says.

"Yes?"

"It's complicated."

"Yes?"

She tosses her hands into the air. "A total squalid mess."

"I'm sorry."

"We're all sorry, Manuel."

"Can your parents help?"

"Of course, they're making submissions to certain people. They're coming over tonight to discuss tactics." She checks her watch, the fake Bulova he bought off a street vendor in Paris. "But because the hotel is owned by Spain, our government ..." She doesn't need to fill in the rest of the sentence. Manuel understands perfectly: the state must show itself to have no patience with illegalities or the resorts might disappear, leaving the island even more destitute.

"What has Eric been accused of?" he asks. The list of possibilities is long: diverting kitchen supplies being the most obvious. Manuel has sampled its offerings many times. But it could be something nastier, procuring women for conventioneers, or robbing suppliers.

"I can't say," Lucia tells him.

That is how he leaves her, a small-framed woman, no longer young, standing in the doorway of the house they once shared.

Guillermo is no help. Manuel's colleague at the Foundation for Filmic Arts stares at the computer screen, hand on mouse, editing his latest masterpiece. "I need two more minutes of music," he says. "Ending's reshot and your score doesn't work."

"Write me a letter I can take to the Department of Immigration," Manuel urges, while his friend presses a key, and swoosh, the figure on the monitor disappears.

Mónica saunters in, holding two mugs of coffee. "You look terrible," she says, giving Manuel a quick once-over. Then to Guillermo: "Delete the reaction shot. No, next one." She leans over his shoulder, sipping one coffee and recklessly setting the other next to the precious keyboard. She points at the screen. "Too obvious. Flash back to the kid instead." She straightens and says to Manuel, "Have you brought us the final two minutes?"

Guillermo, without lifting his gaze from his work, says, "I just told him about it."

Manuel leans against the concrete block wall — this building was built during the Soviet era — pressing his shoulder blades against a poster advertising Neptuna's most recent triumph, a documentary about the revival of certain antique grain cultivation processes. He moans. "No one is listening to me!"

"You're in a state," Mónica observes.

"My flight for Montreal takes off on Monday, but they've denied me a visa."

Guillermo finally twists around on his stool and glances at his colleague. "Tough luck, brother." He uses the resigned tone that is much in fashion.

They work in a converted elementary school classroom that used to be open air on one side but has long since been boxed in. Guillermo and Manuel rigged up the trestle table that the computer rests on.

"Tough luck?" Manuel snorts. "It's a catastrophe!" He hovers over his friends, smelling the coffee no one has offered. "I could be blacklisted, never able to leave. The only reason I can survive in this backwater is because I get out whenever I please."

"Lucky you," Mónica says.

Guillermo is silent.

"You two are used to being stuck here," Manuel rails on. "But I'm not. They might as well haul me off in a straitjacket." He knows how this sounds, but he's too upset to care. They're jealous of his privileges, but he's earned them, and through his travels he brings honour to the country.

Guillermo taps on the keyboard, slurps coffee, and peers at the screen, which is fast-forwarding through the garden scene: Papa and the boy find the bleating goat, look up to see a man with knife in hand. This is where Manuel composed a sprightly arrangement of the children's song "Señora Santana, Why Does the Boy Cry?"

"I've been invited to attend festivals in Madrid, Seville, Lyon, and Zurich next year," he says. "It's inconceivable that they can hold me prisoner here."

He waits for reassurance.

Mónica, without glancing up, repeats, "Inconceivable."

Her tone, inflected with irony, enrages Manuel. "Lucia is gouging me. She must have her trips to the massage therapist and special shoes for arch support. I can't possibly survive on the pittance of my conservatory salary." Realizing that his colleagues are forced to survive on a similar pittance, he quickly adds, "When I go abroad, don't I bring you domestic items and computer software and —" He searches for an item that made Guillermo shout with joy. "This external hard drive, super-megabyte —"

"Which got fried in last week's electrical seizure," Guillermo reminds him.

Blackouts are a regular occurrence, often followed by a sudden disruptive surge as power returns. Mónica rubs her husband's shoulders. "*Pobrecito.*"

Again the resigned tone. It is this attitude that Manuel must regularly flee, or he, too, will be drawn into the sinkhole of passivity.

An idea strikes him, an old one, many times courted and just as many times denied: this time if he wangles a visa, he may never return. It would serve them all right for not appreciating his talents. With Lucia on the warpath, recent life has been a misery. Their daughter is well placed as receptionist at the hotel. His job here as father and husband is over.

Mademoiselle Gagnon from Montreal has been trying to reach Manuel all day. "Is something wrong with your phone down there?" she asks.

Manuel has to laugh. He's talking over the din of late-afternoon conversation at Café Bohemia, a place frequented by tourists that features an operating telephone.

"We've pulled it together," Mademoiselle Gagnon tells him. Her French accent is musical, sliding into his ear like *Afternoon of a Faun*. The knot in his stomach finally begins to uncoil.

"Thank you," he says after a moment, realizing he is close to weeping. His future is in the hands of others. The patrons of the café, mainly tourists and local guides, watch with interest. He's become a familiar figure in recent days, darting in and out to use the phone.

Mademoiselle Gagnon says, "Of course you must finalize things on your end."

Manuel doesn't feel a shred of guilt about Eric's arrest. Until three months ago when Lucia booted Manuel out of the house, his only involvement in Eric's shenanigans was eating the roast chicken that magically appeared on his plate several times a week. Since then it's been rice and beans with a scoop of Chef Ana's unnamed fish when he's desperate for protein. He pictures Montreal's shiny streets and bustling bistros, a riot of flavours. Fortunately, he's been granted a generous per diem. His attendance as judge at the festival guarantees a higher quality of competitors. This is not vanity but simple fact.

Manuel spends the following day cycling between state *funcionarios* in their cubicles, watching them laboriously type the necessities of his case. None seems to share his sense of urgency. Of course, he hides this urgency by sitting with an arm slung over the back of the chair and legs crossed. One must be slightly haughty and never reveal a hint of desperation.

He is sent to the next office and the next carrying his growing dossier and multiple copies of his passport until he ends up in a tiny cabinet where a young man earnestly dabs at a cracked keyboard and stares at the monitor that remains blank. Without speaking to Manuel, he disappears for twenty minutes and returns with a plug-in hard drive retrieved from another office, but soon realizes there is no cord to attach it to his own computer and begins to rummage around in a box at his feet, pulling out wires and cords and tossing them onto the floor. Tourists find such poverty quaint, along with the crumbling facades of the once-noble colonial buildings.

Manuel clears his throat. "I have business with you," he reminds the functionary who has worked himself into a sweat. Startled, the young man pulls himself up. He is light-skinned, almost blond, with blue eyes. Manuel has copperish hair, what's left of it, and freckled skin.

The lad grabs his file, then begins to scrutinize each page for an interminable length of time.

Manuel shifts in his seat. "I understand there will be a further tariff to pay," he says with the proper mix of pride and obsequiousness.

The young man rises from his chair, closes the door, and returns, pressing his buttocks against the edge of the desk. Now he is facing Manuel.

"Fifty dollars," he says, meaning the convertible pesos worth twenty-five times the national currency.

Without moving a hand toward his wallet, Manuel says in an equally calm tone, "Shall we say thirty?"

The youth considers, drops onto his chair, and puts his feet up on the desk. "Forty-five." He stares at the ceiling, the picture of patience.

Manuel peels off the bills and slides them under a coffee cup on the desk.

Suddenly, the computer screen springs to life, and Manuel spots his own name printed on the monitor. A rash of typing ensues, then without a word the functionary disappears from the room, clutching an ancient floppy disk and leaving Manuel to cool his heels for another twenty minutes. Will there be another "tariff" to pay? He's half asleep in the airless little room when his tormentor returns with a freshly printed form.

"Your visa," the youth announces, handing the paper to Manuel with reluctance. The precious *tarjeta blanca*.

NINE

MARK'S UNCLE HAS FINALLY PUSHED OFF. OUT THE DOOR HE goes, spry as a bird, tossing his vinyl suitcase down the front steps, not bothering to thank Lucy or Mark for their hospitality, nor offer a farewell to the boys who'd already left for school. His forehead shines as he smiles. In his mind he's already disappeared from this sorry excuse of a city. The limo idles curbside, plumes of exhaust meeting autumn air while Uncle Philip's suit jacket whips in the wind.

He wears no overcoat, having left this bulky item stashed in the cupboard down the hall. It is an unnecessary burden in the torrid climate he is about to enter. He will return in six months to reclaim it. Mark's uncle insists on limousine service to Pearson International because he likes plenty of leg room before the arduous flight to Southeast Asia. Of course, he was too cheap to pitch in for food or wine when he stayed here en route.

Lucy feels a faint spasm of guilt on thinking these thoughts, for it was Uncle Philip, music lover extraordinaire, who quite unexpectedly mailed her a cheque last year with the note: "If you're going to enter this competition, you'll need an excellent teacher. I hope this will help."

Thanks to him she's been working with the divine Goran.

Lucy watches the driver fit suitcase into trunk, then hold the passenger door open for Uncle Philip who, once settled, rolls down the window and calls out in his sunny voice, "Back in the spring, dear."

As if she'll be counting the days.

She shuts the front door, twists the lock, and breathes clove-scented aftershave mixed with breakfast bacon, a now-familiar brew. With luck there will be no interruptions until four o'clock when the twins amble home from high school. Her husband, Mark, works as a security guard at the Art Gallery of Ontario and doesn't get off shift until suppertime. It's his dream job, or so he claims. He loves standing in the eighteenth-century room surrounded by lacquered paintings by little-known artists, making sure school kids don't jostle or touch anything, or some jackass doesn't take a knife to the brittle canvases. He claims to thrive on the long stretches of nothing, punctuated by bursts of activity. It gives him time to think — about what, Lucy has no idea. She pictures him standing guard in front of the portrait of some long-forgotten Cornish merchant whose manicured hand rests on a globe.

Uncle Philip is on his way to Thailand. He flies first to Toronto from his home in Halifax to break up the trip, and he'll stay here again during his return, only then he will be tanned and relaxed rather than snippy with excitement as he was during this visit. It's Lucy who gets roped into preparing hot breakfast and lunches because she is the one with a flexible schedule. Uncle Philip sits at the kitchen table and reads her copy of *Harper's*, dripping sugary coffee over its pages, making early-morning throat-clearing noises. He combs his hair over the butter dish, and after eating, holes up in the bathroom for a marathon flossing session. She hears pops of loosened string and later finds herself sponging dislodged food particles from the mirror.

Yet Uncle Philip was the one who slipped an arm over her shoulder last night and said, "I have great faith in you, my dear."

But now he's gone, they are all gone, and Lucy has the house to herself. Beginning at noon she will practise her guitar. No point in trying to do this once the boys come home. They play their own music: Megadeth and Slayer at a deafening volume, and bound around the kitchen shoving drawers in and out and snapping open the fridge door.

The competition starts in four days, and she figures she's as ready as she'll ever be. The idea of it sends a thrill of anticipation through her body, so intense she can hardly stay upright. Twenty-five years of playing weddings and bar mitzvahs, reaching an age when most women accept "their limitations," as her own mother puts it, and she is charging into the centre of the cyclone.

Goran told her, "Just play your best."

"But is that good enough?"

Bemused, he looked at her and said, "Good enough for what? You make music, people listen. Why make it more complicated?"

First task is to collapse the fold-out bed where Philip parked his slim and limber self for the past four nights, get rid of all signs of the guest who will soon disappear into the steamy coastal villages of Thailand. He'll return, chipper as always, sporting a grizzled beard and tanned hands, the creases of his palms a dental white: seventy-six years old and going strong.

It infuriates Lucy that Philip refuses to make up his own bed, which means putting the couch back to rights so it won't stick halfway across the living-room floor. She'd asked him to do it several times, as had Mark, and they'd even demonstrated how. Uncle Philip professed great interest in the task, marvelled at the ingenuity of the sofa's mechanism, and never tried it on his own, not once.

Lucy tosses his pillows and blankets onto a chair, then begins to yank off the sheets. She feels something trapped in there, tangled in the bedding. A brisk shake tosses up a manila envelope, and Lucy curses, thinking he's left behind his passport and soon she'll receive a panicked call from the airport and have to drive up there in morning rush hour to perform the rescue. So much for running through her program. So much for dipping into the series of right-hand *rasqueado* exercises, crucial for the first compulsory piece. She dangles the envelope over the exposed mattress and watches its contents slide out.

A series of black-and-white snapshots tumbles onto the bed, images of boys half-dressed or almost entirely without clothes. Boys — she holds the photographs by their edges — about the same age as the twins, approximately fifteen, with developed bodies, yet still lean and innocent-looking. Slick dark hair — undoubtedly Asian.

She carries the photos over to the window and tilts them toward the morning light. Are they professionally posed shots, something one might pick up in a shop, or — and here she feels her mouth pucker — are they Philip's own handiwork, using his vintage Leica?

The top picture is at first ambiguous. A teenage boy stands by a market stall, wearing a decorated robe, one hand cradling a melon. His face is expressionless, although he appears to be gazing at something, or someone, to his left. It's his face that draws Lucy's attention, for he is extraordinarily beautiful, high cheekbones and large eyes possibly outlined by kohl. He holds himself upright, shoulders thrown back and chin tilted.

Oh.

Now she gets it.

The robe has swept open just a little, enough to let an erect penis peek out, sly yet knowing. Suddenly, that castaway glance and jutting chin assume new meaning. Uncle Philip's whorled fingerprints are all over the emulsion, and now, so are hers. She thinks of Philip lying on the hide-a-bed while the rest of them sleep, staring at this picture and — well, yes.

She doesn't drop the photograph. If anything, she holds on to it more tightly. The image looks posed and at the same time carelessly set up, with rudimentary lighting. The exposure is grainy, very fast film that pixilates the subject's skin and robe. The photos are saturated with the same clove aftershave that lingers in her hallway — spritz of the marketplace. She thinks of Uncle Philip's tapered nails and visualizes his earnest unblinking attention when someone speaks. He'd been, until he retired, chief inspector of restaurants and food-serving sites for Halifax and liked to say, "If you've dreamed it, it exists, and I've seen it."

She always thought this referred to rodent hairs floating in the bouillabaisse.

Has he dreamed these boys, or is he on the way to meet them now, the Airbus ripping across continents of sky while his pale hands tap his trousered knees? He refuses to eat airplane food and packed his own bag of fruit and nuts, mindful of his bowels. He won't bother watching the movie. He has his own theatre playing behind those clear blue eyes.

Lucy lets her dressing gown slide to the floor. Under it she wears an old T-shirt and a pair of Mark's boxers. A man walking a dog on the sidewalk below glances up at her, and looks quickly away.

Then the phone rings. It's Mr. Hyke, vice-principal at the twins' high school.

"Am I speaking to Mrs. Dickie, Charles's mother?"

"Lucy Shaker," she corrects him, not for the first time, and feels her stomach lurch.

"I have Charles here in the office," Mr. Hyke proclaims in his plummy voice. "Perhaps he'd like to tell you why."

She reaches for her mug of cold coffee and sets the photos on the window ledge. Charlie comes on, his voice pitched so low she can hardly make out what he's saying.

"What's up, Charlie?" she asks.

"I seem to have forged this person's signature."

Silence.

"Keep going."

"I seem to have forged this teacher's signature on my skip sheet."

There is muttering in the background, a correction being issued. Lucy is pretty sure she catches the word *seem* spoken with inflection.

"Mr. Hyke says I'm suspended. Just for a day."

"Hang on. You forged whose signature?"

"Leftko. Mr. Leftko."

She never remembers teachers' names. "And he teaches …?"

"Math."

Charlie bombed math. On his midterm report he'd received a single-digit mark.

"Then you better come home," she says, choosing a tone of weary patience but actually feeling a wave of panic. When will she practise? For each day missed, a notch of technique slips from her fingers. "Put Mr. … the vice-principal back on."

"Why?"

"Just do it, Charlie."

A few seconds of transfer, background of PA announcing the track meet, city finals. Imagine, Lucy thinks, having sons who enter track meets.

"Hyke here."

"Will this suspension go on Charlie's academic record?"

"I don't know who else's."

The rage nodule leaps up her brain stem and settles like a pulsing coin behind her eyes. "Has he apologized to the teacher?"

"In a manner of speaking."

"Good," she says firmly. Someone has taken charge of the matter.

She dresses quickly, pulling on jeans, a blouse, and a pair of Mark's sneakers. Now she'll have to hang around all day and monitor Charlie, making sure he doesn't fool with his PlayStation or run off to the park for a toke. Not for the first time, she envies Mark as he issues a soft warning into the hushed museum room: "Please stand back from the painting."

She can hunker down at the computer and do the books for her catering business. Not a chance of practising now, not with the mood she's been zippered into. Who's she kidding — pretending to be a serious musician in her forties puts her on a level with those women in floppy hats who set up easels by the riverbank.

Charlie will arrive in half an hour, dumping his pack in the front hall, ranting about the uselessness of school and how teenagers have no status in society. He will glare, daring her to contradict these obvious truths.

One of the boys in Uncle Philip's pictures sprawls outdoors on a wrought iron bench, leg swung over the opposite knee, hand resting on his inner thigh. He stares into the camera, lips parted, showing even, small teeth. The boy wears only a vest, tossed open to display a smooth torso. His genitals are more or less hidden by the leg position, but he looks as if he might shift any minute — this is the magic of the pose, the source of its tension. In another shot the boy appears to be emerging from a bathroom or sauna, towel slung over one shoulder. Is he scowling? Hard to tell, the lighting is so bad. His complexion is pitted, unless that's just dust on the lens. Uncle Philip needs to spring for a digital camera and Photoshop. The next picture is more intriguing: a boy, perhaps twelve or thirteen, crouches naked on the dirt floor of a shack, his baseball cap twisted sideways. He's smiling, and the smile is friendly and unforced. The pose is unselfconscious, the small genitals hanging like baby fruit. Behind him a woman, possibly his mother, reaches for something high on a shelf.

Lucy shuffles the photographs and stares at them again. What kind of life does Uncle Philip lead over there with these boys, their skin glistening as if oiled? Her own body, she must admit, has seen better days.

Is it so strange to search for beauty?

That's hardly the point, she reminds herself.

Charlie kicks open the front door on the dot of the half-hour, drops his pack, then begins to bustle about the kitchen below, at the same time popping a basketball, an activity that makes the whole house shake. The racket is pure theatre. He's proclaiming that he is in no way ashamed of the day's mishap.

In fact, it's a bonus, because he gets the remainder of the day off. He knows she's up here; he's waiting for her to come down and issue the predictable lecture, which he'll mouth word for word in tandem.

The computer monitor displays a breakdown of prices for the job on Saturday, dinner for eight, three of whom are lactose intolerant. Before each job she determines to earn a higher hourly rate, but somehow it never ends up that way. The twins, Charlie and Mike, hover in the kitchen as she carves the elaborate garnishes that are her specialty: olive rabbits, radish flowers, tomato roses, carrot daisies embedded in aspic, and the boys will say, not inaccurately, that it's this manic attention to the "crap no one eats" that squeezes her profit margin. You can say that about Baroque embellishments, the mordents and trills that decorate the musical line. Yet it is precisely because they serve no purpose but to please the eye that she fusses over her food decorations. She snaps photographs of the spreads before delivery and mounts them in a portfolio to show prospective clients.

Charlie launches into singing "Stairway to Heaven" in his newly developed baritone voice that still thrills him, and drums on furniture until the microwave dings. He's slid a pair of chocolate chip cookies in there, liking the way they go soft and gooey, chocolate oozing onto the glass trivet. Lucy knows he's wondering why she isn't there laying down the law.

She won't mention the photographs to Mark, because he'll want to see them, and Mark is a literal sort of man. He'd insist on shredding them into tiny pieces right away, ensuring they didn't turn up in recognizable flakes scattering down the street.

"Disgusting old goat," they'd agree. Then they'd fret over whether Philip had approached the twins in a creepy way during one of his visits. That might explain Charlie's nosedive at school. And why did Uncle Philip suddenly grow this family feeling after years of nothing more than a UNICEF card sent at Christmas? The visits started three years ago, coinciding with his trips to Thailand, but also with the twins' free fall into puberty.

"Hey." Charlie stands in the doorway of her study, gangly five feet eight inches, shaggy hair, ancient Pixies T-shirt.

She looks up, pretending to be surprised.

"I suppose you're pissed off," he says through an elaborate yawn.

"I suppose I must be."

He squints, suspicious. "You don't sound very."

"Other things are on my mind at this moment, Charlie."

He snorts, knowing better. "Hyke way overreacted."

"Did he now?"

"Lots of kids forge signatures. It's practically a religion at my school."

He waits for her protest. When it doesn't come and she merely taps out a code on the computer, he slaps the wall. "I know what you're doing. You're trying to guilt me by not responding."

"I thought I was trying to print out a menu." She clicks "select all," then "print," and waits for the machine to spit out pages.

Their jeans land in sculpted heaps on the floor, surrounded by key chains with industrial-sized links. When the twins were small, they slept in bunks and tortured each other with hand-held lasers. Now they sleep in futons at opposite sides of the room, though Mike keeps threatening to move to the crawl space in the cellar. Mark nixed the idea because the furnace is on its last legs and quite possibly leaks noxious fumes. The boys love fire. They are always lighting incense or dollar-store candles, then sitting in the darkened room listening to spacey electronic music. Lucy wasn't born yesterday. She knows they smoke pot in there and blow the smoke out the open window, even in the depths of winter. No wonder the heating bill is sky-high. She picked a glass tube off Charlie's desk one day: a crack pipe? Confronted with the evidence, he rolled his eyes and said, "Mum, it's a vapourizer."

"A what?"

Lucy loves it when the boys swoop on her, lifting her high in the air and twirling her about. Somehow she's morphed from being an intimidating mother into this cute miniature Mum, and she never fails to squeal with feigned alarm.

She cleans the house, but not often these days. "My practice time is sacrosanct," she likes to say, and watches everyone, except perhaps Mark, roll his eyes.

Why waste precious moments scrubbing and dusting? They'll only mess it all up, grimy fingers stippling a route along the walls and down the stairwell, clustering around light switches. Her anger as she sprays toxic cleanser and starts to mop contains a heavy overlay of martyrdom, which no one notices. It is, after all, not her actual body they trample over in their mud-caked boots, just floorboards and linoleum, symbolic value nil.

The ideal level of tension while playing guitar is four out of ten. Her teacher for the past year is Goran, a Serb from Sarajevo, once a respected performer, who escaped the city's siege with a piece of shrapnel lodged in his shoulder, hence his teaching career. He likes to lean back in his chair in the conservatory studio and say, "Tell me, how tense now?"

"Seven?"

"I think maybe is nine today. You must feel your spine awaken, like a serpent." He's been studying Kundalini yoga to deal with the trauma of his country's civil war.

TEN

RIGHT HAND "M" FINGER FEELS AS IF IT GOT STUCK IN A CRANK-shaft, thanks to the Montreal humidity. It's an old problem, going back to the day when staff dragged Toby onto the base-ball field for first-base duty. The halfway house was very keen on sports participation. Then some bozo popped the ball to right field where Toby made the heroic leap, landed on his butt and hand, and felt the ominous crunch of ligament. He flexes the finger now, gauging degree of loss of flexibility. He is walking along the buffed corridor of the university building past groups of competitors who huddle in excited chatter. They all seem to know one another. Didn't we meet in Aspen? Brussels? Houston? Barrueco's master class? They hail one another in a mishmash of accents, ignoring Toby who tries to look as if he knows where he's going.

No one is watching, a novel sensation in a competition. He tells himself it is freeing, rather than unnerving. The hall steers left, and he follows the rich fragrance of coffee and baked goods until he reaches the cafeteria with its bistro-style tables. For a moment he stands in the doorway and scans the noisy room. A group of competitors has taken over several tables at the far end, their instruments propped against chairs or lying under-foot. Toby left his own guitar in the locked dorm room. He nods at them, but the gesture is unseen, yet that one glance tells him everything: they are unspeakably young, starting with that baby-faced boy sporting a soul patch and a girl with a shaved head. They might take him for being one of the judges. That's why they've turned to stare and are whispering, trying to figure out who he is in the classical guitar firmament.

Toby throws back his shoulders under the vintage Aerosmith tour shirt. The room's concrete walls are painted yellow with windows running down one side, open on this warm day. It's Indian summer, last gasp before winter closes in. Toby grabs a tray. Because this is Montreal, buttery croissants and salads sprinkled with watercress and crumbled chevre fill the glass shelves — no sign of crap sliced bread or troughs of gravy growing skin. Jasper would approve. Pictures of the Laurentian Mountains decorate the walls alongside sepia-tinged photos of Old Montreal. The girl serving hot dishes sports a neck tattoo and a chain mail bracelet.

"*Bonjour,*" Toby tries after clearing his throat.

She glances up and nods, acknowledging this triumph of linguistics, then says in perfect English, "You here for the guitar festival?"

"Yes." Suddenly, he wants to tell her all about it. "I've entered the competition segment."

"*Fantastique!* I hope you will win." Then she slides a piece of cake onto his tray, waving off his protests. "You must eat sugar for energy, yes?"

Women always want to feed him. They spot his waif-like form and start scouting for calories. He grabs a fistful of cutlery and paper napkins and pays the cashier, another languid beauty, another neck tattoo.

In Paris the musicians jockeyed to sit with him, even older guys: they all wanted to catch some of what was roaring off him, a sensation that now seems remote. He strides to the table in the corner, holding his tray high, offering an enigmatic half-smile. The musicians glance up and see his white tag. White signals competitor. Yellow means judge and blue indicates exhibitor, one of the guys selling instruments or sheet music in the salon.

A man with a thin face and not much hair pulls out a chair. "Join us, my friend. I am Armand Stolz from Frankfurt."

Toby reaches over with his free hand to shake Armand's, then hears the flurry of introductions. He repeats each name in turn, knowing he'll forget them in an instant. Everyone's keyed up, a mixture of jet lag and nerves. The small tables feature candles set in the middle, currently unlit. Toby catches a chair leg with his foot and drags it in, manoeuvring around the bulky guitar cases.

"Hausner? So you must be German also," Armand says, genial in his open-neck shirt and pressed jeans. Crow's feet around his eyes indicate he's not so young.

"That's right," Toby says, blowing into his coffee. "Another Kraut." Right away he wishes he could suck back his words. "German heritage on my father's side but born here in Canada," he clarifies, then realizes he's trying to wiggle out of this very heritage. Klaus, when bombed on schnapps, makes dumb-ass Nazi jokes, trying to dispel any imagined tension. When he's not drunk, he'll moan, "Why do they reduce hundreds of years of German history down to twelve?"

Armand's smile tightens. He knows what's going on.

Toby attacks his salad, peeling back the wrapper. Someone across the table is tittering. The cafeteria doors burst open, and a group of army reservists dressed in fatigues enters and marches toward the food trays without speaking, like monks on retreat. Their convention includes seminars in civil disobedience and emergency disaster management. Toby spotted the schedule posted in the entrance of the building.

Without thinking he polishes the tines of his fork on a paper napkin.

"Fastidious," Armand notes, turning to the others. "Definitely German, yes?"

Trace, the girl with hair shaved close to her skull, sits with her feet drawn up on her chair, resting chin on hands. She's built like a boy, no chest to speak of, sharp features, no hint of makeup. Half a dozen beaded necklaces decorate her long neck, and at the hollow point where neck and sternum meet, a tattooed rose winks.

"Aerosmith?" she says, reading his shirt. "Joke, right?"

"Absolutely not," Toby replies, mouth full of lettuce. He eyes her back. "How old are you?"

"Seventeen."

Jesus. "How long have you been at it?"

She squeezes her knees. "Since I was nine."

"This your first competition?"

"Not counting Kiwanis."

How good can she be? Toby wonders. Then he remembers how good he was.

"Where are you from?" He feels like an elder statesman, drawing out the next generation.

"Gulf Islands."

"What gulf?" Geography isn't Toby's strong suit. Jasper claims that he slept through school, thinking only of music. As proof, he'll ask him to recite the periodic table, and Toby will say, "The what?"

"Off the B.C. coast," she tells him. "I live on the smallest island that has actual people, Martin." She pronounces this *Mar-teen*, the Spanish way.

"Lucky you," Toby says, letting his gaze wander around to take in the others: a Japanese guy wearing a toque, a Russian, a Brit, a blond woman whose name he missed.

"Lots of goats and hippies," Trace says. "The most beautiful place on earth. I miss it already."

It turns out she attends a private arts academy on the mainland instead of a regular high school. She tells Toby this in a voice that pretends not to care, yet she soon lets him know the academy holds a rigorous entrance audition. "Like one in fifty makes the cut."

Toby was like this at her age, craving attention and at the same time brushing it off. "Can't wait to hear you play."

"Really?" She's pleased.

This is where she should echo the sentiment, but it takes time to learn competition etiquette.

Larry is from Austin, a skinny guy who doesn't seem faintly Texan until he opens his mouth and speaks. He's a vegetarian; so much for stereotypes.

"Vegan," he drawls. "Makes me popular with the good old boys." He rests his thumb on his belt buckle, which is shaped like a Fender Telecaster.

Toby guesses he put himself through college playing cover tunes in a bar band, one of the brotherhood. Toby played the Yonge Street strip before he was old enough to drink.

Larry peers at his registration package, leafing through the competitors' bios until he spots Toby's name. "You've been away a piece."

"Eleven years."

Larry whistles and waits for an explanation, but Toby doesn't volunteer one: no point in revealing weakness to this lot. They'll hoover it up, then wait to see him crack.

"I have played in twenty-one competitions," Armand announces.

"How many have you won?" Trace asks.

Armand gazes sternly at her. "Young lady, I have earned one participation in semifinals, and this is my aspiration, to achieve that level again."

"One semifinal in twenty-one tries?" Trace doesn't disguise her astonishment.

Armand gives her a doleful look while Hiro, a guitarist from Osaka, giggles. He sports a metallic toque worn over spiky hair and moves with a self-conscious grace, tilting his head just so, adjusting his collar. Toby studies him, the smooth skin, grey linen shirt. Queer? Too soon to be sure, and there are cultural differences to consider.

Toby bolts down his food. When he's on edge, he can't taste anything and it's a struggle to get it down. But food is fuel, a necessary stoking of the furnace, and it prevents death — a fact he once notoriously forgot.

The cadets pull half a dozen tables together at the other end of the cafeteria and sit with their legs swung out, boots too big to fit beneath. Their voices pitch low, as if they're on a secret mission. Armand eyes them and pulls up his collar, pretending to hide. Toby's the only one who laughs, who gets the joke. The other guitarists chatter about the judges, preferences known and rumoured, and possible prejudices: one is a sucker for the lyric line and lush tone, while another craves brash modern dissonance with flamenco trimmings. Information is ammunition.

"What you must understand," Armand insists, slapping the table with his palm, "is that even a fantastic guitarist can have a bad day. So if you genius people make a mistake onstage, I will be waiting in the wings."

"Juerta's here," Larry says, referring to the eminent judge. "He's not going to be put off by a few wrong notes."

"A few wrong notes," Armand interrupts, "is a catastrophe if —" he lowers his voice "— you cannot instantly recover."

A short silence follows this remark as each musician imagines himself flubbing onstage, spotlight burning.

"Those of us who have been around these events for years, the judges understand how we play, what we can do," Armand says, then leans back, hands clasped over his trim belly.

Toby calculates — twenty-one competitions. The man's been at it for years. He must be well over thirty. Unlike most competitions, this one is open to all ages.

Toby's name, briefly known in classical guitar circles beyond Canada, means zip to this lot. Whatever reputation he once enjoyed has long since disappeared into the ether of flamed-out early promise. It will happen to many of these characters, too, though such a possibility is far from their minds now. They trade news of master classes attended, guitar gods glimpsed in the hallways, luthiers who use traditional fan bracing versus radial. There had been a day when Toby was in the thick of it, and he wipes his mouth with a paper napkin and waits for all this to feel different, more how it was.

At the far end of the table a woman with tangled blond hair smiles at him. When he meets her gaze, she glances away, then back again. Shy? Perhaps. What he can see of her face intrigues him: she must be at least forty and is dressed with some care in a yellow blouse and silver necklace.

"Where are you from?" she mouths.

"Toronto."

She points to her chest and mouths back, "Me, too," then indicates an empty chair next to her. Toby picks up his tray with the remnants of lunch and joins her there.

"Another refugee from the virus," she says in a too-bright voice, then holds out her hand. "Lucy Shaker."

They shake, and he sees milky skin under the framing hair and violet rings under her eyes.

"I know you," Lucy says.

"What?" Unsettled, Toby looks down. Here goes — the moment he's been fearing.

"I heard you play years ago."

He recovers, memory spinning. "Where?" he asks, hoping it wasn't that final recital in Toronto at the Women's Art Association, the show he's mostly forgotten. Legend goes that he interrupted his playing to rant to the audience, then launched into an improv that went on so long that everyone tiptoed away, leaving the rented hall almost empty.

"That church nestled inside the Eaton Centre," Lucy reminds him.

Little Trinity, an urban marvel rescued from the developer's wrecking ball, surrounded by a shopping mall. Toby smiles in relief: that concert was a triumph, broadcast on CBC Radio for its Young Artists series.

"I played Boccherini," he recalls. "The Grand Sonata by Sor and a set of Tárrega."

"You were just a boy."

"I was fifteen."

The table has gone quiet as other competitors eavesdrop.

"You were amazing," Lucy says. "In a world of your own."

"Still am." That old self can seem remote one moment, then reappear in dazzling Technicolor the next.

She waits a beat before asking, "Did you ever stop playing?"

"Never." He senses them leaning in, wanting to hear more. Most are too young to realize that a life contains detours, more detours than highways.

"But you didn't perform?"

"That's right."

He feels their attention burrow in and is grateful when Lucy notes his discomfort.

"What number did everyone draw?" She turns to the group, still speaking in a brittle voice. She's referring to the lottery that determines in what order they will play in the preliminary round, a two-day marathon that will weed out most hopefuls.

"Fifty-one," Toby volunteers.

"Out of sixty?"

"Afraid so."

Lucy winces in sympathy.

"The judges will nod off," Toby says, though he doesn't actually believe this for a minute. His performance will shake them out of their torpor.

"Budapest guy number one," Hiro offers in uncertain English. "He finish early, then practise second round. Lucky guy." He nods several times, confirming this opinion.

"If he goes to a second round," Armand points out.

A cloud passes over the crew as each member enters the possibility of being cut before the real competition begins. Months of work, travel expenses, cocky assurances to those back home …

"I can't worry about it," Toby says, feeling worry creep in, anyway.

"Their ears will be numbed by repetition," Larry adds.

Lucy turns to him and asks, "And you?"

"I drew six." Larry smiles smugly, as if this were an achievement, not merely luck. Drawing an early number gives him ample time to work up his program for the semifinals. Everyone must play the same compulsory pieces plus the killer Mark Loesser sonata composed especially for competition. Finally, each artist gets five minutes to strut a favourite from his own repertoire.

Lucy turns to Trace. "And you?"

"I pulled twenty-something." Her studied indifference is a cover.

No one thinks to ask Lucy what number she drew.

Armand checks his watch. "Important technique workshop in five minutes. Myles Boyer demonstrating cross string ornamentation."

The institute is topsy-turvy, and before Jasper can even hang up his jacket, Rachel, the intern, hands him a stack of papers striped with her highlighter pen. Someone wheels in a monitor so staff can watch the morning press conference. It's Dr. Steve Rabinovitch issuing the latest statistical report and — surprise, surprise — their very own Chairman Luke stands on tiptoe at his side, offering a sober face to the camera. The disease may be gearing up into another round as the virus mutates. They aren't front line here at the institute: Jasper and his staff sweep up after the parade has gone by, caring for survivors after discharge from hospital and the first run of rehab. Despite the fraught word *epidemic*, there have been fewer than eighty cases confirmed in total.

Jasper can't contain a snort when the camera lens flies past Luke. Look at his tidy blond hair and moustache and the way he nods whenever the good doctor makes a point. Luke is small but muscular — a ferret, Jasper decides. Soon as the cameras switch off, Luke will pull out his phone to issue directives that counter every decision they've made the week before. Sirens wail up and down University Avenue. Someone is making a fortune flogging latex gloves and surgical masks.

"Hey, Jasper," Rachel says. "He looks just like you."

Jasper glares. "I'll pretend I didn't hear that."

She's not the first to note the resemblance. It was Luke himself in that first board meeting who hung back when the others left and confided to Jasper: "We're much the same, you and I. Bodes well for our future working relationship."

Soon after, the freshly elected chair fired off a memo declaring that the institute must "prioritize its goals" and "the executive director's role must be redefined within the new context." That would be Jasper, and so he found himself thrown into the contest of his professional life.

Now he looks around at his staff members, who quickly avert their eyes; Chairman Luke has got them thoroughly spooked.

Slurp of cereal. Kettle whistles. Toilet flushes from down the hall. Someone farts. Elaborate humming. Please, not that song from *The Titanic* … is it possible to hear too well?

Toby, lying on the narrow dorm bed, tosses an arm over, but Jasper isn't there, and his bare hand slaps against drywall.

Laugher from the other side of the door: his roommates are bustling into the day. He feels a rush of panic, but it quickly subsides as he recalls that this lot plays in the preliminary round today and he's not up until tomorrow.

That must be Hiro keeping his door open a crack so they can all hear as he charges through the allegro at breakneck pace. An old trick. Kid wants to scare them, make them question their interpretations: will the judges be impressed by such a transparent display of technique?

Sure they will.

But Toby won't be swayed. A more nuanced approach is also effective. There is no finish line, no stopwatch.

Except there is.

At twenty minutes they cut you off, a guillotine chop midway through your soul-baring adagio. Not for the first time, Toby thinks — why the hell am I doing this? Hiro lets out a cowboy whoop when he reaches the end of the piece and gives his soundboard a smack — giddy up. Toby rises from the bed, clad only in his underwear, and stumbles into the hallway, rubbing his eyes.

Each man gets a Spartan bedroom with a cot, a single shelf, and a desk. The shared kitchen doubles as living area. Toby grabs a thin but clean towel off the pile and pads down the hall toward the communal bathroom.

When he returns, his roommates have disappeared into their cells, starting to rip through arpeggio and scale patterns. Still undressed, Toby draws his guitar onto his lap and starts to tune.

Back home, Jasper insists on a morning routine of tea, fruit, and whole grain cereal, the proper balance of nutrients and electrolytes. Today Toby will grab a sugary cinnamon bun from the cafeteria and a double espresso. Meanwhile, Guitar Choir is meeting at the church to run through the Thanksgiving program, and no doubt Pamela and Matthew will duke it out for conducting duties. He twists the tuning pegs, easing a set of new high-tension strings into flexibility. By tomorrow's performance they'll be perfect. Glance out the window to the courtyard where the Hungarian guitarist is pacing the flagstones, hands clasped behind his back. He's due to play in twenty-five minutes.

Howl of anguish inside the pod: Larry.

"Fucking Montreal humidity!"

Toby holds his guitar tightly to his chest: too damn easy to get pulled into the drama of others.

"What is the difficulty?" Armand calls back.

Excitement drills through Toby: another man's calamity might protect him from his own.

"My soundboard split!" Larry cries. "And I'm booked to perform in an hour."

"Let Uncle Armand take a look." There is the sound of footsteps, and a door pushes open, followed by a series of taps as Armand inspects the damage.

"I believe I can fix this small but unfortunate problem," he says. "We use temporary adhesion."

"Yes?" Larry frets. "How?"

"I will press sides together —" A grunt of effort is followed by a click, then tense silence.

Toby leans forward in his seat.

"Better now, yes?" Armand says.

"Maybe," Larry says, hardly daring to hope.

"And because I am organized German, I will obtain a tube of glue from my suitcase."

A friendship is being sealed along with the busted soundboard. Toby lays down a chromatic scale with crisp articulation. He won't allow a hint of longing or loneliness to enter the room.

ELEVEN

IT'S BEEN YEARS SINCE LUCY TRAVELLED ANYWHERE ON HER own. Faced with her departure to Montreal, the twins buried their faces in her shoulder and pretended to sob, then pleaded, "Don't go, Ma. We'll be good."

Despite the clowning, she knew they sort of meant it.

"I've made a buddy," Lucy speaks into the phone. "A sweet fellow with small hands."

"Small hands?" Charlie echoes. "Why are you checking out this guy's hands?"

"Because he's the competition," Mike reminds him.

Phone pressed to her ear, Lucy perches on one of the concrete benches in the courtyard that separates the two dormitory wings. "I'm the oldest person here." A pair of reservists wearing berets and baggy uniforms strides across the yard, shoulders rolled back, spines erect. They can't be much older than the twins, her two wan boys on the other end of the phone. "And I haven't a hope in hell of making it past the first round. All I care is I don't make a fool of myself."

"Whoah, Mum," says Mike. "Sounds like you've already quit."

"Sure does," says Charlie. By his distracted tone, his mother guesses he's texting one of his juvie pals.

Where's Mark? Does he have a clue what's going on in the house?

"Don't be so down on yourself," Mike says in a surprisingly mature voice.

"Ditto," says Charlie. "Crush the opposition."

"I'm sure you're better than most of those crumbs," Mike adds. He's been watching old gangster movies lately.

"Thanks, guys," she says. Then she adds, "Where's your father?"

The boys confer.

"Down cellar," one says.

"Something to do with laundry," adds the other.

"Why aren't you boys doing that?" she says, hearing her voice squawk like the starlings overhead. "Shame on you, letting your dad wash your dirty clothes." Lucy is on her feet now, pushing past the fountain with its murky doughnut of water.

After a brief pause, Mike says, "Don't you have anything better to think about?"

The two judges rise from their chairs when Lucy enters the cramped studio. She bids them good afternoon, noting the glance that passes between them. Who's the old bat? they're wondering. She barely slept, burrowing deep into the hard cot, hearing every sound in the pod and beyond, every clatter of elevator, every siren and screech of brakes. Nina, the Mexican girl on the other side of the residence wall, spent half the night whispering to her boyfriend on her cellphone.

Quick scan of the studio, because Goran's final piece of advice was: "Take time to settle in." She notes the chalkboard with a harmony lesson intact and five empty Styrofoam cups. A piano has been wheeled to the corner.

"You two must be exhausted," she says, lowering her case to the floor and snapping open the latches. She flashes the judges a concerned smile. "What a horror, listening to the same pieces over and over. I'd go mad."

Stop, she tells herself.

Juerta looks pointedly at his watch.

Smyth, the young British judge, keeps yawning as if oxygen-deprived. They just want this to be over, scratch one more name off the list.

Crush the opposition. Charlie's advice darts into the room. Lucy lifts the guitar out of its case, sets it on her lap, and then it happens, a supreme furnace-stoked hot flash, a jolt of hormonal heat funnelled to her extremities, lashed by her now-fiercely beating heart. Her gleaming face must be the colour of the fire alarm set high on the wall. A tremor seizes her hands, and it's all she can manage to adjust the tuning pegs.

So it will be a disaster, a train wreck.

Mark will welcome her home with a sympathetic hug, the boys will be amused by her description of the episode, and life will go on: catering receptions for the association of architects, plucking "Greensleeves" at weekend weddings.

Flames lick both cheeks, then subside.

"What will you play first, dear?" Smyth asks in his London accent.

Dear? She takes a breath. "I'll start with the Mark Loesser."

"Second movement only," Juerta says, glancing again at his watch.

She is surprised. "You don't want me to start at the beginning?"

"Not necessary."

The allegretto is a bitch to launch into without the first movement lead-in. If she'd known, she would have requested to begin with the more straightforward Italian piece. Maybe it's not too late to change. She opens her mouth to protest, then sees two weary masks facing her. Last thing they need is a middle-aged woman who can't make up her mind. What is she afraid of? Compared to the time she was robbed by a Bolivian taxi driver in 1985, this is nothing. Compared to clutching a bracken-hued Mike when he stopped breathing after kissing the neighbour's cat, this is a walk in the park.

She lifts her right hand over the sound hole — and begins.

Jasper reaches Toby, who has finally consented to turn on his phone.

"You haven't played yet?"

"I'm about to," Toby says.

Jasper waits to hear more, but there is silence. He's used to such pauses in his life with Toby but still can't help charging in with: "Not too late to change your mind."

More silence. Toby hangs up.

Room bloody C. Door's locked, which is weird, and pressing his ear to the wood, Toby hears nothing at all. It's well past noon, and the guy before him should be finishing his audition. Time to warm up but no place to do it except this bare hallway of the Nathan Gold Fine Arts Building. Should have stayed back in the dorm, soaked his hands in a sink of warm water. Instead he's pacing the empty corridor, a strategic error. The call from home messed him up. Jasper can never hide the edge of worry in his voice.

He checks his schedule: the 12:30 slot is in the west wing. A diagram shows where that is. Take a left, down the hall, make a right turn and cross the overpass. He stares at the diagram. What overpass? He's in the wrong bloody wing. There's another room C. He grabs his guitar and darts off. Last thing he needs is to arrive at the session sweaty and out of breath. If Jasper were here, he would have scouted the location the night before. This insight doesn't help.

He jogs down the corridor, makes a dash left, then right, then left again, heartbeat ramping up. Moments later he surfaces into the glass-enclosed overpass that joins the two wings of the building. In the parking lot beneath, cadets guard a pair of relic tanks. His guitar case kneecaps him, and he swears, then continues through the overheated bridge toward room C. In this newer wing the doors are cream-coloured with frosted windows and the hallway smells sweet, like French toast. Room C announces itself with a gold letter stamped above the window. Toby pauses to compose himself, tucks hair behind one ear, and waits until his breathing slows.

The door swings open, and they call him in at the same time as an Asian youth in a blazer scurries out, not meeting Toby's eye. Two judges sit cross-legged on chairs and don't look up right away, being busy writing notes. No window, just the hiss of underpowered ventilation. A piano bench is set next to a footstool — that's it, no music stand. Competitors must play from memory.

Toby smiles fixedly as he enters, sets his case down, and flings it open, miming a confidence he doesn't quite feel. This isn't the time for lame jokes or false bonhomie. The hinge of the case catches on his forearm and leaves a tiny bite. It could have nicked a fingernail, which would have been disastrous. Sometimes it comes down to such small misadventure. He inhales the familiar intoxicating fragrance of his instrument's wood and varnish.

"Make yourself comfortable," commands Manuel Juerta, the noted Cuban guitarist, a chubby man with a shock of reddish hair. Castro lets him out of the country for recitals and conferences because he always returns with a sheaf of ecstatic reviews. The other judge is a couple of decades younger — Jon C. Smyth, a Brit of determinedly plain name and phenomenal technique, already chair of guitar studies at a major U.S. university. Juerta consults his clipboard as Toby settles on the upholstered bench, adjusting its height while the guitar seesaws across his lap.

"Mr. Hausner is from Toronto," Juerta says, reading off his list as Toby tunes. "You're not such a kid, yes?" he chortles, trying to lighten the mood.

Since Toby's hairline started to recede, he looks at least thirty. The room is airless and rank with the nervous sweat of earlier contestants. The judges have been at it for a day and a half, and they're waiting to be astonished. This is what Toby tells himself as he cranks up the footstool to its highest position. He likes the fretboard to skirt his left ear. In his view there can never be a bench too low or a footstool too high.

First up is the Fandanguillo, a wicked piece full of tricky inversions and heroic leaps up the fretboard plus an endless barre-chord that leaves the wrist weeping. Toby visualizes the opening phrase, exactly where his fingers will plant.

The judges yawn and stretch and sip water from plastic bottles. At his age, Toby realizes, he could be sitting alongside them, presiding over the future of the next generation.

Juerta glances at the wall clock. "When you are ready."

Toby figures they've heard the same three pieces so many times that they're not sure whether to laugh or scream after encountering the full range of interpretations, too few offering glimmers of originality, let alone genius. He shuts his eyes, for music has a precise moment of entry: in his mind he hears the opening measures played sublimely, a perfect wave he must catch just as it begins to curl. How do you know if you are playing well? Only by listening, and Toby does nothing but listen. He could hear a mouse gnaw a piano string two studios away.

He begins, evoking the sound of Andalusian streets and baked land — no, nothing so literal, for music creates its own form. He dampens notes to avoid harmonics that might bleed into the next chord. Phrasing and breathing are inseparable, for without phrasing there is no life in the music, just a parade of notes, and without breath, well, we all know where that leads.

Toby glances at the judges as he finishes the piece with a long ritardando. They sit in identical postures, legs crossed, pads in hand, expressionless. No acknowledgement that he has just played his heart out.

Second piece is by a little-known Italian composer from the Romantic era. Musically second rate, but a technical obstacle course that makes it a competition favourite.

He announces its title in a hoarse voice.

The judges nod.

He wipes his hands on his trousered knees, takes his time. The mood will change drastically, and he must set it up. The first bar involves a series of quick chord changes, and a pratfall at the start is never good. He feels a whistle of panic, a sensation that is almost nostalgic: only performance creates this feeling that every second matters.

Opening line speeds by, though not without a slight drag in the bass, then suddenly he is creating music, not jumping hurdles — and he dares to relax a fraction.

Mistake: a performer should never feel safe. As if to demonstrate this truth, he fumbles a simple transition. The mishap catches him off guard, though Juerta, if he notices, doesn't make a mark on his sheet. Smyth's lips tighten.

Toby attacks the rest of the work to its edges, aggressive, proving he is in no way scared by his flub. Finishing, he wipes his forehead: one more piece, then it's free choice, his beloved Sarabande.

But first the Mark Loesser modern work. The lattice of styles is incoherent to the uneducated ear, and he soon fills the studio with a crunch of atonal chords. The judges nod, impressed, for this musician doesn't hide and hope for the best, like some they've heard over the past two days. The piece closes with rapid fire harmonics, caught at the last minute before they capsize into silence.

"Thank you, Mr. Hausner," Juerta says, not waiting until the performer lifts his wrists.

And so the Sarabande.

Fall back into time — eighteenth-century Germany. Toby unrolls the Baroque embellishments without going overboard. He's the master of tasteful mordents and trills, poring over original lute manuscripts, tracking down the composer's intention. He can't help the expressions that cross his face: a tightening of the brow, a wince. He is fully exposed, that tenderness twinned with complete control of tone and tempo. So many artists rush the stately dance, not trusting the guitar's meagre ability to sustain sound, but Toby pulls it off, in part by tricking the audience through body language. His hand hovers over the strings to contain the notes, even as their sound fades. The memory of sound completes the phrase.

The instant his hand plucks the final note, Juerta says, "That will do, Mr. Hausner. Please pick up your things as quickly as possible. We're running late."

"Names of successful participants will be posted this evening," Smyth adds.

Not a word of encouragement or appreciation. Have they any idea what it costs a man like Toby just to step into this room?

Jasper slips out of his good jacket and hangs it in the closet before placing the bag of takeout pad Thai on the kitchen counter. He eats slowly, taking care to thoroughly chew each mouthful. Like all restaurant food, it's over-salted. With his free hand he punches Toby's number. He feels oddly calm. Today the executive of the board demanded a blow-by-blow catalogue of Luke's misdeeds since he began his tenure as president. Jasper fished through agenda books and emails to organize them thematically, then made multiple copies of the finished document, plus another on disk, just to be sure. Rachel escaped early, creeped out by his vengeful enthusiasm.

Toby picks up on the fourth ring.

"So?" Jasper asks, mouth full.

"I'm in."

"They've posted the names?"

"I'm in," Toby repeats.

"Congratulations," Jasper says carefully.

"To be confirmed tonight," Toby allows.

Where does this surge of confidence come from? Jasper wonders. He doesn't know whether to be relieved or alarmed. "I dropped by Lakeview to see Klaus."

"You didn't tell him about the competition?" Toby sounds unnerved.

"I did not. He's looking awfully thin."

"Of course, he looks thin. He *is* thin."

"You see what you want to see."

This irritates Toby. "Klaus is getting old."

"Gaunt, that's the only word for it," Jasper says. "Maybe he doesn't like the food at Lakeview."

"What's wrong with the food?"

"Your father has changed, Toby." Sometimes the obvious has to be pointed out.

The kettle, plugged in at the beginning of this conversation, begins to whistle. Crooking the phone against his ear, Jasper pours boiling water over a green tea bag. The smell of it soothes, and he's transported inside a haiku.

"He kept looking over his shoulder," Jasper says, "as if he expected some other visitor."

Toby seems to relax. "That's it then, one of the old girls. They love him there, one of few men with all his marbles."

Frankly, Jasper felt hurt, seeing as he'd made the effort to travel across the city in the rain.

Toby starts to work up a thesis. "The place is full of Mama's presence, which is why he moved in."

"He's holding something back," Jasper says, taking a slurp of tea. "One senses it in his furtive manner."

They could spend hours discussing Klaus's peculiarities.

A monsoon of arpeggios issues from Hiro's room across the hall.

"Gotta go," Toby says.

"Wait." Jasper lifts off his chair, then says, "I love you, dear boy." He stares at the kitchen chair where Toby normally sits.

Toby waits a beat then says, "I know."

The conversation, such as it is, grinds to a halt.

"Manuel, *amigo*, we must talk."

It's Portia Vanstone, just flown in from Berkeley, California, to take her seat among the judges. She sweeps past the final contestant now scuttling out of the cramped studio and pounces on Manuel. Literally. She spreads her batwings, garbed in an array of shawls, and touches his shoulders with her fingertips.

"I have thirst," he says, pointing to his mouth. During the last rendition of the Fandanguillo, he nearly expired from dehydration.

She follows as he hastens toward the drinking fountain in the corridor of the Fine Arts Building. Pressing the chrome lever, he watches the water gush in a satisfying arc — so quickly does one become accustomed to responsive plumbing. Portia taps her hip impatiently as he takes long, soothing drafts.

"Where can we talk?" Her tone is urgent.

"Now?" Manuel sighs. "I am fatigued and hungry."

The other judge, an English kid named Smyth whom Manuel once taught in master class and now sits pretty on a college job in the United States, dashed out of the room ten minutes ago, suggesting they meet in the pub across the street.

"I can fix hungry." Portia sinks a hand into her cloth bag and draws out an apple, which she holds out to Manuel, waving it in front of his mouth, as if he were a dog.

He takes the fruit and rolls it against his throbbing temple.

"There's much to discuss," Portia says. She grabs his elbow, then leads him in a trot down the hall.

"Where are we going?"

"Outside."

Thank God. What he craves is air untouched by anxious music.

She propels him down the labyrinth of hallways to a door that warns, in French, that it must be opened only in the case of fire. Without hesitation she pushes it open, and the musicians step outside onto a spongy carpet of moss. They've entered a tiny precious green spot, flanked on three sides by institutional buildings. Someone has planted herbs in a clay pot and dragged out a pair of plastic garden chairs. Portia lets go of his arm and rustles in that oversized bag until she finds her cigarettes. She holds out the pack, and Manuel shakes his head, tempted as he is, for he means to quit for good.

"Promising crop?" she asks in that distinctive raspy voice.

Manuel understands she means the musicians. "Some very good ones. Perhaps no one outstanding. We will see."

She taps the end of the cigarette on her wrist and lowers herself onto one of the chairs.

Portia's a force at these competitions. One year she insisted on a Belgian guitarist being promoted to the finals, a girl who was in way over her head and went running back to her provincial conservatory, never to be heard from again. Then there was the Welshman who seemed out of his element, rough clothes and a beat-up guitar, but Portia kept urging the other judges to "Listen hard. This is something new."

Alun Carew just finished recording his third CD with Naxos.

She plants herself on one of the chairs and leans over to remove her sandals, giving a little moan of release as her feet flex. Manuel glances away: he'd seen the dry, scaly skin.

"I can't talk long," he warns her. "Smyth and I must meet to choose who will continue to the semis." Yet he sinks onto the other chair, feeling his lower back relax. Two solid days in the studio and he forgets where he is, what country, what year.

"I've agreed to run for the position of president of our august organization," Portia declares.

Manuel straightens. "Again?"

Five years ago she campaigned to oust old Gregorio and failed.

Undeterred, Portia says, "Several eminent members have begged me to toss my hat in the ring."

"I see," Manuel says. Guitar federation politics bore him.

"But if I'm to be successful, your help is essential."

Manuel, despite his fatigue, is flattered. He takes a bite of her apple.

"The organization must be dragged into the twenty-first century if we're to survive."

He hears a lot of this sort of thing in his travels, always from people whose countries satisfactorily completed the twentieth century.

"Of course," Manuel says, hoping he sounds firm and decisive.

"The website is a mess." She sits up straight and pauses, allowing him to contemplate this sad fact. "We must allow prospective competitors to send first-round programs via digital file. Initial vetting is done by a select group of judges around the world, working from wherever they may live." Her hair, entirely grey now, flings about as she gestures. She's gained a few pounds in recent years, but so have they all.

Manuel feels himself resist the suck of energy.

"Moreover," she continues, leaning so that the front of her blouse flaps open, revealing a freckled cleavage, "the finals must be recorded on video and posted on our site. People can wager on the winner. We'll create intense excitement throughout the guitar world."

Manuel feels his forehead pulse: protein, that's what he needs.

"Progress is impossible as long as Gregorio steers us toward his lost valley." She waits for Manuel to agree, which he does, because that will make the lecture shorter. "We'll create a pedagogical destination, with classes delivered by our most eminent members ... a digital conservatory."

Her teeth are unnaturally white. His tongue darts in the gap between his own teeth, still a shock to discover the absence of the upper cuspid. He wants to sit in a cool, dark room with a towel over his head and a cold beer in hand.

"This is where you come in," Portia says. "You shall be in charge of hiring teachers and devising curriculum and thus confer instant prestige on the venture. Please say yes." She lifts her shawl around her shoulders and beams at him.

Manuel is thinking. That pretty middle-aged contestant from Toronto — he liked the way she played the Italian piece, very crisp and musical. He actually leaned back and listened, forgetting he was meant to judge. But he could tell Smyth was horrified by her very presence; a young man, he flinches from the contamination of age.

"This will transform our lives, Manuel," Portia natters on. "You could stay home in Havana soaking up the rays, and still earn money."

When he seems less than thrilled by this proposal, she lowers her voice. "And here's the cherry, the icing on the cake: we organize hologramic recitals of our most august members."

"What?"

"Think of it: eliminate jet lag and billeting with local guitar society members, family dog jumping on your bed in the morning. I see this as an ecological statement. Imagine, Manuel, you play your program from the comfort of your studio where it will be transferred hologramatically to audiences around the world."

Manuel's mind fixes on his current, post-Lucia studio — a corner of the cramped bedroom, which is in turn situated in a corner of the living area, where, if the Venetian or New York audience were to peer closely, a glimpse of his hot plate might turn up in the background.

"Can I count on your support?" Portia asks, sitting erect on the chair, waiting for his blessing.

Manuel summons up his last bit of strength. "This must never happen," he says, rising to his feet, aware she is frowning as he disappears into the building.

TWELVE

MANUEL GUESSES THAT THIS CORNER BAR WITH ITS PRESSED tin ceiling and ceramic floor tiles is considered chic. He hesitates inside the entrance, watching the gangly Jon Smyth perch on a bar stool, his long neck pink from the barber's razor. A man dressed in black with a white cloth slung over one shoulder greets Manuel, "*Ça va?*" to which Manuel replies with a dismissive wave. He'll make his own way, *merci*, which he manages, grabbing the stool next to Jon's at the mahogany bar.

"What are you drinking?" Manuel peers at the glass of red liquid.

"Bloody Mary, minus the blood and minus Mary," Jon says. "The liver's become a conscientious objector."

Manuel straddles the padded stool, but only the tips of his toes reach the floor. This country is full of such small humiliations. Electronic music pulses in the background, a computer mimicking oboe and strings, even brass. The barkeep brings him a pint of ale.

"That last girl ..." Jon winces.

"Nina," Manuel says, remembering the fine-boned Mexican girl, pride of the University of Veracruz, who fell apart during her recent performance in the studio. She played the first piece like an angel, but during the modern work she lost her way yet insisted on ploughing on, a shambles, until to their horror she began to weep. She kept playing while tears splashed onto the soundboard, and Manuel hadn't dared order her to stop, any more than he would have jumped in front of a runaway train. The episode left both men feeling mean and ill.

"Remind me never to sign on for this job again," Jon says. "We should be like Portia, swanning in to judge only advanced rounds."

They chink glasses as Jon stares gloomily into the mirror at his own hunched form. Manuel remembers the teenage Jon wearing an oversized jersey from his beloved Manchester United, playing Granados under a tree in that hillside town in southern Italy where a festival convenes each summer. Smyth had been the star that season, performing with obvious joy. Today his face looks haggard, his eyelids heavy, that fine hair beginning to thin on top. When young people start to grow old, it is particularly sad.

"Does sweating through a competition make you a better musician?" Jon asks. Without waiting for a reply he barges on. "It's about building a fucking career."

"As you did," Manuel points out. "And so you have this excellent position at the university —"

"A position, right," Jon cuts him off. "Seventy percent tedium and politics." Their eyes meet in the mirror. "Even my most gifted students crave safety. They talk about landing jobs at colleges and universities with pensions and health plans. That's what this generation desires, Manuel. They're not willing to knock around the world, playing recitals in gymnasiums, carving a reputation from pure gut and talent, not like you, Manuel. You're a dying breed, my friend."

"They are sensible," Manuel says.

"Sensible," Jon agrees. "'What must I do to get a job like yours?'" they ask. "'What are the most important competitions?'"

"Another round?" The bartender flicks his towel over the counter, and the men nod a synchronized "yes."

No matter how much Manuel drinks, he is still thirsty.

Smyth draws a crumpled sheet of paper from his pocket. "Whom are we going to sprinkle with fairy dust today?"

Manuel digs out his own list, knowing there will be arguments about the contenders. He reads off several names, and when he reaches Lucy Shaker, the other man snorts.

"Are you joking? We're in the business of launching careers, not rewarding middle-aged hobbyists."

"There was something interesting in her playing," Manuel protests.

"Really?"

"She wasn't mimicking a performance." That isn't quite what Manuel means.

"Ah." Jon lifts one long leg to cross the other and smoothes the material of his khakis. "But is that enough?"

"I only know what I hear."

Jon clears his throat. "Of course, I trust you implicitly. If anyone's got sharp ears, it's Manuel Juerta."

Manuel acknowledges this flattery with a nod. Jon isn't the least bit convinced, of course, and so the deal-making begins.

An hour and a half later they've whittled the list down to twelve, and the two weary judges have polished off another round along with a platter of *tourtière*, the tasty minced beef pie native to the province. The bar has filled with office workers: women in short skirts and high heels, men sheathed in skinny pants with open-collared shirts.

Smyth chips away at the last of the meat pie. "We'll get you down to my college to teach a master class. Interested?"

"Certainly," Manuel says.

"The dean will spring for a modest recital fee, but we can lay on extra for expenses and teaching a master class. What do you say, *amigo*?"

"I say yes."

Jon slaps him on the shoulder. "Consider yourself booked."

They are silent for several minutes, the letdown after strenuous negotiations.

Manuel got through to Lucia late last night. She'd gone to visit Eric at the detention centre, taking him sandwiches and fruit. "He was so pale," she said over the crackly phone line. "Papa promises he'll be out by the end of the week, but I don't know. Papa isn't so powerful now."

Listening to this plaintive description, Manuel sat cross-legged on his bed on the seventh floor of the boutique hotel, eyeing a room service trolley that held two steaming platters covered with metal lids.

"Where is your college?" he asks Jon.

Jon names a state in the Southwest.

"Maybe you can create a permanent position for me at this college," Manuel says.

Smyth peers at a handful of Canadian bills before selecting one and placing it under his glass. "Tell me you're not serious."

"I am always serious."

"You don't want to even think of such a thing, not at your stage of the game. It would absolutely mutilate your soul."

"My soul is already mutilated."

They walk out together into the early evening, sunlight careening off the flank of the high-rise across the street.

Jon looks around in all directions, his small head bobbing. "I'd love to have you join us. What a dream." His long nose makes him seem like an elegant mammal, perhaps an antelope. "Your technique is brilliant, but —" He pauses to whistle in admiration as a yellow sports car roars past. "Fucking brilliant, but not precisely what we teach in our academy." He grabs Manuel's elbow, and they dart through two lanes of traffic to the opposite sidewalk where Jon stands, barely winded, and Manuel feels his chest tighten and wheeze.

"If we teach opposite forms, the poor creatures will be even more confused than they are now," Jon says, waiting for Manuel to agree. When this doesn't happen, he continues. "It's a bloody bore being chair of the department. All these accommodations and decisions. One is more politician than musician. But you'll come to visit us next term, yes?" He dives into his pocket to retrieve his phone and scrutinizes the tiny screen. "Interdepartmental meeting postponed," he reads aloud. Then he adds, "One is cancelled, but another appears. Such is my life."

"Names are posted!" Larry races past Toby's door like the white rabbit, leaving his scarred guitar lying across his bed. The others pop out of their cells: will they be invited to join the semifinal round, or will they return home, stricken with shame and excuses?

Toby pulls out his ear buds, rolls off the bed where he was napping, and slowly buttons his shirt. So this is it. This is why he came. That sharp metallic taste in his mouth appears again. He skips the elevator, which is going crazy jumping between floors to pick up contestants, and lopes down the fire stairs.

Sixty-five members of the guitar congress mash around the bulletin board in the foyer of the Fine Arts Building. Only twelve names are posted, twelve names printed off a sheet of white paper. Urgent castings for glitches in alphabetical order are fruitless — there are no such errors.

Toby doesn't stampede to the front. Instead he holds back a dignified distance and runs over the way he played in the preliminary round, and for the life of him, can't imagine anyone did better.

"Dumb fucks," someone moans. A fist slams the wall. It belongs to Marcus, a young man from London. With his cropped hair and spotty face, he looks like a soccer hooligan, not one of England's finest young interpreters of the pre-Baroque repertoire. He didn't make the cut. Even the best can have a bad day.

Trace appears at Toby's side, reeking of bubble gum. "Hausner, right?"

Toby nods.

"I saw your name up there." She waits for his response, but Toby betrays nothing, though inside the beast stirs. "You don't look exactly thrilled."

Trace doesn't understand that he's been measuring out the scene in spoonfuls. "Give me time," he says.

She pops a bubble. The tough girl exterior can't hide an orthodontist's pricey work.

"What about you?" Toby remembers to ask.

"Ditto."

He stares at her. "Ditto you made it?"

She shrugs. "I thought it would be way harder."

The crowd begins to thin as the lucky ones head for the exit to practise like demons for round two while everyone else makes for the pub to drown their disappointment in beer.

"Fifty-three people tanked," Trace proclaims in awe.

Toby cringes: does she have no pity for the poor devils slinking off? Many will roll back to the dorm at two or three in the morning, making plenty of racket — a tiny but satisfying revenge on the successful. He inhales the whole sweeping drama, and only when the foyer is nearly clear does he walk over and read his name in bold type. It's like breathing snow, and he feels the back of his throat tingle.

"And now you must go fishing."

Toby spins to face Manuel Juerta, who stands before him holding his upturned Panama hat full of bits of folded paper. Juerta gives the hat a shake, and Toby plucks a number. He's never seen the task done in such an improvisatory way. The draw will determine playing order for round two.

Unfolding the bit of paper, Toby makes a face. "One," he reads aloud.

Juerta makes a cooing noise, possibly sympathetic.

So he will play first. He's barely finished the opening round and now he must dash back to the dorm to prepare for the second program, a different set of pieces. In fourteen hours he'll be onstage again. It's all happening so fast. After years of waiting, it's full steam ahead.

Trace steals up, sandwich in hand, and Juerta jiggles the hat near her nose. "Determine your fate, young lady."

She dips her greasy fingers into the hat, lifts a chit and

unfolds it. Six. "Is this good?" she asks.

"Ideal," Toby reassures her. "Centre of the pack." He watches her face soften.

"A guy your age must be pretty relaxed about all this," she says.

A guy my age, thinks Toby, can go days without sleep when necessary, can live off hardtack and water, can bathe his sorry fingers in saline solution.

Back in the dorm he plunges into a run-through of the new program before supper, setting the alarm to remind himself to eat.

Later, Toby joins the thinned-out crowd in the cafeteria for supper, selecting a protein-rich soup with no drowsy-making carbs. When he sets his tray down at the communal table, everyone applauds. It's a nice moment.

Armand hasn't made the cut. "They do not like my style — too romantic," he says, sighing. "Also, maybe I have a small problem with the repeat." He's donned a Greek fisherman's cap and looks pale.

"What was your free choice?" Toby asks.

"Third cello suite, first two movements."

Bach is dicey, especially the cello suites. Every student plays them, and there are so many transcriptions, all contentious.

"I was sure I would convince them with my interpretation," Armand says, but he sounds discouraged.

The statement cranks everyone into an animated discussion of different versions of the suites. Do you listen to cellists? If so, which bowings do you prefer? No one wants to deal directly with Armand's disappointment. He is thirty-five years old and has never made it to a competition final. Does he have a family back home? No point in checking for a wedding ring, for his fingers are bare. Think of swimmers with shaved heads, no extra weight, no drag.

"Bach is supreme king!" Hiro cries and everyone agrees with this indisputable fact. Having made the cut, Hiro is regarded with new interest.

It turns out that Javier has also made the cut. He's the silent Argentine who sits at the end of the cluster of tables. Since day one, he's held himself apart from competition fever and gossip. And there have been rumours about another guy, possibly from Winnipeg, who hides in his room, practising and sleeping, only stealing out after dark for food.

Texas Larry bites down on a vegetable burger, glancing neither to the left nor the right. Was his name posted? Toby can't remember.

"I still can't believe it." Lucy pulls her chair next to Toby's, and he gets a whiff of tea-rose fragrance.

"Believe what?" he obliges.

"I'm so amazed and honoured." She touches his wrist. "Am I shaking? Have I entered a state of delusion? If so, please give me a sharp kick. I need to know."

Her head tilts against his shoulder, and he feels the heat of her, the pulsing flank of a small, nervous dog.

"You made the semis?" he asks.

She seems hurt: he should know this. "Unless there was a typo."

Armand reaches into his pocket and removes a pewter flask. "Next I will enter the Barcelona competition," he advises the group. "World-class judges, huge audience, such aficionados you can't believe." He drinks quickly and wipes his lips. "If you make it in Barcelona, you establish an instant career. You know Stanley Blake?"

Everyone nods. Of course, they know Stanley, or rather, they know *of* him.

"Barcelona, grand prize, 2003." Armand smiles, point proven, and takes another pull of whisky.

"Larry ran aground," Lucy whispers in Toby's ear.

Toby swings to face her. "What happened?"

"He was playing during some breakdown with the ventilation system, and Smyth actually jumped up in the middle of the

Loesser first movement to fiddle with the thermostat. So Larry stopped playing, thinking he was meant to — and they wouldn't let him start over."

Toby glances at the Texan, who is peeling the label of a bottle of mineral water.

"Remember the year Christophe Poulin walked off with the Miami prize?" Armand is getting excited. "In 2001 I was in exactly the same competition."

"Who's Poulin?" Hiro asks. He sits on the edge of his seat, wearing a flaming orange singlet.

"Nobody! The guy played like shit, but his teacher was related to one of the judges, *ja*?"

Toby nods. He is perhaps the only one here who remembers the scandal.

"At the gala the jury didn't arrive for two hours," Armand goes on, becoming even more animated. "Because they were hauled on the rug by the organizers for total incompetence. Everyone knew the best players didn't make it past round two."

Hiro scrambles to his feet and excuses himself. "I run," he says, and escapes into the night, trotting into the crowded sidewalks in his shorts and singlet.

The institute is driving Jasper stark raving mad. Toby pretends to listen to the phone rant, but Jasper feels his lover's patience wear thin.

"Okay, not mad," he corrects himself, for it isn't a word one should toss about. "The institute is a thing of beauty, but Luke must go."

"Of course," Toby agrees with a yawn.

"He's brought back an ex-officio president, and the two of them are attempting to hijack the place." Toby still doesn't get it: not only is Jasper's job on the line but the future of the institute. "They're plotting to get rid of me. It's a strategic ouster."

This snaps Toby to attention. "Can they do that?"

"Luke is omnipotent."

Toby doesn't believe a word of this, for it is Jasper who is omnipotent.

With his free hand Jasper throws the boy's dirty socks into the laundry hamper. Before tossing his jeans into the same pile, he slides an empty box of Smarties from the rear pocket. Not quite empty: a solo red bead sticks to the bottom. When Toby arrived at the halfway house all those years ago in the middle of winter, he pulled his guitar out of its battered case and launched into the mournful Sarabande while snow melted in his hair. Jasper stood in the doorway holding the discharge file while residents trickled in and out of the room, oblivious to the divine sound that had entered their realm. The boy was achingly thin after his hospital stay, a frail bird waiting for Jasper to rescue him.

"How do your colleagues sound?" Jasper asks.

"I avoid listening."

"You don't want to be influenced?"

"I don't want to be scared." Toby gives a crackly laugh.

"Are you eating well?" Jasper probes.

"Like a field hand."

Jasper feels the boy holding back information. This is not a good sign: his secrets are such a burden to him.

"I'm perfectly all right," Mrs. Ivy Cronin assures Jasper. "It was just a nasty bout of the flu."

Jasper nods in an encouraging way but says nothing.

"Monkey flu," she says. "It jumped species. Don't you find that interesting?" She stops for a moment to marvel. "I was on a ventilator for ten days, but you know all that."

"You've had a rough time."

"And look at me now," she says, spreading her arms wide.

What Jasper sees is a handsome but gaunt woman with coifed hair whose voice, still hoarse from the ventilator tube, is bravely chipper.

"Let's start with a few questions," he says, pen poised over the clipboard. They're sitting in the lounge area of the institute overlooking the boulevard many floors below.

Mrs. Cronin hasn't touched her coffee or the bowl of nuts, but then neither has Jasper. It strikes him that she might have difficulty swallowing, and he makes a mental note to offer yogourt from the staff fridge. Choking disorders aren't uncommon in these cases. New Age, vaguely Indonesian music, a mistake to his mind, wafts from overhead speakers. Luke cites research on its tranquilizing properties.

"Ivy, do you know what day of the week it is?"

His client smiles evenly. "Do I care?"

Jasper presses on, used to such evasion. "Let's just say that I do."

"Is this a trap?"

"By no means."

"Because I'm not going back to that place. Wild horses can't drag me."

"Don't worry," Jasper assures her. "You've graduated with flying colours." This is true. Ivy was a woman fighting for her life and mind less than a month ago.

"So ask me something interesting." Ivy leans forward in her chair. "Given the fact that I've stared death in the face." Her eyes are milky with medication. She left hospital fifteen days ago, her departure a media event, cameras recording each movement as she was helped from a wheelchair into a waiting car.

"All right, where were you born?"

She lets out a barking laugh, a sound that causes the intern, Rachel, to poke her head around the doorway.

"I've been reborn," Ivy proclaims. "From the chrysalis of pain to my present state."

"Why do you think you're here?"

For a moment Jasper fears she isn't going to answer, but she releases a long breath and says, "Because I've forgotten nearly everything. I can hardly dress myself in the morning, and they won't let me near the kitchen."

"I can help," Jasper says, "if you'll agree to work with me."

Ivy looks dismayed. "You have no idea, do you?"

"We've found notable improvements in such cases."

"What I really long to remember," Ivy says, "is being sick." She hesitates, then offers with a burst of intensity, "Where was I then?"

The panicked stare is chillingly familiar; Ashok, the Emergency Room physician, gazes at Jasper the same way. The illness takes them on an arduous journey to another country, and when they return, they've forgotten how things are done here. Mrs. Cronin, according to her file, ran a garden nursery before getting ambushed by the virus.

"How can I possibly return," she says, "if I don't know where I've been?"

When Jasper suggests they develop a recovery plan, she gives him a pained look.

"We might start with a short routine you can easily follow," he says.

That look again. Some might call it blank, but Jasper knows better. Ashok says he lost his limbs and was just a floating head during his illness, surrounded by string instead of air. Another time he was an aquatic creature nosing at his own inert body. No one came to see him for months, years.

"Is there something in particular you'd like to learn to do?" Jasper asks.

Ivy brightens. "I've never been able to remember a joke and tell it right."

———————————————

Toby practises his bows in front of the dormitory mirror, bobbing up and down like a manservant. Ten points will be awarded
for presentation, and bowing is a minefield of potential indig-
nity. You don't want to look like a fool before you begin to play.
He grabs the guitar by the scruff of the neck, then bends deeply
beside it, demonstrating the dead-chicken bow. Next, as practised
by the dazzling Romero brothers, he stuffs the instrument under
one arm like a surfboard and strides across the floor, smiling and
nodding at an imaginary audience.

Bad idea. The mirror reflects a taut, crazed expression that
would spook anyone. He circles the common room, edging past the
weathered tables and scuffed chairs, then returns to the ad hoc stage,
this time mimicking Scottish virtuoso David Russell. He holds the
guitar horizontally in front of him like a magician about to perform
a levitation caper, then rotates the instrument so the sound hole
faces outward and — here's the tricky bit — he bows behind it.

Way too complex. You don't want to use yourself up before
the first note sounds.

Armand stomps in, wet hair with towel flung around his
neck. "That's not how you do it, esteemed colleague. You'll fall on
your face. Permit me. I have perfected the ultimate stage bow." He
reaches for Toby's guitar. When Toby doesn't deliver it immediately, Armand's smile grows rigid. "I may not be such a genius as
you who have achieved the semifinals, but I do know how to bow."

Toby relents. "Show me."

Armand seizes the instrument, lifts the sound hole to his
nose, and peers inside to examine the maker's name. "Who is
this guy?" he asks.

"Luthier from Quebec," Toby says.

This was his standby instrument, until he lost his main
performance guitar. Yes — lost.

Armand clutches the guitar mid-neck to his side and bows
evenly, the instrument following the tilt of his body, and hovers
there for two beats before rising at the same leisurely pace.

"You see?" he says. "No rush. This is a very elegant gesture."

"Work of art," Toby agrees, taking the instrument back, then retreats to his room, feeling a tingle of irritation. It's so easy to get lost in curtains of detail.

Across the hall, Hiro stumbles over the tremolo passage in the compulsory piece and swears loudly in Japanese. If you can't manage a whirlwind tremolo in the privacy of your room, what hope do you have when nerves bite down? The technique relies on a form of fraught relaxation, achieved after years of practising slowly, then working up to hummingbird speed.

Toby shuts the door, then rolls a towel along the bottom to mute his playing noise and that of others. The single chair faces the porthole window overlooking the courtyard. He switches the chair around so it now faces the door, then kicks the footstool over to its new position: this rearrangement is a trick to keep him from getting comfortable in one spot. Toby has to be able to mount any stage and posses the new space within seconds.

He practises until midnight, then falls into bed, lying there visualizing the way his left hand slides up the fretboard, fingers planting. Toby knows this passage as if it were imprinted on his eyelids, but something is wrong. He jackknifes up in the bed, body licked with heat: it's the wrong damn piece! All he can see is the music he played in the first round, but that's over, finished. He strains to pull his mind to the next morning's program, mere hours away, reciting the name of each work in sequence, what key it's in, and how the first bars sound. Yet the moment he sinks back into the pillow it's the freaking Fandanguillo and Sarabande that appear in photographic detail.

In that week of madness leading up to the Paris trip, he'd practised in his rented room ten hours without a break until day bled into night. Fingers grew numb, calluses shredded, and his wrists seized up, deep down the carpal tunnel. Red stop signs must have flashed, but he refused to see them. A spirit state is where it took him, lips cracked, dropping pounds by the day.

He was pure mind and ringing tone, a lean mystic of the guitar, death a heartbeat away.

Well, it always is, isn't it?

No time to shop for food and no desire to break the spell. That's what no one understands: the so-called black hole was anything but. Nothing could interrupt him, no phone or door-bell, just brother Felix who found him lying on his cot with saliva caked to the corners of his mouth — dehydrated, for starters. It was Felix who lifted him onto the back of his Harley and roared downtown to Emergency. How long was he in the hospital? Four days? Discharge to the halfway house where a man called Jasper greeted him at the door. Lucky to get in such a place, everyone assured him. They'll soon get you on your feet again.

"What would you do if I hadn't entered your life?" Jasper likes to ask.

Toby answers the question with a mysterious smile, convinced that once Jasper is sure about him, sure that he's healed, those sharp eyes will move on.

The first time they became lovers he felt Jazz pucker like a snowflake under his touch, and for more than a year the guitar stayed locked in its case, a pet they weren't sure about.

It's almost 3:00 a.m. and Toby's mind is doing cartwheels. Frantic, he pops a sleeping pill, one of four he sneaked out of Jasper's toilet bag before leaving home. Jasper will notice, of course. He will have counted the tablets.

At last Toby feels his limbs grow heavy on the mattress as the little blue pill folds him into its tent.

Poor Nina, the Mexican girl. Lucy finds her hiding in the dorm bathroom, one foot propped on the sink, painting her toenails. The cellphone lies next to her naked foot.

"You headed home soon?" Lucy asks in a carefully neutral voice, waiting before darting into a cubicle. Everyone knows how Nina wept through her performance.

The girl glances up, brown eyes pooling water. "I am so sad," she says, sighing tragically. "My boyfriend is angry. He pays for my flight, for food, for everything." She goes back to dabbing her nails with the tiny brush.

Lucy places her hand on the girl's shoulder. "I'm sure he'll forgive you." She hopes that's true.

The girl finishes off one nail and proceeds to the next. "His mother and father are professors, very intellectual family," she says. "I thought if I do well here, maybe —" she turns to look Lucy in the eye "— they will respect me."

Lucy feels sorry for the girl, but this is quickly overtaken by a lick of euphoria, for what really stirs her is her own success. She enters the cubicle and dangles her purse from the hook, feeling her heart kick. It's all she can manage to calm down enough to practise for the next round, fending off a crazy fantasy where she's wearing a sparkly top and a long drapey skirt, peering out from behind the curtain as the concert hall fills with admirers. It's the finals, and Goran has flown in to witness the historic occasion.

"Do you believe you will win?" the girl calls from the other side of the door.

"Of course not," Lucy assures her.

Later Lucy perches naked on the rim of a steaming pool while women of all shapes and sizes tiptoe across the tiled floor. The spa smells hygienically clean. Nearby an ancient Korean woman crouches on a low bench and, using a pail, sluices water over her mottled shoulders.

Lucy starts to slip into the bath, but the old woman waves at her urgently.

"You help me," she orders, thrusting the empty pail toward Lucy. This is followed by a crusty loofah sponge.

"What do I do?" Lucy asks, lifting her legs out of the skin-puckering water.

The woman points at the empty pail and the sponge, then makes scrubbing motions. On the other side of the pillar another much younger woman is scrubbing a girl's back with a rough sponge. A film of steam covers flesh and hair, blurring the edges. Mimicking what she sees, Lucy scoops up a load of water and coasts the wiry loofah across the old woman's back in small, tentative strokes. The crepey skin seems translucent, as if it might easily shred.

The woman cries, "No good! Harder!" and shakes her shoulders in obvious frustration. The loose flesh of her back sinks to broad hips and a soft flat bottom, pleating like drapery.

Lucy obeys as soapy water flows down the gutter into the drain.

A young woman wearing a sparkling white bra and underpants appears on the pool deck and calls Lucy's name: it is time for her massage.

This luxury was Mark's idea. "Treat yourself," he said, hearing the clang of nerves in her voice. He was racing off to work where he was in charge of security for the Treasures of the Silk Route exhibit.

A naked Lucy follows the girl into a windowless room where she hoists herself onto the table, fitting her chin into the pocket. Scented oil squirts onto her back and is worked into her skin by small, firm hands.

"Shoulders very tense," the Korean girl informs her.

"Yes," Lucy murmurs, feeling a pair of sturdy thumbs burrow toward her brain stem.

Uncle Philip trots down the noisy street toward a back road lined with shops offering sweets and knick-knacks. He leaps over a ditch, gracefully landing on the other side. He's become a sort of dragonfly, and everyone smiles at him, this old white guy wearing neat shorts and a polo shirt. At the edge of this colony a pair of brothers lives, ages thirteen and fourteen, with excellent teeth. Uncle Philip understands this indicates superior heath. His step is light, his heart a reliable drum.

Lucy moans.

"Too hard?" the girl asks, but doesn't let up the pressure.

A silver disc rises inside her head.

Uncle Philip hears the whistle and stops in front of a small wooden house. A girl is selling cigarettes in the doorway, and behind her a portly woman beckons him in. Suddenly, he's swept past a beaded curtain and experiences a flash of panic: is this how it's going to end? Fear jazzes him up, and he notices everything, the jars of unknown substances laid neatly on a shelf, pots and pans nailed to a slab of plywood, and a peeling poster of the Backstreet Boys.

The woman speaks quickly, holding out her hand. Uncle Philip digs into the pocket of his shorts and finds his wallet. He can hardly breathe.

Lucy touches her forearm with the tip of a finger and shivers with pleasure. Basted with fragrant oils, she could almost taste herself.

THIRTEEN

NOTHING IS GREEN IN THE WINDOWLESS GREEN ROOM. INSTEAD, its walls are painted a soft rose. A bouquet of irises decorates the ledge — a gift to competitors from one of the small army of volunteers.

The first round took place in closed studios, but the semi-finals are real performances. Toby flexes his hands, then each finger in turn, special attention paid to the one damaged in his baseball-playing mishap. The hall's plush seats and concrete-clad walls will create bright acoustics, and this early in the day the audience will be tiny. Breakfast was a banana and a glass of water: banana for its hit of soothing potassium and water to keep hydrated. He ducked into the shower long enough to wash the sleep out of his eyes but not so long that his skin dried out. Such calibrations come easily after all these years.

He chips the tuning fork against his knee and sets its stem on the soundboard of his guitar to resonate: pointless to overtune, since stage lights will ramp up the pitch within seconds. Toby is old school about tuning, using his ears rather than electronics. He straightens, rolls his shoulders, and inhales deeply. Control the mind, banish distractions. He squeezes a millimetre of Vaseline onto his finger and dabs it in the crease of the instrument where neck meets body. During pauses in performance, he'll smear his fingers to keep them moist. The thumbnail of his right hand is bevelled from practising so much, though not worn enough to justify gluing on a falsie. Too much flesh creates a soft, undif-ferentiated bass sound. He'll make a slight adjustment with the angle of his wrist.

Breathe. Focus. This is what he tells members of Guitar Choir when they titter nervously backstage, wiping slimy palms on their dress-up clothes.

Five minutes until showtime.

He grins, feeling the surge of elation that precedes performance, but it too must be tamed.

Setting the guitar back in its case, he tugs off his shoes and, using the wall for leverage, teeters up into a headstand. Blood soars, filling his scalp and ears, flushing out the Eustachian tubes. Broadloom presses into the top of his head — *eau de* nylon and stale cigarettes. In the hallway he hears a door swing open and the barking voice of Manuel Juerta demanding sugar for his coffee.

A volunteer taps tentatively on the door. "Toby Hausner?"

"Yup," Toby grunts, lowering himself vertebra by vertebra, feeling the rush of blood disappear from his head. Bits of carpet fluff cling to the knees of his dress pants, and he brushes them off before tucking in the tails of his shirt. He gives his shoes a once-over with his sleeve, not a recommended method, and glances at himself in the full-length mirror. Jasper's right — he's going squinty, a sort of Mongol thing happening with his eyes.

"One minute," the volunteer cries.

Create your own courage, insist on it. Toby grabs his instrument and begins the march down the corridor. The volunteer leads the way as they sweep past framed photographs of little-known musicians.

"My magic hands will leave them breathless," Toby intones, a recitation geared to deflect any last-minute panic, the hound of doubt that may seek a final lunge.

The girl pulls back the curtain.

His buttocks clench as he strides onto the stage.

Trickle of applause from the sparse audience.

Doused with light, he leaves the cool forest to emerge into a sun-drenched meadow. The wooden floor feels springy underfoot, and when he spots the padded bench waiting down-stage, his heart jumps, a sci-fi horror that threatens to burst out of his chest.

Jasper stands next to the window of client room B on the upper floor of the institute. A teenage girl called Moxie tips back and forth on her chair and refuses to talk. She's been sent over from Eating Disorders for a life-skills orientation. Her hair is dyed albino — think of the ammonia leaking into her porous young scalp. Moxie's days revolve around not eating, and one of Jasper's tasks is to help structure her time so that a range of activities will offer the promise of a full and interesting life.

Jasper gazes down at the city boulevard with its hot dog stands, groomed civic gardens, and a godawful sculpture of one of the province's founding fathers perched on a concrete plinth. It is possible, Jasper knows, even inevitable, to be two places at once, his world and Toby's, which is both blessing and curse. At this moment Jasper has no choice but to imagine his lover as he approaches the bench in Montreal, sweat soaking through his laundered shirt.

"You okay?" Moxie finally asks.

The comment startles Jasper. "I am quite all right." She must have spotted the flush of excitement on his cheek. He wishes he could say that it isn't every day you play your heart out for a team of international judges — you with your twig limbs and sunken chest can't know about the ecstasy of the artist. But perhaps Jasper is mistaken. Moxie is a devoted and tireless sculptor of her own body, and there is elation as well as fear in those overly bright eyes. The artist is never understood by conventional citizens.

Toby reaches the bench where, clutching the neck of the guitar, he bends deeply from the waist toward the unseen audience.

At the back of the hall a door clicks open, letting in a sleeve of light — Lucy, with two other competitors have come to watch.

Toby adjusts the bench to its proper height. The guitar fits with its waist on his raised left thigh, the footstool cranked as high as it will go. He launches into the tuning dance, popping harmonics, checking one string against another as heat bears down from the spotlight, changing the strings' pitch. At the same time he listens to sound reverberate in the hall, gauging acoustical brightness and rate of decay.

First up is the Tárrega, which begins slowly, then builds to a hectic middle section. Important not to think ahead and thus infect the early part with intimations of anxiety.

He lifts his hands and peers into nothing; plenty of time to gather the sound in his head before beginning.

Moxie is seventeen. Jasper checks her chart. No, eighteen. Lives in an Iranian community in Thornhill, north end of the city.

"My parents don't know what to make of me," she says in a voice tinged with pride.

Literature professors in pre-revolution Tehran, the couple now runs a mail-order office supply business.

"They believe they're modern," Moxie goes on, "but they want to control my every move. I freak them out because I have actual friends." She brushes aside that haunting white hair, such a contrast to the olive skin. That's when Jasper spots the raccoon rings under her eyes and the taut cheekbones. Her teeth are almost transparent, enamel scoured by gastric acid, and he guesses the girl is bulimic as well as anorexic. She could die of this horror.

Toby enacts a bit of flim-flam near the end of the piece. Not exactly a wrong note, more of a fudging through a tricky transition. Only people who know the work intimately will guess, which means everyone in the hall. Key thing is to continue and not break the spell. He dabs the Vaseline and rubs it into his fingertips, a slick wakening of the flesh.

Someone coughs, another blows her nose. Judges take the opportunity of the brief break to rustle papers and make notes.

Toby holds his hands over the strings, a signal for silence, then launches into the next piece, feeling it soar as his fingers anticipate each nook and cranny.

On the upper floor of the institute, Jasper leaks a relieved smile. Moxie is diligently writing down a list of leisure-time activities, most of which involve text-messaging or downloading music. In her dreadful thinness there is beauty, but one mustn't speak of this, though it's what she loves most in herself, even as it frightens her. Her delicate wrist sweeps across the page, and the crown of her head is almost bare, for the malady causes hair to fall out. Does someone kiss her there? Jasper wonders. A boyfriend, a sister, or perhaps the mother who hovers in constant worry.

Spanish composers are Toby's specialty, and he's proud of this, given his Teutonic ancestry. It is unexpected, this proclivity toward the romantic and glissando passages.

Next up is the final piece of the compulsories, a wicked tour de force by Toronto composer Jay Krehm. His "Pounce in E-Flat" is a competition favourite because it runs the gamut of virtuoso techniques, including a series of polyrhythmic whacks on the soundboard.

Toby retunes, basted by the spotlight, while the judges scratch so many points for tone quality, for artistic merit, for presentation — and technique.

Jasper claims to love this piece, but then he makes a point of loving anything difficult and up-to-date. Toby's hands shake

— too late to pop beta blockers. This is the treacherous moment, just before attacking the opening bars. He looks up at the audience that he can't see and forces a smile: he's a message in a bottle tossed into an invisible sea.

Moxie blithely continues to print in capital letters the story of her life. After school she'll Skype the boyfriend in Peterborough that her parents disapprove of. Before rising each day she'll write down her dreams. "I have astonishing dreams," she insists, waiting for Jasper to pursue this, but he doesn't.

The first minefield in the Krehm pops up: a barre chord that crosses all strings but one, and that one is in the middle of the fretboard. Toby lays down his index finger, leaning into it, and luck swarms in. The notorious bar passes with just a hint of string buzz. Quickly, he creates a new memory that supersedes the old; it's music's great gift of temporality.

The middle movement is a hailstorm to be played, according to the composer's instruction, "as fast as possible."

Hold on to your hat: Toby dashes into the flamenco-styled *rasqueados* that lead up to heroic slaps on the soundboard.

Bravo, Toby. *¡Olé!*

"Know something?" Moxie stares at Jasper with her sunken eyes. "Everyone thinks I'm making myself puke, but that's not true. This is the way I'm supposed to be."

"I'm not your therapist for the eating disorder," Jasper reminds her. "We're here to concentrate on life skills and organizational issues."

No wonder she sniffs with contempt. She's finishing up her list and has managed to write "homework" in the slot just before "bedtime." Her high school marks have been in the doghouse, she confesses.

Scheduling saves us; without it there is no way of living inside time, feeling its edges. Toby claims this is what music does, creates bar lines and distinct phrases and rhythm, pressing time into a logical sequence. He likes Jasper to believe that music is a steadying influence, both feet on the ground, but Jasper isn't fooled. It's a parallel universe reached via a home-made rocket.

Krehm's middle movements are ultra-short: one is thirty seconds long, the other less than a minute, both percussive, sounding like cutlery jiggled in the drawer. In the final movement, regulation length, comes a passage of great tenderness and retro-charm, played in creamy *tosta* tones over the sound hole — the composer's nod to tradition. Toby starts in, but he's going way too fast, caught up in the wild ride of what preceded. The judges must be scratching their heads: is this an interpretative oddness, or a misstep?

Jasper feels his shoulders tighten as he stares out the window at the boulevard streaming with morning traffic. Noise is muted by double-paned glass. Something is going wrong.

Toby expels breath, and when he goes back to play the repeat, he's sweet as birdsong. With luck the judges will think he meant the contrast.

"Want me to fill out this part?" Moxie tilts the page, index finger pointing to "sports."

"Please."

Jasper watches as she checks off football, ice hockey, and ping-pong: she's been lying from the start.

Toby doesn't know what he's going to be asked to play for his free choice until the last minute. Competitors email a list of possibilities, and the judges announce their pick on the spot. The performer must be ready to enter any of several musical worlds without hesitation.

Manuel Juerta calls out, "Sor's Grand Sonata, please, Mr. Hausner."

Toby tugs at his cuffs. "Excuse me. That's not on my list."

Juerta peers through his reading glasses at a sheet. "I see it here, son."

"That piece was on my first list," Toby says, clearing his throat. "I sent you a replacement list last month. Didn't you receive it?"

The auditorium becomes very quiet, then there is a whispered consultation among the judges and a shuffling of paper.

Juerta glances up. "We have located it. But this is not a good plan, my friend, to change your mind."

Toby bows his head in acknowledgement of this indisputable fact. Jasper would have told him it was a daft idea.

"Let's hear the Giuliani," Juerta says, easing back into his seat.

Toby's face relaxes. He could play this in his sleep.

"I like the way you don't get on my case about eating," Moxie offers, tapping the pen against her injured teeth.

"That's not my job."

"Everyone else does." She considers Jasper with big amber eyes.

"So I don't have to."

She doesn't buy this. "You probably think I want to disappear, so I starve myself. That my dad or some gross uncle had sex with me when I was little and that I hate my boobs." She rises to her feet, teetering with the vertigo that accompanies her condition. Jasper holds out a hand to help, but she waves him off. "Everyone's making such a big deal about it. Why can't they just go back to their own lives and stop gawking?" She points to her medical chart. "Write something true for a change."

"What might that be?"

She looks as if she's going to bark at him, but instead she sits down again with a light thud. "I wasn't always like this," she says after a moment. She's plucking at the material of her skirt. "Something happened. It took on a life of its own."

Jasper has read her chart before the session: this behaviour began when her sister left home to go away to college two years ago. A fact that tells him nothing.

The life-skills chart spills off Moxie's tiny lap onto the floor. "You actually believe in this crap? Tell me you don't. It's too pathetic."

The sardonic tone is back, but Jasper isn't deceived. She tries to wipe away tears without him noticing as she leans over to pick up the paper. The abrupt change in position makes her dizzy again, and she grips the side of the chair. He moves in; he could reach her in one step if necessary. She's supposed to be drinking Ensure Plus twice a day.

"I believe in your ability to turn your life around," Jasper says. "A plan can help you get started."

This solid life Jasper presents to her, measured off in teaspoons, holds little appeal. The institute's room is two-dimensional, a cubist spray of lines and colour. She sees what other people can't: hunger gives her special powers.

Jasper points to the chart. "I wasn't born yesterday, Moxie," he says good-naturedly. "Erase, please, and start again."

She mimes indignation, and when Jasper doesn't respond, she laughs and says, "Tough crew here," then hunches her brittle shoulders for the task.

How her mother must despair, watching her daughter's flesh fall away. The woman crowds in at every meal, adding a dollop of sour cream or extra meat, then watches anxiously to see what Moxie does with it, every bite and swallow a victory. After the meal, she stands next to the closed bathroom door, ear pressed to the wood, listening to every sound that breaks through the swoosh of the running tap.

"This is so sick," Jasper's client informs him. "You want to know what I'm doing every minute of the day."

"It's not for me, Moxie. It's for you."

She doesn't fall for this line, either. But instead of attacking him, she changes her tone and speaks in a low voice, barely audible. "I can't stop."

He waits, then says, "I know."

"Every morning I wake up — it's there. First thing I think about, even before my feet hit the floor." She shakes her head. "You can't imagine."

But he can.

"Everyone wants to burrow inside me," she goes on. "The hospital? They can't get enough, poking around measuring potassium levels, glucose, antibodies, blah, blah heart rhythm, blah, blah thyroid, blah, blah kidney function ..." She seesaws back and forth on the chair, voice rising with outrage.

"What if we all went away?" Jasper asks. "Then what would you do?"

She seems to be having trouble catching her breath: lung function poor. Maybe feeling an arrhythmia, though the immediate crisis is supposed to be past. Her bony fingers tap her sternum, as if encouraging the engine to rev up. Her whole body seems to quiver from within. "That's not going to happen," she says. "I got appointments into next year." Her fingers now curl over the rim of the chart — such old hands.

"You've heard about the virus," Jasper prompts.

"No way I'm going inside an airplane. Those things are bacteria bombs."

"This wouldn't be a good time to end up in hospital again," Jasper says.

She rubs her mouth, which is itchy, possible case of thrush.

Jasper gazes over her head at the wall, the framed photo of Monet's pastel-hued water lilies.

Toby is well into the Giuliani by now, a charming piece but hardly the pinnacle of artistic expression. Prickly heat soaks his armpits, masked by the trim blazer he's bought for this event. Then he finishes, wrist lifting to let the last of the sound float away.

"I practically died last year," Moxie says. "They said a couple more days and my kidneys would've shut down." She crosses her legs, making no attempt to mask their alarming thinness: she is in awe of her achievement, even inside her terror.

"We don't want that to happen again," Jasper says.

"And this list is going to help?" she asks, holding up the chart.

"What do you think?"

"Don't feel bad if you can't get through to me," Moxie says. "Because *I* can't get through to me, either."

The timer starts blinking: session is over.

"Take the chart home and give it another go," he says, then holds out a hand to steady her as she rises. She clings to his elbow as they make their way to the door, but already with her free hand she's searching in her bag for her phone. No doubt she believes that Jasper is ill-defined, that most people stumble through life as deaf as furniture.

Rachel is talking on the office phone as they enter the reception area. When she spots her boss, she waves and continues to speak to the caller. "I get the picture," she says with a gesture of exasperation, and Jasper understands it is Luke on the other end.

"What did our friend want?" Jasper quizzes when she hangs up.

"Oh, you know." Rachel assumes a conspiratorial tone. "Making nice before the meeting, hoping I'll let some tasty bit of news slide out." She leans back on the swivel chair and plants her feet on the desk. "Don't worry. I'm a paragon of discretion."

Sometimes Jasper regrets confiding details of the current mess: the girl believes it gives her privileges.

"I need a copy of this document." He releases Moxie's chart.

Rachel hesitates before lowering her feet, as if the mundane task were beneath her.

When Rachel disappears into the copy room, Moxie says, "She doesn't like you much, does she?"

"What makes you say that?" Jasper doesn't conceal his surprise.

"That weird look on her face."

For a moment Jasper is rattled. He recalls Rachel's expression while talking on the phone before she spotted Jasper. You can't say it was gleeful. That would be an overstatement.

Pens squeak as the judges scribble notes and scores on their clipboards.

"Thank you, Mr. Hausner!" a voice booms from the wilderness. No hint in its tone as to how he has played. Toby beats an escape to the wings, breathing hard.

"Outstanding!" Lucy says, touching his back.

His heart is an ungated pony. "I was okay?"

"More than."

"I stampeded through the last movement of the Krehm."

"But you pulled it off." Lucy clings to his elbow in a proprietorial way as they move down the corridor toward the green room. "Dazzling!"

"Really?"

"Where have you been hiding all these years?" she asks.

"Hiding?" he repeats like a half-wit. He's running through the program in his mind, focusing on bits where he'd inexplicably strayed from decisions worked out hundreds of times in practice. "I could ask you the same thing."

"You could, but you haven't."

The Argentine sits on the chair in the green room, hands breezing through the opening bars to the Tárrega. The man is dressed like a movie star — steel-grey jacket with black shirt and turquoise tie. He glances up as Toby enters, nods once, but keeps playing. Feeling his impatience, Toby packs quickly and darts out of the room, not noticing that Lucy has disappeared. He's ravenous, a tight muscle of hunger, and fixes his mind on a platter of steak frites, the sort of thing Jasper never serves at home.

Lucy waits outside the recital hall in her summery dress, hand planted on one hip as Toby steps into the daylight. "They tell me," she says gaily, "that if you play well here, you might get laid."

"Good incentive," Toby says.

"I go on in forty minutes."

"Then you should be busy prepping, not hanging around here."

The smile leaves her face, and he can see the lined skin, the brave red lips. He guesses she has allowed thoughts of home to invade her mind, a substitute anxiety that is more familiar than performance.

They move toward the dorm, which is a long block through the campus. A slick modern building housing the medical school blocks light in one direction while a dour Victorian edifice crowds the western side. An outdoor art exhibit is underway, and the courtyard is packed with booths displaying watercolours of Old Montreal and marine life, the vendors parked on camp chairs. Lucy threads her way between them.

"I never practise just before going onstage," she says, brushing past a booth selling handmade puppets. "What if I blow a passage, or forget it entirely?"

This is where Toby should reassure her, but he doesn't, his mind still wrapped around his own performance. As they near the dorm building, Hiro bursts through its double doors and cries, "Absolute disaster!" He waves his hand in front of their faces. The nail of the ring finger is torn, leaving a jagged edge. "I hit on fucking shower tap."

Toby lifts the wounded hand and inspects the damage. "Got a Nittaku back in your room?"

Hiro nods. Nittaku is the Japanese ping-pong ball favoured for cutting into crescents to serve as emergency nails.

"But I absent special glue," he says.

"Fetch the ball and I'll enact my magic," Toby instructs. "But first I must eat."

As Hiro disappears into the elevator, Lucy says, "Don't do too good a job."

Toby is genuinely shocked. Not enough glue, and the nail will go flying, like a hockey player losing a blade mid-stride.

Lucy is stricken. "Scratch that last comment," she says, hurrying toward the elevator leading to the women's wing.

The Krehm piece went off the rails with that weird slur he added out of nowhere; it threw off his fingering until the end of the phrase. Can't let each tiny flaw chisel into his confidence, for something else, almost magnificent, stole in when he was onstage: he knew he belonged up there.

After lunch, after demolishing a platter of steak and fries, Toby bends over the nail repair job, manicure scissors in hand, Hiro's elegant finger waiting to be saved. He remembers his mother clipping his nails when he was little, tenderly pushing each soft cuticle out of the way. When he was very small, she chewed off his nails with her teeth. Hiro sits quietly during the task, as if afraid he might distract Toby. It's an intimate procedure, and Toby inhales the kid's aftershave and minted breath as he slides the tiny slice of celluloid over the nail and presses it flat. The two men eye each other, and it's Toby who breaks the silence, saying, "Don't drink hot fluids or eat for an hour."

Hiro looks anxious; he doesn't get the joke.

"You'll be fine, my man," Toby reassures him. "This is your lucky nail."

Luck is a word Hiro does understand, and he grins with relief.

Something's taken hold of Lucy's body and colonized her mind, an unstoppable force. She's leaped from being ecstatic at not making a fool of herself in the opening round to actually thinking she might win.

When she first met Mark, he was a compact man wearing khakis and one of those Picasso striped shirts, and she decided they would create a bohemian life together. Each month they would host a salon where poets could read their latest masterpieces, musicians would play difficult experimental music, and Mark's big, expressive paintings would hang from the walls to be viewed and discussed by all. Lucy would play a sonata or two, when she wasn't refilling the cauldron of chili. Something like this event did happen once or twice. Then one day Mark came home announcing that he'd landed a job at the Art Gallery of Ontario as a security guard and was about to be fitted for his uniform. He took to the job and claimed he was in no way restless or unhappy, although weeks went by where he didn't set foot in his studio. In the evenings he'd fool around with his collection of vintage lunch boxes and Big Little Books. She never dreamed she'd end up living with a man who enjoyed hobbies.

"Draft Agenda." Jasper types these words under the subject heading, then taps send. Luke likes the word *draft* because it's an invitation to muck about and change things. Jasper fully intends to edit the sequence himself before tomorrow's meeting, and he'll do this without alerting Luke. The fiendishly expensive dinner party Luke arranged for potential donors, without consulting the executive, will be brought up under "other business." Jasper has arranged for Ruth Baxter, treasurer, to raise the issue: she's livid. Luke took his cronies to Flood, the fancy oyster bar, and put it on the institute's tab. They can ill afford such reckless extravagance. Luke will squirm in his seat and bluster on about how they were discussing "key elements of our fund-raising mission," but no one will buy it. When the issue is raised, he'll act startled, then say with a grandiose wave, "If I've lost the confidence of this board, then I offer my resignation …"

Not for the first time.

Except instead of the ritual chorus of objections, there will be a tense silence, then Ruth will ask for a show of hands.

Jasper lowers his wrists, flexing them according to the ergonomic exercises he's followed religiously since that spot of trouble last year. He feels like a hunter closing in on his prey after a long and exhausting chase — don't snap a branch now.

FOURTEEN

TOBY SLIPS INTO A SEAT AT THE BACK OF THE RECITAL HALL TO catch the rest of the semifinalist performances. As each musician finishes his set, he disappears into the wings, then re-enters the auditorium through the rear door.

When a young Mexican plays with a strained expression on his face, Larry the Texan whispers, "Too much *frijoles* for breakfast. The kid's holding back an epic fart." Bumped from competition, Larry has been on a bender and reeks of the bourbon he carries in a Perrier bottle.

A Brazilian plays recklessly, and Armand leans over to titter, "He comes too fast, yes?" The German musician, who also struck out in round one, is making copious notes about each guitarist, convinced this will help him in future competitions.

When Salvatore, a diminutive Italian, performs an extravagant bow full of unnecessary flourishes, there is general merriment at the back of the hall. He plays with self-conscious beauty, lifting his hands to let the chords ring, extended rubatos that verge on corny, all of it a shameless romanticism that sets Toby's teeth on edge. He even plays the modernist Krehm piece as if it were a late-nineteenth-century *Fantasia*.

Javier, the Argentine, slips in two seats down. He's changed into a polo shirt and velvety chinos. Toby eyes him more than once and waits for a mirroring gaze. No dice — Javier is a straight arrow, despite the fussy cufflinks. "Italian guys play cantabile from cradle to grave," he whispers during a pause between movements. This is true. Salvatore finishes each phrase with an arpeggiated chord, a mannerism that his fellow guitarists term "a Segovia" — a tip of the hat to the great pioneering guitarist who played in a different era. Such easy sentimentality won't fool the judges.

Toby rests one sneakered foot up on the seat in front. Lucy waltzes onstage next, wearing a long black skirt and a gold blouse.

"The old babe," Armand says, making no attempt to lower his voice.

Suddenly, Toby is rooting for her while Armand slumps in his seat, reminded that he has been humiliated by a woman. Lucy has piled her hair on top of her head in a weird way and fastened it with a clip. Toby watches as she aims her hundred-kilowatt smile at the judges, though there is no way she could see them in the blare of the spotlight, and her bow is a modified form of dead chicken with an odd jerk at the end, as if she's lost her balance.

If Lucy heard Armand's nasty comment, she isn't letting on. She arranges the material of her skirt, then cranks up the piano stool and the footrest. Her guitar has a reddish soundboard, not the best instrument in the world but a decent copy of a fine luthier's work. Lucy has promised that if she makes it to the finals, she'll put a deposit on a Clifford Fairn concert model, though it takes seven years for delivery, given his backlog of orders. By then she'll be — good Lord — fifty-three.

Her tune-up is discreet, apologetic pings that only the first rows can hear. She wipes her palms on her skirt, then steps into the opening bars of the Tárrega.

The piece unfolds in a version so opposite from the Italian's overblown romance that at first Toby recoils. Decent tone, but it all sounds diligent to his ears, each phrase carefully articulated, each nodule of expression prearranged — nothing left to chance.

Toby glances at his colleagues down the row and notes the skeptical expressions, and let's face it, obvious relief. Nothing here to fear. Yet by the time she's halfway through, Toby is almost convinced. This Tárrega is brainy, perhaps brainier than the composer merits. He claps harder than he needs to when she's done.

Next up is the Krehm marathon. Lucy skims her palms over her draped knees and gazes at some point at the back of the hall, then plunges in. Whispering ceases. Javier, about to beat an escape, stops in his tracks. The Tárrega has in no way set them up for the performance that is underway. She attacks the piece with her whole body, fingers snapping off the fretboard, head bobbing, shoulders pressed forward — the performance of a lifetime. Chords unroll with deadly accuracy, and she mutes vibrating strings with her wrist, her thumb, anything that moves. It could fall apart any second, but it doesn't.

Toby slips his foot off the seat and leans forward, hardly daring to breathe.

The final notes die away and only then does Lucy release her shoulders. How fragile she looks, as if the air has gone out of her.

"Jesus," Larry breathes, "she plays the rest of the program like this then the rest of you crew might as well pack it in."

Javier stiffens. He won't give up so easily.

"Where did this *hausfrau* come from?" Armand wonders aloud. "I have entered twenty competitions, and this is the first time I've seen her."

Falling back into the seat, Toby begins to share the tango of panic: Lucy doesn't need to win the way he does. She waltzes in with her disguise of middle age, pretending she's some housewife, someone's mother.

Next up is the suite.

———————————

Lucy squints blindly into the auditorium. Something inside her chest is doing handstands. Beyond the lights they note her bleached hair, a body that has borne children, and they are inventing a hundred stories to explain her presence here.

Delete Mark's recent phone call.

"Just spoke to the Canadian consulate in Bangkok," he said in the flat voice he uses when agitated. "Uncle Philip's been busted. Turns out he's a sex tourist."

If I can get through the gavotte, she decides, the largo will be clear sailing. She can play the gavotte perfectly ten times in a row, then have it splinter during the eleventh. A slight drop in concentration causes havoc. If she stops for a moment to think, then she'll capsize. Uncle Philip stashed in some third world jail, an old man in a hot country, so fastidious, flossing his teeth three times a day, those manicured nails. They will have confiscated his camera: Exhibit A.

Nothing lasts, least of all this heated stage and her pulsing nerves, nor the anticipatory stirrings of the audience. This is what the young ones don't know; they have no perspective.

The guitar settles in her lap, a familiar weight.

Uncle Philip, she decides, smiles at a woman with a red purse and tells her, "I'll look after your boys." The woman nods, and without glancing at him, holds out her palm. He counts out a wad of *baht*, the national currency, and watches as the bills disappear into her purse.

The man will be kind, the woman thinks. He'll give the boys treats, more than she can ever offer. Tonight she'll cook fish and see her sister-in-law, who is pregnant again.

Her modest house is the site of a pleasure Uncle Philip has been imagining for months, a bouquet of anticipated tastes and smells, his papery skin yearning to be touched, as he touches now, pulling the boys into his chest, burying his face in their sleek hair.

Lucy lifts her hands to play. The tug of string against flesh and nail is welcome relief.

When she finishes the piece, she cradles her guitar tenderly as if it were a child she's rescued from great danger.

In the back of the hall, Hiro caresses his new fingernail, giving it suspicious glances in the dark. He needn't worry, for Toby is an honourable man and used plenty of glue.

Like the others, Lucy has mailed a short list of repertoire to the judges and awaits their selection, not knowing what piece she'll be asked to play next.

Nerve is nothing new to her. Try fishing a toddler out of a swollen river or marching into a hospital room to demand they not resuscitate your own father. Nerve is what you get by living a life.

An older judge rises to her feet and peers through spectacles at a sheet of paper. Visnya Brocovic achieved second place in this same competition during its inaugural year, and she returns every fall to help select the new generation. She examines the printout and says in a heavy Balkan accent, "We will hear the Briscoe, please."

"The what?" Larry whispers from the back of the hall.

No one in the row of musician spectators has heard of a composer called Briscoe. Will Lucy get extra points for this departure from tradition?

Toby smiles tightly. He knows that Charles Briscoe taught Brocovic decades ago in Sarajevo and that Visnya, in turn, taught Goran, Lucy's current teacher — a biblical order of transference. This is no coincidence. Lucy has done her research.

Turns out that Briscoe is hardly a crowd-pleaser. The first note rings as an harmonic and the sound decays into silence before the piece gets going, to be followed by a series of tone patterns overlaid with otherworldly key changes. Jasper would like this — dissonance excites him — but it's a lousy choice for competition. Toby relaxes his fists until they fall open.

Jasper and the rest of the institute staff gather around the monitor. The city has flown in a noted epidemiologist from Calgary who stands outside Toronto General, surrounded by a squadron of reporters. Wind blows his hair across his face; he looks as if he packed quickly, wearing a scruffy shirt and windbreaker. It's Bob Howell, the physician who firewalled Foothills Hospital with a series of screening procedures and protocols considered second to none.

Microphones bob while the doctor holds forth. "You know how this beast operates?"

A rhetorical question.

"A virus can't do its business until it binds to a living cell," he continues breezily. "The host cell is tricked, can't sort out its own protein from the invader's. The virus replicates thousands of times in less than an hour. While you ladies and gentlemen sip your morning coffee, a virus has already done a day's work."

Nervous laughter greets this observation.

FIFTEEN

"MANUEL, DEAR FRIEND AND COLLEAGUE, YOU HAVE A SOFT heart," Portia says, dropping an arm over the back of the leather couch.

Manuel Juerta stiffens, feeling himself shrink from the heavy limb behind his head. "I insist we consider promoting this woman to the finals."

"We consider everyone."

"It's our job," Jon Smyth adds.

Why does Manuel feel they're ganging up on him? The judges have gathered in the faculty club lounge, a low-ceilinged room featuring leather furniture and walls of white pine. He feels as if he's in a fishing lodge, not in the middle of a large urban university.

"Her performance was original and not ordinary," Manuel says, hearing his voice rise.

"I agree," Portia says, sliding a finger down to touch his shoulder.

"It was certainly both of those things," Smyth concurs.

"Visnya, what do you think?" Manuel turns to the Croatian guitarist, her face, as always, set in a worried frown.

"An interesting case," Visnya says, reaching for one of the digestive cookies on the tray. "In my opinion this performance had great vitality and originality, but it was the work of a gifted amateur."

"A moderately gifted amateur," Jon corrects, wielding one knobby knee over the other. He's changed into a pair of cargo shorts and has been scarfing cookies since the group adjourned here half an hour ago. "What do we know about her?"

"She studies with Goran Petrovich, a student of mine in Yugoslavia before the war," Visnya says.

"What does Goran say?"

"We haven't spoken in years. He lives in Toronto. I live in Belgrade."

Manuel interrupts this exchange. "What do we care about the viewpoint of her teacher? Are we not here to judge a particular performance?"

There is a short silence, then both Jon and Jean-Paul, who is head of the guitar department at this Montreal university, start to speak at once.

"We must determine who is most able to launch a solo career," Jean-Paul insists. "I would have to agree with our British colleague that this woman is a moderately gifted amateur."

Jon jumps to his feet, spilling crumbs onto the floor. "I can't believe we're even considering promoting this woman to the finals!"

"Settle down," Portia warns. Then, in demonstration of her conciliatory powers, she turns to Manuel. "Tell us more what you are thinking."

What is he thinking? Manuel hardly knows. Perhaps Mrs. Lucy Shaker is exactly what they say, no more, no less. He heard how she played, saw how she caressed the instrument in her arms, an intense, hunched figure whose hands shook, yet he couldn't keep his eyes off her. After so many years of judging countless musicians, how many times has he felt compelled to listen to every note?

"I suspect it's the narrative possibilities that appeal to our friend," Portia says. "What a marvellous gesture to lift this woman from her regular life. We all want to be given a second chance — God knows I wouldn't mind a crack — but is it realistic?"

They turn to Manuel and wait for his reaction, for he is the most eminent musician in the room.

Of course, he feels compelled to defend his choice rationally. "Her rendition of the Krehm was the most coherent and passionate of any competitor."

"I grant you that," Jon says, "but we must speak of the rest of her program."

Manuel starts to list sideways on the couch. He's exhausted after another sleepless night, not helped by someone pulling the fire alarm at 3:00 a.m. The truth is that he can't remember much of the rest of Mrs. Shaker's performance. His own scribbled notes reveal unspectacular scores, a fact that he shields from the others, but knows he must eventually share.

"What Manuel means to say," Jon ventures, "is that we must realize this musician has achieved a personal triumph."

"Well put," Portia says. "Alas, we have no form of adjudication to reward such an achievement. Of course, I intend to take her aside and congratulate her."

A note of relief enters the room — sanity has returned to the judging process. Only Manuel remains silent. His coffee cup is empty, and when he peers in, he sees a tiny insect drowning in the dregs. Behind a pacing Jon Smyth, a pristine log lies on the hearth, waiting for the bitter Canadian winter to land.

Jon can't let go of the topic. "Is it feasible to believe this woman is on the cusp of a major performing career?" he asks, though it isn't a real question.

"Why not?" Manuel asks.

Jon spreads his arms. "Because she's forty-six years old, man!"

An antiquity, barely clinging to life. Manuel reaches into his coffee cup, retrieves the corpse of the gnat, and flicks it onto the floor. "Is it our business to forecast future performances, or to reward the recital we have just heard?"

"Come on, Manny," Portia sighs, reaching under her blouse to give her bra strap a tug. "You're being philosophical rather than realistic."

That word again.

"I only know what I have heard and seen," Manuel insists. "Not what I might hear at some point in the future. Who can predict this?"

Portia comes to the rescue again. She'll make a fine president of the federation. "Let's proceed to the next name on the list," she suggests, peering over a pair of flaming red reading glasses. "We can revisit Lucy Shaker's case at the end. Agreed?" She fixes her gaze on each judge in turn until she receives a confirming nod.

"Toby Hausner." Jean-Paul adjusts his own glasses to read from the list. "Name rings a bell."

"Indeed it does," Portia says. "Do we all recall Paris? Jon was present as a youthful competitor."

"Which year?" Jon asks. He entered the Paris competition twice.

She reminds him.

He sighs. "Never made it past the preliminary round. Small problem with tone and warped fingerboard."

"Toby Hausner made it to the finals."

"He did?" Jon seems mystified, then gradually a look of astonishment crosses his face. "Christ! That kid in dreadlocks who scorched through the semis, then came out barefoot for the final?"

"The very one."

"He self-immolated out there. It was a horror."

There is a short silence as they digest this sorry tale.

"He played magnificently today," Jean-Paul eventually says. "This is an artist I'd pay to see."

"Yes, but ..." Portia ventures. "Do we dare promote him?"

"Come on, lads an' girls, let's hear it for our courageous driver!" This is Marcus holding forth as he lunges down in the aisle of the rented bus.

"Rah-rah," someone says.

He slaps his hands together. "Who knows a song? C'mon, you lot. I want to hear boisterous singing."

The bus brakes sharply, and Marcus tumbles forward, grabbing the back of Trace's seat for balance. "Fucking shite!" He's been hammered since being dropped from round one.

Pine trees spin by on the old highway, a river route following the crevice of a glacier-age gorge. Let the judges deliberate, Toby thinks. You can't sit on your ass waiting for your future to arrive. Worse, you can't let your recital haunt you, endlessly replaying the program in your mind, each hiccup going stereo, every misstep and string buzz pressed into memory. "A hundred bottles of beer on the wall!" he roars, and everyone joins in for a verse.

"Sit down!" the long-suffering driver pleads.

Acting like a bunch of unruly camp kids, the gang's on furlough from the competition, trying to pretend it doesn't exist for a few fragrant hours. Air streams through the open windows, message from the larger world.

Marcus, the Brit who was expected to ace the first round but didn't, ignores the driver's instruction. "What's our national anthem, mates?" He starts ripping an air guitar version of the opening chords to "London Calling."

The rented school bus crests into the final leg of the journey, then drills a sheer downward slope to the launch area next to the riverbank. A picturesque log cabin is set up next to stacks of kayaks, canoes, and rubber rafts.

The group clambers out, stretching and yawning after the hour-long ride on hard seats.

"Fuck those," says Marcus, pointing to the row of kayaks. "Eskimo tippies. I want something with a nice fat arse."

"You must wear PFDs, sir," the youth in charge of rentals insists. "It's the law."

Marcus lifts up one of these objects. "Did the mighty voyageurs wear lifesaving vests? I think not."

Lucy and Armand haul the cooler of beer from the bus as the door swooshes shut, and they all watch the rattletrap vehicle take off, due to return in two and a half hours.

Many competitors elected to stay back in their dorms, continuing to practise, not allowing their precious focus to soften. Toby was like that once, but now he grabs a beer and clambers up on a rock — Champlain discovers the new world. It pours in from all sides, the rolling foothills of the Laurentians, the river curling below, and behind them the highway buzzing with traffic. The universe is a bigger place than an airless room and a guitar.

Hiro, looking capable in track pants and purple tank top, scrambles down the hillside and lifts the bow of a kayak, testing its weight. Toby leaps off the rock, beer can in hand, and skips after him to the launching area. They could be a normal group of pals on an outdoor lark. Daniel, a francophone guitarist, negotiates with the youth in charge, and soon a pair of kayaks slides into the water, Hiro deftly stepping into one and Trace in the other. The girl lives on an island, so she swings away from shore with an effortless tug of paddle. The rubber raft bobbing dockside is for everyone else. They pick over the stack of orange vests, and Toby pushes his arms through one bulky number, not bothering to fasten the ties. He can almost see Jasper pointing a warning finger. Rolling up the cuffs of his jeans, he steps into the unsteady craft, clambering over the benches toward the bow.

The gorge is a placid waterway this time of year, long past the unpredictable surges of spring. Armand, followed by a musician from Belgium, then Marcus and Lucy, all settle into the raft, lurching as they find their seats.

"Who's in charge here?" Lucy frets.

"Call me skipper," says Toby, lifting a wooden paddle. "Cast off!" He takes a final gulp of beer before stashing the can under his seat.

The craft rocks as Baldo, a Serbian guitarist with shoulder-length hair jumps onboard, cigarette dangling out of his mouth.

"No smoking!" the Belgian shudders, and the others chime

agreement until Baldo is forced to extinguish, shooting the spent cigarette toward shore.

They're all wearing ball caps emblazoned with the vanished Montreal Expos team logo — even Lucy, who looks like a kid in her capris and T-shirt. She shrieks with glee as the craft enters the current and picks up pace, cruising down the centre of the river, cliffs rising on both sides.

Toby paddles like crazy, then remembers that this is no time to mess up a shoulder and eases off. Two kids working a plastic paddleboat chug past, knees cranking, and everyone waves, fellow mariners. Smoke trickles into the sharpness of sky: trash burning on the far side of the hill. There's something manic in the group's mood as the raft noodles midstream. They've been cooped up too long in small rooms. Marcus finally gets everyone singing sea shanties, and Toby reaches over the side to drag his hand in the current. The water is coated with fine pollen dust, luring dragonflies that dart and hover. Sun bathes his skin, ultraviolet rays be damned, and he feels the tension of the past few days exit his body.

Hiro adeptly steers his kayak around sandbars and rocks, marking the route ahead. Back in Japan he's on a rowing team that gets up at the crack of dawn to practise.

Marcus, despite his extensive knowledge of shanties, turns out never to have set foot in a boat smaller than a car ferry. "Whoah, man, look sharp!" he shouts. "Rock to starboard side."

"Port, actually," Lucy corrects him.

"Will ya get your paddles out and work now?"

"I'm skipper," Toby reminds him, though he didn't notice the rocky patch and it's the current that saves them from mishap as it loops around the boulder back into the deeper water.

Lucy points: is that a hawk soaring over the firs?

"No, dear, it's a cormorant," says Marcus, taking a snort of beer.

Armand reads aloud from his guidebook, translating from German. "Watch for the narrows. In early spring, high waters rage through the sudden narrowing of the gorge." He points a finger upward. "Limestone walls heave as the river surges toward the sharp bend, transforming the placid river into a turbulent froth." He twists so that he's looking back at Lucy and Baldo. "You hear this, my friends?"

"No!" they chorus.

"A turbulent froth. But —" Armand peers at the page "— this danger disappears by midsummer when the run reverts to being a suitable family activity, ideal for novices and children." He beams. "So, precious musicians, your search for glory is not in jeopardy, *ja*?"

Toby stashes his life jacket under his seat when it starts to bunch under his chin. He's an ace swimmer, and these are hardly class three rapids. Klaus drove Felix and him to the Y every weekend for lessons and made sure they earned their badges.

Trace shoots ahead in her kayak, then paddles back to report on what's in store, making fancy manoeuvres, switching direction on a dime. This time she waves her paddle and shouts mutely into the breeze.

"She is trying to warn us," Armand cries, lifting up from his seat to see better. The raft shudders with the abrupt shift in ballast.

Hiro sets his paddle across the gunnels and makes a gesture with his hands, palms pushing together as if he were playing accordion.

"Channel narrows," Lucy interprets. There's a charge of excitement in her voice.

"Of course it does," Armand says. "This is exactly what the guidebook explains."

He starts to read aloud again until Toby barks, "Shut up."

Trace is back-paddling. Her jaw works as she shouts, words lost in the freshening breeze. Behind her the hawk thing swoops over the treetops and disappears behind the cliff.

"What do you want us to do, boss?" Baldo asks in that laconic voice that always sounds as if he's half asleep.

There is an odd silence, a reprieve, then suddenly everyone calls out in tandem, "Whoah," as a calamity enters their field of vision.

The crew lifts out of their seats, hoisting paddles aloft as if fending off a monster. The banks of the gorge rise as the river jackknifes, the placid water now on the boil. Their raft careens toward the flank of bare rock while Lucy cries, "Hold tight!"

"Paddle backward!" someone yelps.

Toby stares in horror at the wall slamming toward them. Better to jump, he quickly decides, and catapults into the water while the raft shoots out from beneath him.

Cry of shock as his chest freezes. River the colour of brine.

Water is your element, Klaus used to say, but this isn't the measured metres of the YMCA pool, and Toby feels his body suck deep into the murk. Any moment he'll pop up like a cork. No one drowns at a guitar competition — the idea is halfway comic. Keep pulling at the water and its skin will break, but it's taking a long time, so much longer than expected.

He'll open the final program with the sonata, classic mood, very controlled and nimble. He can almost taste the audience's attention as he can taste this brackish water. Not much air left in his lungs, last pocket dialled to empty.

Jasper will be so sad. He would say, "What kind of nitwit leaps into rapids without a lifejacket?"

The tug comes hard, a sharp pain. Toby is snagged by his hair, then he's staring into a pink face under a ball cap.

"Got him!" Lucy cries, leaning over the rim of the raft, arms strained to the max. Toby feels himself tear through to open air, skimming across water while she heaves him onboard, a massive trout.

Back on the shore the kid who's minding the shop keeps walking backward as if he expects the musicians to attack him. He's talking a mile a minute, not that Toby is counting. He's too freaking cold, clothes glued to his body, shoes squeaking out aquatic smells and weeds.

Daniel translates, "The Quebec government in conjunction with the local Indian band has built a dam upstream to control water levels."

"Now he tells us," Marcus says.

Another cascade of French, then the translation. "You did not listen." Pause. "The upper river run is closed." Daniel frowns. "There were three warning signs." He looks up. "Anyone see those?"

Lucy creeps up behind Toby and puts her arms around him, and he jerks, as if to be touched were lethal. He's so cold he could shatter.

"Put this on," Lucy says, slipping out of her sweatshirt.

Toby pokes his chattering arms through the sleeves, then draws the garment over his head. For a second, as darkness closes in again, he panics.

He emerges to see the rest of the group clustered on the rocks, subdued after his misadventure.

Baldo flips a butt into the innocent-looking river. Marcus lies on his back, face baking in the sun. Trace swats flies. Where's Hiro? Is anyone counting heads? There he is, tank top peeled off and hanging on a bush.

"You gave us one hell of a scare," Lucy says.

Marcus lifts his head. "Why did you jump ship, son?"

"It was a lousy idea," Toby agrees.

"I was ready to dive in after you," Lucy says. She sounds breathless, as if she'd actually performed this heroic act.

Toby says quietly, "Thank you," the words she is waiting to hear.

Trace steps across the rock and crouches next to him, runs her hands up and down his arms, chaffing them back to life. "What was it like going under?" she wants to know, a flare of excitement inflecting the question.

"Bracing," he says.

"Whoah, Nellie." She grabs his forearm. He was about to keel over.

A crunching sound signals the arrival of the bus as it steers off the highway onto the gravel shoulder.

Armand jumps to his feet, waving wildly.

SIXTEEN

LUCY'S TWIN BOYS, CHARLIE AND MIKE, ARE PLANNING TO get their own place as soon as possible, the only setback being that neither has a job or savings. Mike says that students can apply for welfare. The boys can tell you exactly what their basement apartment will look like: a stack of vinyl records, old-school turntable, handful of clothes stuffed into cardboard boxes, mattresses on the floor — life reduced to its essentials. Maybe a high-def television. A decent set of speakers. Mike wants a dog, a Rottweiler or Doberman. Shame that pit bulls have been banned.

Lucy was in the kitchen preparing lunch for Mothers of Gifted Children when Mark wandered in, eyes bleary from a long shift guarding art. She was in the midst, recipe book cranked open, julienned vegetables everywhere.

"Pass the cumin seeds?" she said. "Top shelf."

"Hmm?" Mark never heard what she said the first time.

"Cumin!" she snapped. Then she added, "Please." She must make an effort.

Mark obeyed, or tried to, scrutinizing the row of spice jars, twisting them around so he could read the labels. Finally, he handed his wife the jar marked cumin.

"Uncle Philip will have touched ground by now," he said, leaning against the fridge door so that she had to ask him to move. "Bunking into some seedy hotel to save money."

This conversation took place a week ago.

"Probably," agreed Lucy, mixing chili oil into the spices.

"Not such a bad life," Mark continued. "Taking off for months at a time. We could do that."

Lucy looked up. "How?"

Mark made a dismissive gesture toward the sprawl of dirty bowls and spatulas. "Just walk away. Take the boys with us, or leave them with my sister."

"With Rosemary?" Lucy snorted.

"Why not?"

Wild Rosemary, whose own daughter waltzes in and out of rehab? The same Rosemary whose current boyfriend sports a three-inch knife scar on his cheek after a skirmish "inside"?

She knew that look on Mark's face: wistful. He was missing who she used to be when they were younger. Well name that tune! She missed herself. She didn't want to take off for months at a time like a pair of retirees. Her life was just beginning to get interesting. Last night her teacher, Goran, set his hand on her wrist and said in that smoky voice, "You are surprising me, Lucy. You are surprising yourself."

She'd just played her entire program in the conservatory studio. When she was done, he stared at her, those almond eyes filled with actual tears.

Three hours of practising, wearing a visor in the dorm room because the overhead light hurts his eyes. Toby is still shivering, but he won't give in to it, no whisky for this boy. They are all waiting to hear who's made the cut, who will enter the finals. The pod is oddly sombre, the now-famous river catastrophe a sobering reminder that life holds surprises. Toby's mind wants to go back to the crisis, as minds do, into the dark cold water. Brain scrambles even as his fingers plant firmly on strings and fretboard.

At 8:00 p.m. Toby drops his competition badge into his pocket, noting that the others don't. They're proud of their status. Montreal's *Gazette* ran a feature on the congress, calling this gang the cream of the classical guitar world, the upcoming generation. The musicians step into downtown Montreal, aching to be together again. The waiting is a kind of torture: when will the judges make up their bloody minds? A tour bus rambles past, headed toward historic Old Town, its loudspeaker noting features in both official languages.

Hiro points to a sign over a café door: LES COPAINS.

Toby nods. Sure, he'll go anywhere. The musicians enter the bistro and hover in the vestibule, waiting to be noticed. Everyone in the joint is earnestly talking while dance music blasts out of a cut-rate sound system.

"We better scram, Junior," Larry says, digging him in the ribs.

"Why?" Toby asks. The place looks perfect, very Left Bank, elegant young men propped up against the bar, soft lighting, pressed tin ceiling — this is why people travel.

"Fag bar, you dumb Canuck."

This is how they end up in a faux-Irish dive called Brasserie Molly Bloom, full of French-speaking students perfectly at home with posters of early-twentieth-century Dublin, cobblestone streets greased with rain and soot. They find a pair of empty tables at the rear of the cavernous bar and push them together.

"I'm not drinking tonight," Toby announces when Larry and Armand try to ply him with beer.

"Come on, man, you're celebrating a near-death experience."

If he starts drinking, he won't want to stop. Coldness sucks at his entrails, a thirsty creature.

"I saw his hand," Lucy says, settling in across the table. "It was poking out of the water, very creepy, then it disappeared. So I snatched what turned out to be hair and pulled like crazy."

Toby reaches up to touch his scalp, which is still tender.

"Such an episode underlines how meaningless this competition is," she says, her voice seeking to be heard over The Chieftains soundtrack. "Who bloody cares about music when tragedy beckons?"

Toby stares at his fingertips, still crinkly from river water. This isn't what any of them want to hear. The competition must matter more than anything. Once they stop believing that, their performances will wilt.

He wants a drink. Now.

It's Armand who makes a point of switching topic. He's tired of Toby grabbing the attention, and he leans into the rim of the table, forearms planted on its sticky surface. "The man is amazing."

"Who?" someone asks.

"Williams."

He's referring to John Williams, the British guitar god.

"And I don't mean just technically," Armand adds.

"Too amazing by half," Larry says, pouring himself a pint from the pitcher. "I swear he never plays at more than sixty percent. He doesn't have to."

Growing more animated, Armand says, "In master class in Frankfurt he remarks that my playing reminds him of Fisk."

Eliot Fisk, that is, American guitar whiz, said to be a carrier of the Segovia torch. This boasting is routine, especially for a man who didn't make it past the preliminary round.

"Give me the wild guys, like Käppel or Barrueco," Larry says, hoisting his beer in salute to those who aren't present. "They take risks."

"I know a guy who had a tendon removed," Armand says, holding up his fretting hand, touching the web of skin between his third and fourth fingers. "So now these fingers move independently."

Everyone winces.

"That's crazy," Toby says, but he's impressed.

The waitress brings a mountain of nachos and a platter of fried clams. Ever since he played in the semi, Toby's been hungry in a way he recognizes as being adolescent. Lucy rises from her seat and heads off in search of the washroom.

"Did you check out that girl's instrument?" Larry asks, sour cream oozing out the side of his mouth. He means Trace, daughter of a schoolteacher and a tugboat driver, too young to join them at the bar. "Perfect copy of a vintage Smallman, for fuck's sake. I'd give my right testicle for one of those."

Smallman is the Australian luthier favoured by John Williams and other top-flight players.

"Who'd she have to fuck to get that?" Armand asks, but his heart isn't in it. Just thinking about the girl possibly going on to the final round makes him sick.

"I hate my instrument," Larry says, his voice rising over the Irish music. "Piece of shit, late Hernandez."

"What model?" Hiro asks.

Larry tells him.

"They are crap for thirty years," says Hiro, his head bobbing out of an oversized collar. He plays an instrument fashioned by an obscure Belgian maker.

Larry looks glum. "You got an extra twenty grand?"

"If I win …" Toby says, grabbing a pint of ale from the cluster of glasses in the middle of the table. This after swearing off until the end of the competition. "I'll track down a Fleta '65, or maybe an early 1970s José Romanillos."

"And for this you offer one testicle or two?" Armand asks.

Toby knocks back half the beer, and his body jolts. This is what counts, the camaraderie and guitar talk; this is what he lives for, what he's been missing too damn long.

"You hear Trace play in semifinal?" Hiro asks.

"Missed it," Toby confesses.

"She is dangerous, my friend."

Toby keeps a game smile on his face. "She's just a kid."

So was he, back in the day.

"One fucking amazing kid," Hiro adds. He's picked up their way of talking.

"Who does she study with on her island?"

"Some guy no one's heard of."

They all stare into the table with its botched plates, worrying about this girl who is too young to drink with them. The poster of James Joyce with his bad eyes glares down: just when you think you're safe again and happy, the old enemy, fear, creeps in.

Lucy returns from the washroom, wiping her hands on her slacks — the dryer was on the fritz. When she sits down, she inserts herself next to Toby, so that he has no choice but to slide over the banquette and press next to Hiro. He feels the young man stiffen. This is probably a social horror in his country, to mash next to someone you barely know.

Hiro fixes his eyes on the TV monitor, Yankees versus Red Sox.

"How's the nail holding up?" Toby asks. He feels Lucy staring at him, searching for symptoms of delayed trauma.

Without changing the direction of his gaze, Hiro splays his mended hand on the tabletop. "You are excellent craftsman." Before Toby has a chance to examine the perfectly glued seam, he lifts the hand and indicates the screen. "See that?" he cries, pointing. "Fantastic Japanese guy!"

The pinstriped player, Hideki Okuda, slides into third base, then rises, grabbing his batting helmet off the dirt. Yankee Stadium erupts as two men cross home plate.

Hiro is delighted. "Okuda is big star in Japan. My college is named after him. Every kid wants to be Okuda."

"My ideal job?" Larry says from the other end of the table. "Grad students pop into my office two days a week, summers off for touring."

"I teach part-time," Armand says. "Frankfurt college, adult education. They promote me last year, for I am respected for pedagogical skills. So, my friends, you see that not always the most fantastic musician makes the best teacher."

Hiro drops back into his seat. "I will not teach," he says. "If I cannot make employment as solo performer, then I give up guitar forever."

His statement silences the group, and Hiro never takes his eyes off the television monitor.

SEVENTEEN

HOW MANY GENERATIONS OF STUDENTS HAVE WORN DOWN THE furniture in the lobby of the Fine Arts Building? Trace heaves herself onto one of the sturdy tables, hitches her pants, and sits cross-legged, so lithe and flexible that one can only remember what it was like to have a body without joints. The box office is closed for the day — no performance tonight. The girl who runs the café is swabbing down the counter, switching off the espresso machine, all animation sucked from her face after an eight-hour shift. Trace thinks, I'll never have to do a job like that. She watches the staircase at the north end of the lobby. She is waiting for someone and trying to look as if this isn't so, running a hand over her bristly head. With her long neck and fine features, she manages to appear both street urchin and feminine.

There is the sound of a door shutting on the floor above, and she jerks to attention, hearing a pause followed by the clip-clop of shoes while a man hums to himself. She recognizes the tune: "Amor de mis amores" by Veracruz composer Agustín Lara. There's the snap of a briefcase closing, then Manuel Juerta appears at the top of the staircase. He's wearing a Cuban shirt, the kind you don't tuck in, and he dances down the stairs.

Of course, Manuel sees her sitting there; he may be tired, but he isn't blind. The empty foyer belongs to a world that will return to its clamour in a few hours, before there's a chance for a proper airing out. He notes Trace, her naked head vulnerable as a newborn's, her scruffy feet jammed into flip-flops.

"You," Juerta says, pointing with a hand clutching a can of beer. He glides like a skater across the tile floor.

Trace pretends to look surprised.

"Where are your colleagues?" Juerta asks.

"At some bar."

He nods sympathetically, then heads for the front door, hesitates, and turns around. "So you are alone."

She doesn't reply. He's working it out.

"Come," he beckons.

She dangles one foot.

"Come here."

She slips off the table, shrugging, as if she might or might not obey, then traipses toward him, aggressively tomboy, so attractive in a natural beauty. He slings an arm over her shoulder and directs her outside into the Montreal night. Juerta doesn't give a damn who sees them. There are implied rules about fraternizing with competitors, but rules are meant to be broken, and this little girl was waiting for him.

"We will go and visit my good friend Ernesto," Juerta says, guiding Trace toward the intersection. "You know Ernesto?"

Trace doesn't.

"Then you will have an adventure." His arm droops from her shoulder, and they canter across the busy street. Trace wonders if Ernesto is a famous guitarist who lives in Montreal. This city is pandemonium compared to her quiet island village — horns toot, tires squeal, everyone trying to run you down. She peers into open doorways and sees the press of people and cigarette smoke, hears throaty laughter and thudding bass beats. Trace tells herself she'll find a way to move here or to some other big city. Not a chance she'll turn into one of those island women growing organic vegetables, selling handcrafted yoga mat sleeves at the fall fair.

Juerta flags a taxi, they jump into the back seat, and Trace thinks, I have no idea where we're going. The idea excites her. As the cab darts in and out of traffic, Juerta touches her cheek with the back of his hand.

"How old are you?"

"Eighteen," she lies.

Ninety minutes later Trace yawns, glances at the wall clock, and yawns again. There's no water left in the cooler — she checked — and she's studied the framed anatomy chart a dozen times and flipped through copies of *Body Mind Magazine* with its weird articles on animals as healers and liquid fasts. She gets up, bottom sucking away from the vinyl chair, and walks over yet again to the closed door and listens, ear pressed to the wood. She hears a soft moaning inside followed by a whimper, then another moan. In the background shimmers a soundtrack of fake rain forest, electronic howler monkeys, and digital squawking parrots. She wonders if she should leave, that maybe it's what he expects. Could be he's forgotten all about her as he sinks into his treatment.

A burst of laughter erupts from the room, and she pulls back from the door, stuffing hands in her pockets. Should she call him Manuel or Mr. Juerta or even Señor Juerta? Some of the other competitors call him Maestro, a term that thrills her, but she can't imagine uttering the word.

Are they going to head out to dinner once this is over? Will he pay? She checks her wallet — twenty bucks and it has to last through tomorrow. Maybe he expects her to pony up, he being from a third world country. Don't think too hard about the naked man on the other side of the door getting his puffy ass kneaded by the muscular Ernesto. What if something creepier is going on in there? Maybe this clinical setting is a front, part of an international operation where they pull in naive girls and it's the last you hear of them. Trace paces the waiting room pausing only to gaze out the window, fourteen floors above busy St. Catherine Street. This office building must be empty so late in the day. Even if she let out a scream, would anyone hear above the street noise? What if they drop a black hood over her head? She'd hate that.

By the time Juerta pushes open the door, patting his bits of hair down and buttoning his shirt, Trace is in a full-blown panic.

"Señorita," he says, ignoring her nervous state, "the mighty Ernesto has rearranged my anatomy and now we must eat. Have you had supper?"

How could she have? She's been hanging out here all this time. Without waiting for a reply, he picks up his briefcase and leads the way down the gloomy corridor toward the elevator. Once inside, he rests his cheek against her shoulder.

"We have survived another day," he says, and she feels the weight of his head as the elevator lurches down to the lobby.

Dinner is in a Mexican restaurant run by a woman from Durango who keeps bringing on courses of spicy food. No one asks what Trace might like. Juerta helps himself, then urges her to do the same. "In my country it is not easy to eat this well."

All she knows about Cuba is that Castro is on the brink of death. Maybe he's dead already. She'd like to ask but doesn't want to appear stupid. Don't they drive old cars down there while ancient men sing on street corners and play marimbas?

Manuel seems to be having the time of his life chattering in Spanish to the waitress. The decor of the tiny restaurant consists of a three-dimensional scorpion gripping the stucco wall, its deadly tail pronged upward.

"Do you know what we are talking about?" Manuel asks suddenly.

She reddens. "Not a clue."

"We are discussing how Lucia, my wife, who is perhaps no longer my wife, says I should stay in this country. Defect."

"Well you should," says Trace.

He laughs too heartily, the way people do when something is the opposite of funny.

"Only if you want to," Trace adds quickly.

The laughter stops, and he leans forward, seizing her hands. "Tell me, young Canadian friend, why I should eliminate my life, my friends, my family, in order to wash onto these shores like a piece of driftwood."

"You wouldn't be driftwood," she protests. "Just about anyone here would hire you to play concerts or teach or —"

He squeezes her hands once, still holding on. "This is very interesting. Tell me more."

Is he making fun of her? "You could write your own ticket."

Abruptly he lets go. "A one-way ticket."

The waitress hovers, lowering a basket of hot tortillas wrapped in a checkered napkin. Manuel says something, and the waitress replies in a way that sounds as if she's reciting from a poem or a song.

Trace picks at the tube of squash filled with some kind of white cheese. When is he going to say something about her playing? She knows she's good. She won the Kiwanis Festival, regional division, last year and played at the lieutenant governor's New Year's levee. Certain people understand music from first breath; she could sing before she could talk.

The waitress reappears to set down jumbo-sized margaritas on the table, and no one asks if Trace is old enough. After running her finger around the rim of the glass and licking her salty fingertip, she takes a generous sip. Tart lime and tequila pucker her mouth into a gasp of pleasure: her first cocktail. Back home it's straight rye or gin, stolen from some parent's stash.

"If I don't return on the date of my visa, maybe I can never go home again," Manuel says. "Tell me what I should do."

Trace says, "It would be amazing if you moved here."

He waits a beat, hops off his chair, and slips in beside her on the banquette, then starts stroking her fuzzy scalp. He's wanted to do this all evening.

"I could do this all night," he says.

Staring straight ahead, Trace says, "Prove it."

The hand stops moving, and he tips her chin to study her face. "You mean this?"

For a moment she wavers, then says, "Sure."

Trace slouches on the bed in Manuel's room at the fancy hotel where he insists on being put up, disdaining the cheaper B and Bs where other judges stay. He moves about the space restlessly and pours Trace a glass of water, then one for himself.

"Are you drunk?" he asks.

"No," she says, though she is a little.

"Too much alcohol since I arrived in this country," he says, loosening his collar.

He's wearing a gold chain, like baseball players or rappers. He paces and drums his thigh as if girding himself to say or do something. That's his guitar case propped in the corner, loaded with airline stickers from all over the world. You'd never guess by the banged-up container what lies inside, the succulent rosewood-and-cedar instrument, chaffed honey-brown by decades of performing. She wonders if he'll bring it out and play a private recital for her. She decides she will be calm, and that this will be the most amazing night of her life. The buzzing in her head is new. She's not much of a drinker, not like some of the kids back on the island.

"Water is good?" he asks.

She lifts her glass in salute. "Primo."

Then he stands before her, knees pressing against hers. "Such a long day, yes?" he says.

Trace smiles, not understanding that he hopes she will go now. She has followed him around all evening and now she's in this man's room, the same man everyone watches as he struts down the hallway or huddles in conference with the other judges: Manuel says this, Maestro says that. While other contestants prowl around downtown Montreal, she's been spending hours solo with Manuel Juerta.

"This is a dangerous place for you, young lady," he says.

"Yes?"

"Alone in a hotel room with a man you barely know."

She shrugs, pretending to be unimpressed.

"You should be back in your own room practising."

She sucks in a breath. He wouldn't say this if she hadn't been chosen to head into the finals. No need to practise if she were to be sent packing. Maybe he'll tell her she's a rare talent; that's what people say after they hear her play.

But Manuel's plump face sags with weariness. Dampness soaks through the cotton shirt that sticks to his muscled back. On his island, buildings never have windows sealed shut. Back home, fragrant sea air follows you everywhere.

He takes her head and squeezes it into his chest.

This is it, she thinks, this is how it begins.

"I am going to telephone a taxi and send you back to the *dormitorio*," he says.

But he doesn't push her away. Instead, his hand lowers to her shoulder blade, and she feels him shift, some adjustment being made.

"So you think you want to stay with some old Cuban guy?" he asks.

She looks into his puffy eyes and wonders how old he is — forty? Fifty? She always knew her life would never be ordinary.

"Answer me," he says.

She says nothing.

He disappears into the marbled bathroom, and soon she hears the faucets drill water against the tub, then a clank as his belt hits the floor.

She picks up the TV remote and waves it at the screen. It's that crappy movie where Jennifer Lopez pretends she's a maid. She turns the sound way down so that she'll hear when the faucets stop running. New York City must be great, she decides, watching JLo waltz along a Central Park trail in midsummer. If she wins the competition, she'll make sure they book her into a New York recital hall, one of those fancy places with chandeliers. People will flock to hear a kid from a Canadian island. Well, they might. Her teacher, Trig, will fly down for the event even if she has to pay his fare. She'll keep her head shaved and won't slink onstage in some diva gown. She'll stay authentic to herself.

When the bathroom door creaks open, Trace waits for the Maestro to stride out naked. She tells herself she won't blink or act surprised, but the truth is she hasn't exactly done this before.

She snaps off the remote and the movie dies.

He's hairy, she notes, with stocky legs that he's crouching to towel dry.

"Now we go to bed," he says, very matter-of-fact, then reaches over to switch off the light. As he does this, she sneaks a look. Somehow she thought it would all be more pink.

The mattress heaves as Manuel rolls in beside her. "Take this off." He tugs at her shirt sleeve.

Maybe she was supposed to have done it already, while he was in the shower, and she obeys, turning away. Suddenly, she's not feeling so great. Perhaps she shouldn't be here. Not too late to escape. Street light begins to seep through the curtains, and she feels him watching. Off with the shirt. She unhitches her bra, which is a little grotty on day four, then pulls at the hemp pants, lifting her bum so she can slither out without rising from the bed. Underpants, she decides, can stay on for now.

God, it's actually happening, the mighty deed.

"You headed for breakfast?" It's Larry the Texan making for the cafeteria, sticking his hands deep in the front pockets of his jeans.

"Not yet," Trace says. She hardly knows where she is, what day, what month, what year. Her face must be flaming, and her feet coast over the pavement, light as feathers.

Larry squints, trying to stare her down to where he can see her plain. It's the lobby of the dorm building. She found her way here after sharing a cab with Manuel, after saying goodbye at the iron gates. Her teeth are crud, tongue coated with last night's meal. Tex has no idea. But he cocks his head and asks with obvious curiosity, "You just coming home?"

Let them think what they think.

Manuel's chubby leg dropped over hers, a dead weight, and for a minute she thought he'd nodded off. But soon he lifted his head and peered into her face; he smelled of soap and toothpaste.

"I apologize, my young friend," he said.

For what?

"I think you have not done this before."

She was quiet, then said, "Not exactly."

That was when he rolled off and lay staring at the ceiling in the dark hotel room.

"I have," she said quickly, "but not very often."

He ran a hand over her bare belly, the calluses on his fingertips pebbling her flesh, making her gasp.

"This is not the scene I compose for you," he said. "It would be a disappointment."

Round cheeks, snub nose, curly reddish hair, not what you'd call handsome, but his eyes were beautiful, fringed by long lashes.

"I have a better idea," he said, looking at her with what might have been amusement. "Play for me."

"Now?" She sucked in a breath.

"Certainly now. Tomorrow we might all be dead."

"But I didn't bring my instrument."

"So you must use mine."

She slipped out of bed and pulled on her shirt, not her pants, and unsnapped the locks on his case. The guitar was heavier than hers and beat-up after twenty years on the road. Sweat marks stained the fingerboard, and there was an obvious repair on the back. This was a guitar that had seen the world, had played in every concert hall she'd imagined and more. She stroked it as if it were a cat, a creature with a beating heart.

Manuel propped himself on the pillows, then clasped his hands behind his head. "It won't bite. Please begin."

Scooping up a chair, she started to play.

"Ah," he sighed as she swung into the opening bars. "The partita. So beautiful."

Later, as she lay beside him while he slept on the bed, he slipped a hand between her legs. He's dreaming I'm his wife, Lucia, Trace thought.

Entering her monk's cell this morning, Trace plucks her guitar from its case and perches on the edge of her cot, feeling cool wood press against her thigh and forearm. The instrument smells of abandonment. Without her it's a dead thing, pieces of wood glued together, but the moment she touches the fingerboard and rolls her thumb across the strings, the beast stirs back to life.

EIGHTEEN

TOBY'S SEMI-DRUNK WHEN A KNOCK ON THE DOOR ROUSES him. Peek at the clock: just midnight, but it feels as if he's been awake for hours, cursing the greasy pub food and beer. Since everyone else in the dorm is dead to the world, he rises groggily, wraps a sheet around his midsection, and heads out of his room to investigate.

Lucy looks as if she hasn't slept, either. She's wearing the same clothes she wore at the bar and waves him into the foyer with an urgent gesture.

"What?" Toby rubs his mouth. His breath must be Middle Earth.

"They posted names."

He feels a shudder of anticipation. "The finalists?"

She nods. "I don't dare look on my own."

Toby tugs at his hastily assembled toga. "Let me change."

"You'll be fine. Let's go."

They ride the creaky elevator to the ground floor, then step into the deserted foyer, Toby clutching the improvised garment to his chest.

Lucy points to the daily board where someone has pinned a sheet of white paper containing a daunting short list. "I don't know if I'm more scared to be left off or to make the cut," she says in a pinched voice.

Toby approaches the board, chin high. With each step the print grows larger until he can read the eighteen-point caps at the top: FINALISTS.

Rise of sour puke to the throat — blame nachos and the second round of Guinness.

"Seems like you're one of the chosen few," Lucy says. She's crept up beside him.

He stares at his name. Cascading euphoria, a wild sensation that roars through his body, and he has to close his eyes for a moment, then just as suddenly, joy's boxcar arrives — doubt.

There's been a mistake. He's some lunatic who thinks he's the pope or Napoleon.

"Congratulations," Lucy says. "Well deserved. I thought you played beautifully."

"Thank you." His voice echoes inside his head.

"Might as well head back to my room and sleep," she says, and he hears footsteps disappear behind him, the elevator door swing shut.

Four names appear in clear type.

His own.

Trace.

Javier the Argentine.

And Hiro.

Salvatore, Mr. Bel Canto, has been dropped.

No sign of Lucy. He looks around, but she's gone.

She may sleep, but he will work.

Toby soaked his battered fingers in a bowl of salt water. This took place in the room he'd rented, first home away from the childhood home. Eighteen years old, practically a genius, people were saying. Yes, the word was used. He was training full-time for the Paris competition. He'd been playing so long without a break that his calluses cracked, hence the blood and stinging saltwater bath. In the early hours of a marathon session, he was on edge, too much energy; his nervous system was his enemy. He'd discovered the solution: subdue the animal via repeated exercises while watching himself in the mirror. As time crept by, he seemed to enter a state of bliss where the rest of the world fell away. He'd been reading documents by certain Christian and Eastern mystics, so the sensation was not unexpected.

What did it feel like and how exactly did it come upon him? This is what he's been trying to remember all these years. Was he playing better back then, more poetically — not a word he would normally use — or did it just seem like that?

How could he ever know for sure, since nothing was recorded and all he knew then was that he wanted to stay divine, so he removed his bloodied hands from the water and went back to work.

Brief pauses to sip cold tea and eat biscuits until both ran out. Did he sleep? He had no memory of it.

The next stage slunk in like a troll, bringing a drenching fatigue. His mind seized up and was unable to look upon itself, to reflect. Sleep was death; food was death; water was liquid kryptonite.

This lasted how long? He wasn't sure, because he continued to play, hardly knowing what he was doing, until one evening the fatigue lifted and he found himself performing the most difficult piece of the looming Paris competition flawlessly, not a hint of tension in his body.

If this was ecstasy, then he wanted more of it.

Rapture and genius were twinned, though this was no place to linger, more like a hot stove touched and escaped from.

Jasper's opinion was that he'd been deceiving himself in a hypoglycemic trance.

Brother Felix found him slumped over a chair, passed out, and hauled him down to Emergency. The object was to re-hydrate, re-salinate, orchestrate potassium, electrolytes, and urine production. He'd lost his way, everyone seemed to agree, because he'd forgotten the basics: eat, drink, sleep. It came from being a young man living alone.

Ten days later Toby clambered aboard the airplane to Paris — wild horses couldn't stop him. The so-called breakdown, he figured, was a minor setback. He barely glanced at the City of Light as he set to work, and very soon the judges were scared and excited by him.

On that June evening of the final recital, he crossed the stage in front of six hundred people, sat down on the quilted stool, lowered his right wrist, still scarred from the IV, and began the variations.

Then the horror started. A composition that he could, and did, play in his sleep unravelled, then vanished without a trace. He improvised in a quasi-classical mode until a voice called out, "Thank you, Mr. Hausner. That will be plenty for tonight."

Valium injected in the left buttock brought him back to the recognizable world, while Klaus flew over the Atlantic to fetch him home.

"Was that you I saw sneaking into the university this morning?" Portia fixes Manuel with her eyes. She wears a military cap today along with some sort of sailor getup, complete with bell-bottom trousers.

They stand holding takeout coffees on the sidewalk below the entrance to Jean-Paul's brownstone. The judges and a select group of federation members have been invited for a breakfast meeting.

"Excuse me?" Manuel says.

"With our youngest competitor in tow, both of you looking worse for the wear?"

"Excuse me?" Manuel crafts an indignant tone, but he is hoarse, his throat not yet lubricated by coffee.

"You should know better," she adds before edging past him and mounting the iron staircase.

The front door is already open, and Jean-Paul greets her with a kiss, then waits for Manuel, who ducks the kiss but receives a comradely embrace.

"I hope that you have slept well," Jean-Paul says.

"I can only speak for myself." Portia raises her crescent eyebrows, then sails past both men into the high-ceilinged room where she pirouettes, taking it all in. She strokes the dining table that is set up as a buffet, then runs her hand over an accompanying chair and notes, "Hans Wegner wishbone chair, very nice." Without a trace of self-consciousness, she lifts one of the asymmetrical plates. "Vintage Russell Wright. Jean-Paul, you suffer from impeccable taste."

"Blame my wife." Jean-Paul stands in his collared shirt and pressed black pants, looking embarrassed.

"And where is this celestial being?"

Before Jean-Paul can answer, the doorbell rings and he hastens to greet the newcomers — the judges Visnya Brocovic and Jon Smyth, both looking achingly chipper.

As greetings are exchanged, Manuel rubs his eyes with his fists, grinding the optical orbits until he sees flashes of light. The front door continues to swing open and shut as federation members arrive. His head throbs — nothing to do with last night's romantic fiasco.

"Do not come home," Lucia ordered during his morning phone call to the weary homeland. "There is nothing here — zero." Then she pleaded, "Stay, Manuel, and send money."

"Pastry?" Jean-Paul offers a tray of delicacies.

Portia makes a little gasp of pleasure and coasts her hand above each item on the platter until her fingers seize a miniature brioche.

The guests draw file folders from a stack and sit on folding chairs that have been set up around the perimeter of the spacious room. The walls, Manuel notes, are decorated by abstract paintings, the artist's palette knife yielding layers of colour and unusual dumpling shapes.

Seeing his interest, Jean-Paul says, "My wife is the artist."

He looks proud, so Manuel quickly mutters words of praise.

"I hiked up Mount Royal as the sun was rising," Portia announces to the gathering as she brushes pastry crumbs off the flap of her nautical shirt. "From which vantage point I watched the city spring to life."

Visnya appears cross. She finds Portia's athletic feats undignified in a woman of her age.

"Time to call the meeting to order," Jean-Paul says, clinking a spoon against his water glass.

Twenty-two musicians and teachers have gathered this morning to attend to the important question: who will succeed old Gregorio as president?

Portia teeters at the edge of her chair, face bright and expectant, folder set on her lap. Gregorio himself is not present. A reoccurrence of an unpleasant disease keeps him home in Milan under the devoted care of his wife and widowed daughter.

"Who's running for election besides Portia?" Jon Smyth asks.

"I see three names on our list," Jean-Paul says, directing him to the material they are supposed to have read and carefully considered.

"I'd just like to add," Portia says, clearing her throat, "that I feel confident that any one of the nominees would do a fine job, and I will happily bow to whomever gains your favour."

Still, she can't restrain herself. "As we are well aware," she continues after a tiny pause, "the organization has become an old boys' club and technologically backward. I aim to change this."

There are mutters of agreement and even a trickle of applause. Then Jean-Paul taps his glass again. "May I remind you that elections are the *final* item on our agenda. I draw your attention to the first point of business — how shall we thank Gregorio for his decade and a half of careful stewardship?"

There is a short, troubled silence. Everyone has a Gregorio story, often involving some small humiliation or misunderstanding.

"Lifetime honorary membership," someone suggests.

"Scholarship in his name?"

"We commission a guitar-shaped pin."

"Cufflinks."

Someone snickers, then cufflinks versus tie pin occupies ten minutes of heated discussion before Jean-Paul cracks the tabletop. "How many in favour of a scholarship?"

A few hands shoot up.

Meanwhile, Portia is mouthing something in Manuel's direction; an instruction is being issued. An ominous feeling creeps into Manuel's already churning gut, for Portia remembers things with hideous clarity. She will have recalled, for instance, that episode in Mexico City, not his finest hour, and now this new slanderous accusation caws into his morning brain: *Was that you I saw sneaking back this morning with our youngest competitor in tow?*

What right has she to monitor his actions?

He nods back, very curt, inviting no further communication. The voting continues, and Portia slips out of her chair to perch on the arm of Manuel's modernist settee. She whispers in his ear, "Can I count on you?" and places an icy hand on his shoulder.

He stares straight ahead, pretending to be intent on the business of the meeting. Cufflinks are surely more useful than a tie pin. Gold is too expensive and would deplete the coffers of the federation.

"For the proposed virtual conservatory?" The hand sinks farther into his flesh.

Jean-Paul glares at the pair of them as he tots up numbers of raised hands.

"I need you," she breathes.

"Why?" Manuel can't bear women who drag him into their personal dramas.

"No private cabals during the meeting," Jean-Paul says, staring at them with a fixed smile.

Portia glances up. "Carry on, love. We'll be done in a flash." She presses her magenta lips to Manuel's ear again and confides, "Without you onboard the idea will be DOA."

After this pronouncement, she pulls away and returns to her chair, bowing apologetically to Jean-Paul. Everyone notes the way she dangles one long leg over the other, sailor on shore leave.

Manuel steams: why should he lend his name to her enterprise? He won't agree to be her hand-picked director of the Internet conservatory, an unpaid position. Yet if he doesn't, he understands, last night's girl will be brought into the picture. A disaster for Trace, as his vote would be cast off as tainted. There could be a nasty scandal, one he can ill afford. So unfair. After all, he tried to persuade the girl to go back to her *dormitorio*.

Perhaps not hard enough.

The front door of the apartment kicks open, and Jean-Paul glances up. His face changes. He looks startled, then wary.

A stout young woman appears in the doorway. She is a mess, hair uncombed, jeans slung low on full hips. Jean-Paul speaks in rapid French, which the girl ignores. Instead she examines the scene in the room and demands in unaccented English, "What are these assholes doing here?"

Jean-Paul's expression freezes, then he speaks quietly to the assembled group. "I apologize for the manners of my stepdaughter."

"Don't apologize for me."

Jean-Paul's face blanches. Or rather it loses its colour and white is what remains.

"Come." Portia seizes Manuel's hand. "Now's our chance."

They retreat to the room behind the kitchen where coats hang next to a stack of neatly tied newspapers. Daisies wilt in a pair of window boxes, the petals brown so late in the season. Beyond the window is the fire escape decorated with a compost bucket.

"Tell me why you're not supporting my initiative," Portia demands, pressing her hip against the ledge. "It's not my nature to twist arms, yet I'm fully prepared to do so, for the sake of the organization."

"I understand," Manuel says.

"And yet you claim not to be in favour of the virtual conservatory."

"It is so."

She can't bear his bland tone. "It's the only way we can grow into a global organization."

He thinks of Guillermo and Mónica back home, content to live their lives staring at a computer monitor, never setting foot outside the country, hardly moving beyond the confines of the decaying capital city, lulled into a hypnotic trance they mistake for life.

More stormy words issue from the front room, followed by Jean-Paul's measured tones. The man is a paragon of self-control. After this exchange, they hear a stomping noise as the girl makes her way upstairs, then the bone-rattling slam of a door and the rumble of a bass beat — the universal language of adolescence. Even his beloved Gabi exhibited such behaviour once or twice.

"I will return to the meeting now," Manuel says, not about to be bullied by this woman who sweeps her hair behind her ear, a woman who thinks she is still beautiful.

She ignores his small threat. "Do you really think Aaron Whatshisface from Tel Aviv is a possible leader? The man can't be bothered to show up for meetings. And Harry from the Florida Panhandle? Nicest guy on earth but —" She raises her palms. Words fail her. "I've led Berkeley Integrative Strings to its present stature, sat on every committee in the federation." She stops. "Why am I working so hard to sell myself?"

"I don't know," Manuel says.

Her expression shifts, all trace of pleading gone. "If you don't sign on, your indiscretion of last night will become public knowledge. How many more competitions do you think you'll be invited to judge?"

The woman is a warrior, and Manuel likes warriors. He is one himself.

"Perhaps I will support this plan," he muses aloud, "but first I have one favour to ask."

"What?" she asks, already suspicious.

"Can you create an artist's position for me in California?"

As soon as he speaks, he feels a surge of excitement. Lucia will whoop for joy at the news. He'll send home envelopes, via Western Union, full of crisp money orders that she'll dangle in front of her family. Morning fog rolls into Berkeley, California, the city where Nobel Prize winners meet over coffee to discuss the birth of the universe or urban ecology, and where he, Manuel, might finally cease the daily struggle.

NINETEEN

So it's over. No need to make a fuss. It's a miracle she made it this far.

Lucy plants herself in the middle of the dorm room, open suitcase on the bed, train ticket in hand. She could make the 2:10 to Toronto and be back in time for dinner. Wadding up soiled underwear and socks, she stuffs them into a plastic bag, which she tucks into the bottom of the suitcase. Hope springs eternal, as her mother would say, but now she is merely tired and wants to be home. She'll phone the empty house and leave a message, hint that Mark stick a roast in the oven. The boys could help — peel carrots and wash lettuce for salad and thaw the berries for dessert.

Here she goes, planning her own welcome-back meal.

"What are you doing at home?" she demands when, to her surprise, someone picks up the phone.

It's Mike, mid-morning on a school day.

"Who's this?" he asks groggily.

"Your mother."

"Oh, right," he says. "Hi, Mom."

"Is this a PD day?"

"Yeah. That's exactly what it is."

"Charlie's home, too?"

"Charlie's wherever Charlie is."

"And where is your father?"

A long pause with the sound of feet padding to the window. "Car's gone, so he must be at work."

"Does he know you're home?"

"I can't be expected to intuit what Dad knows or doesn't know."

She recalls how the boys looked lying side by side in the dresser drawer when she first brought them back from the hospital before Mark assembled the crib. Charlie had cradle cap, scaly skin on his bald head, while Mike was pink and clear from the start.

"Did you win?" Mike remembers to ask.

"God, no."

"Hey, that's too bad." Mike seems to come alive. "How come?"

"I'm not good enough." This is a useful lesson for the boys, Lucy thinks. It's not always enough to work hard and to want something badly. "I didn't make the finals."

"No way!" Mike is indignant. "Who do I have to come and kill?"

She laughs, feeling oddly pleased by his impassioned response. "I'm headed home now."

"Don't you have other stuff to do there?" he asks quickly.

He refers to the schedule of workshops, recitals, presentations.

"I guess I've lost heart."

"Don't utter such words," Mike says. "Don't be a quitter."

He sounds so firm and mature.

"You really think so?" she asks, pretending to defer.

"You've been looking forward to this event for months. Live it out, Mum. We're counting on you to set an example. Charlie and me, we could use some uplift."

She slips the phone into its case, her eyes shamelessly red, and picks up the program. If she hustles, she can still make Manuel Juerta's Baroque Ornamentation workshop.

As she splashes water on her face, other thoughts elbow in: why doesn't Mike want her to come home? And what's this hedging around Charlie's whereabouts? PD day, my foot. Isn't Mike supposed to be at band practice this morning, allegedly playing saxophone?

I am becoming mentally ill, Lucy thinks.

Uncle Philip, neatly pressed clothes soaked in sweat, pulls the two boys close to his body. His nostrils flare as he inhales deeply, as if he could draw them inside himself. They are lying on a bed in the room at the back of the hut, dirt floor and no glass on the window, just a sheet of newspaper taped up, and through it he can hear the sound of the street, the put-put of a motor scooter, mothers calling to children — though not these children.

He props himself on one elbow and gazes at the boys, whose eyes remain closed as they pretend to sleep. Their narrow chests rise and fall in perfect synch. He doesn't hear the grinding of a car as it pulls up, nor the popping of doors as two men in uniform slide out and take their sweet time making their way to the entrance of the hut, hands grazing their holsters as they always do when they approach such a dwelling. They nod toward the stout woman who fries meat in the outdoor kitchen, and she nods back. The reward money will pay for a concrete floor, and later, maybe running water. Meanwhile a new flush toilet waits, as it has for five years, in its cardboard box in the corner.

The judges cluster at the foot of the stairs of the Fine Arts Building, weary from hours of heated arbitration. No sign of Lucy's colleagues who must choose this morning between a demonstration on French polish technique in the atrium or Manuel's ornamentation workshop upstairs.

Lucy holds back, pretending to adjust the strap of her guitar case, and waits for the judges to mount the stairs.

Disappointment ambushes her again. This crew eliminated her from the last round, which means there was discussion over the merits and demerits of her performance. Flaws in technique and interpretation were pointed out, mishaps of presentation, the whole bloody shooting match.

"Ms. Shaker?" It's the judge from California, Portia Vanstone. "I was so impressed by your performance." Her teeth are unnaturally white. "Especially the Mark Loesser piece, which you pulled off with great style and brio. Well done." She lifts her hands to shoulder height and claps three times, a lonely sound in the nearly empty foyer.

"Thank you," Lucy says and feels her heart ping-pong in her chest. She's probably flushing, the hormonal goddess never quiet for long.

Portia and the other judges are climbing the stairs when Lucy hears herself say eagerly, "I do prefer the modern repertoire. Purely guitaristic, so much more interesting than arrangements of old work sucked from keyboard and violin."

Did she really say that?

Jon Smyth, the tall young man with morning beard bristle, pauses on the steps to stare down at her, for he is a noted arranger from the romantic and classical keyboard repertoire.

Too late to grab her words back. "I heard Toby Hausner play when he was very young," she says, watching as all five judges gaze down at her, waiting for more.

"He was brilliant even then." Lucy hesitates, then charges on. "Perhaps something has been lost."

"Lost?" Jon Smyth asks. "What might that be?"

She pretends to think. "Reckless confidence found only in the very young."

Manuel begins the demonstration session by playing two variations on the opening movement of the Bach suite: first version unadorned, the second featuring full Baroque embellishments. His hands float through the elaborate trills, mordents, and turns. Lucy plucks her guitar out of its case and joins the other musicians in imitation of the master.

None of the competition finalists made it to the tutorial. They're hunkered down in their rooms, practising while their glorious futures bob within reach.

TWENTY

LUKE HAS LEAKED THE WHOLE BUSINESS TO THE MEDIA AND sponsors, which means the phone has been ringing off the hook all afternoon. The first call caught Jasper off guard: Is the institute, a nonprofit organization that depends on the goodwill of government grants, attempting to jettison its highly respected volunteer president because of some personal vendetta?

How the hell did that version get out there? Jasper stares at each staff member passing by his desk — who is the traitor?

Jasper's gym crony, Al, emails to say he watched a clip of Jasper on the midday cable news. Al tells him that he sounded calm and articulate, but "For God's sake, flip your collar down."

What Jasper is, is careful. Careful not to say that Luke is a chronic liar disguised in the mien of backslapping loyalist. No one would care if it weren't for the virus. The institute is the location of choice for extended rehab.

Write everything down and record each phone conversation. It's key to keep each member of the board onside and informed before Luke sways them. The institute must not be allowed to capsize because of one errant member. Presidents come and go, but Jasper has been here since the beginning. The fur is flying: Jasper must confess to a certain heated excitement. Not so long ago he and Luke were the best of friends. Luke would sidle up before meetings and flatter his executive director with his easy confidence, pretending to defer on matters of institute policy. There were those long shared lunches at May's where Luke would order lychee nut martinis and pledge that together he and Jasper would lift the institute to "a whole new level." He was a man of vision and optimism, just what the old joint needed. Or so he convinced Jasper.

Salon B in the mezzanine of the Fine Arts Building streams autumnal light from a bank of windows. Before entering the cavernous room, Toby must show his conference tag to prove he's paid up. Luthiers have set up booths to display cutaway models of internal bracing systems next to finished guitars waiting to be taken through their paces. A television monitor shows the artisan tramping through a forest in search of just the right tree to be felled and milled, voice-over with overlay of peeping birds and the crunch of boots on rough trail. Placards contain endorsements by famous guitarists. Other booths display custom stands and stools and other props. One stand folds ingeniously and fits in your pocket; another is guaranteed to prevent back strain. The usual Mel Bay mini-store of sheet music takes up the back corner.

Toby makes his way toward XTract Music, a small publishing company run by judge Jon Smyth that specializes in transcriptions from other instruments and Jon's own eccentric compositions.

"One of our bright young men," Jon hails Toby with enthusiasm, for his booth has seen little action during the competition.

The two musicians slap palms, and Jon hustles him onto a chair. "Fresh from the printer," he says, offering a thin folder. "I've sampled Dowland, though you might not recognize the old boy. The trick is finding a meter and sticking to it." He drops the score into Toby's waiting hands.

Toby gives the piece a quick scan: Jon uses conventional notation with a hodge-podge of time signatures.

"Perfect encore piece," Jon says, hovering. "Bravura, yet compact at three and a half minutes."

Toby taps his toe on the floor as written notes translate to sound in his head. Perfect pitch arrived at birth, but rhythm comes from the heart's own beat.

"Give it a go, will you?"

Toby smiles. "Sure."

"Horace!" Jon barks at the luthier hunched over half asleep in a neighbouring booth. "Lend the man one of your gut buckets."

Horace Manners, who builds concert-level guitars and Celtic harps, wakes up with a snap and gestures toward Toby. "Take your pick."

Silky smooth grain, spruce top with a yew body made from timber milled on Horace's property near Lake Simcoe — waiting list for an instrument at least five years. Toby grabs one off the stand. A guitar's not a newborn. You can bash it around a little. It improves the sound.

Horace winces. Toby grins, but he does remove his zippered jacket and drape it over the back of the chair. He's the prince of sight-readers. Give him anything and he'll rip it off the first time, not just correct notes but phrasing, expression, the whole nine yards.

This guitar, redolent of seasoned wood and coats of meticulously applied polish, nestles against his body, a perfect fit. He inhales, and the instrument breathes with him. Run his hands over the smooth neck, then try a chromatic scale: boomy bass notes, brand-new strings too crisp. It takes at least a year to break in a new instrument.

Toby launches into the skittish piece.

The trick is not to over-think, just enter the bloody thing, one eye out for the next corner. First few bars conjure up a tilted version of Dowland's famous "Lady Beatrice's Jump," but isn't that a Latin beat starting in the bass? The instrument is loud and full-voiced, crafted to reach the far corners of a concert hall without amplification.

A small group gathers around the booth as the music erupts. Enter Javier, then a couple of other luthiers emerging from their booths, followed by students from the local conservatory, all pressing in to hear the world premiere of "Dowland's Backbite."

Toby nails the complicated patterns, the zigzag of counter-rhythms and nasty transitions, his jaw tight and shoulders hunched, bronco rider taming the beast.

When he finishes, giving the final chord ample time to ring, he lowers his hands.

Someone says, "Holy shit."

There is a smattering of applause and even laughter.

Jon Smyth's eyes burrow in on him. "I know you."

Toby recoils. This is not what he expects.

"I remember this bloke." He points at Toby, then glances around at the gathered crowd.

Toby squeezes the guitar into his chest — body armour.

"Paris," Jon announces. "You went off the rails. But first you ambushed everyone in the semis. After hearing you play, I nearly packed it in." He's extending a hand, and Toby understands he's meant to shake it. "I offer you this work for your repertoire."

Toby remembers to smile — a dragonfly lighting up at this moment, wings shot with gold. He's always known this about himself, that he'd rise higher, faster, translucent.

———————————

The composer must have sat at this window looking down at the bustle of St. Lawrence Boulevard, working at this beat-up desk, really just a table with a drawer. The room is small but bright, and Leopold Hirsch was already feeling the effects of the osteoarthritis that crippled him in later life. His last couple of decades before dying of emphysema were spent back in Europe where he scraped by thanks to earlier achievements. Didn't he conduct a regional orchestra in the Netherlands?

Toby is alone in the museum room except for Lucy, who cranes her neck to read the titles on the top row of the bookshelf. He runs his hand over the bumpy surface of the table despite a sign that warns: DO NOT TOUCH. But he is here to touch, to inhale, to enter the life of this man.

Leopold Hirsch, born 1900, lived in this third-floor apartment with his family for close to twenty years. The notebook splayed under glass was fashioned by the composer, heavy paper sewn roughly into leather covers, and it's clear by its concave shape that he must have carried it around in his back pocket. There's a scattershot of notes pencilled on hand-drawn staff lines, the stems unanchored to note heads, flags tiny as commas. This is the man's mind in action, untethered, the actual record of his musical thoughts as they tumbled out. The label describes the journal as being "preliminary fragments" of what became "Triptych for Guitar and Orchestra" — here, a gleam in its creator's eye.

Toby can feel the weight of the man's arm as Hirsch leaned over the desk, while elsewhere in the flat his wife cooked up a batch of sauerkraut as she ducked between roughhousing children: "Shhh, your father is working."

Toby's head jerks up.

Did someone speak?

Just Lucy who is still on tiptoe, reading. "They're all in Polish or German," she says. "Beautiful bindings. He must have brought his library with him on the steamer. And look, Toby, this toy is handcrafted. Do you think Hirsch made it for one of his children?" She holds up a small wooden tugboat painted red and black.

Toby hears but doesn't listen. His heart has tapped open. He's fallen back into time and can smell the long-vanished bakery below with its old-country sweet buns, and when he pulls at the sleeves of his jacket, it's the ratty suit coat that Leopold Hirsch wears in the photograph above the desk. Another richer fragrance of pipe tobacco permeates the room after all these years. Hirsch got his favourite brand shipped to him from overseas, except during the war years when he lost track of most of his relatives, some of whom moved here for weeks or months, crowded into the bedrooms, rolling cots up the narrow staircase.

The room is a blur. Toby tastes salt, tears streaming down his cheeks, and he stands helpless and watery, half drowning in his own fluid.

Lucy notices and quickly reaches to touch his hair. "It is your great luck to feel deeply. Which is why you play like you do."

The book of études was composed earlier, back in Europe when Hirsch was still a student at the conservatory, but the gorgeous "Triptych" was formed in this room. The work begins with that lush romantic melody, and you think you're in for a good time, then it kicks open and you don't know where the hell you are.

Lucy drops her hand and nods toward the corner. "Do you suppose there's a real guitar in there?" she asks. A battered instrument case leans against the wall. "Or is it just for show?"

Toby says, "One way to find out." He strides across the room. Leaning to snap open the case, he suddenly stops himself. He doesn't want to know. If this case is empty, a sham, better that it stay shut. He rises to his feet and backs off.

"While he was beavering away at his scores, his wife was peeling potatoes and caring for the mob of children," Lucy says. She slips into the hallway where the walls are decorated with photographs and framed programs going back to the late 1920s.

Swiping his face with his sleeve, Toby composes himself — what an odd turn of phrase.

"These must be his parents," Lucy calls back. "Fine old gent with heroic sideburns. His mother looks like an unforgiving creature, sucked-in cheeks. Mind you, photography was a big deal in those days."

When Toby doesn't speak, she pokes her head back into the studio. "His mother's family was in the shipping business back in Poland." She stares for a moment when he doesn't respond.

Toby practised for four hours this morning. His hands are supple as heated putty.

Hirsch wrote that music came to him as dictation from a mystical source. He studied the kabbalah and other texts and even met Krishnamurti one summer.

"They held salons for artists and musicians on the last Thursday of each month," Lucy says, returning to the hallway. "Here's a tiny drawing by Paul-Émile Borduas that must be worth something. Madame Hirsch, quote, 'cooked massive stews for the hungry children and artists.' I bet she did."

Leopold might be out in the park with the children when sound came to him, sidelong, like the cranked-up music box of the ice-cream vendor or pretzel sellers. He could work anywhere at any time, because, as he famously wrote, music emanates from the world around us, from trees and sky to machine noise and the whirr of telephone wires. To receive these sounds, Hirsch trained his ears and mind to enter a state he termed the Receptive Cone.

Toby has experienced it in himself, a sensation both glorious and unnerving. He feels the enchantment grow in him now, so close to the master.

Lucy cries with delight. She's found the nursery. Reluctantly, he leaves the studio with its moist smell of tobacco and old books. Lucy stands in the middle of a room with a sloped ceiling and a mitred window that looks onto a brick-and-glass building that wouldn't have been there in Hirsch's day. A rough-hewn cradle sits on the floor, plaster doll tucked under its miniature quilt. She picks up a pint-sized hairbrush from a shelf and slowly whisks it across her forearm, then lowers herself onto the rustic bed, perching next to a teddy bear, minus most of its fur.

"The little ones are so dear," Lucy says, glancing up at Toby as if waiting for him to echo her sentiment.

When he doesn't respond, she appears almost cross, an expression Toby recognizes: Jasper gets this way when he thinks Toby should act more interested in what is going on around him.

Lucy asks, "Do you know who else lived here?"

"Relatives from the old country."

"Polish and Russian Jews fleeing the pogroms, escaping their ghettos before the Nazis blew through."

A cold snake enters Toby's gut. He knows this change in tone. Usually, it comes from old people. To this point they've been cordial, but once they discover he's got measurable cc's of German blood in his veins, he's implicated in the crimes of the century.

Lucy rises slowly from the bed and wanders over to the flip-top desk where she lifts a piece of sky from a jigsaw puzzle and ticks it against her teeth. "Think of the terror that made them leave and how difficult it was to land here with just the clothes on their backs."

"My sympathies are with the ones who *didn't* escape," Toby says.

"Quite so."

"I contain the whole range of human feelings," he adds, unable to mask the defensive tone.

She runs her minesweeper eyes over him, then sets the puzzle piece down. "Of course."

Why does he feel accused of something?

Leopold Hirsch tiptoed in at dawn to gaze at his sleeping children, three girls curled up on the one bed, and he listened to the raspy chest from the littlest child who would later die of pneumonia. It can be a curse to hear too much.

They step out of the haunted room into the corridor. This part of the hallway is decorated with faded manuscripts displayed behind glass, most too spotty and stained to recognize, though isn't that the opening fragment to the adagio?

"Bathroom," Lucy says, stating the obvious as she peers into the adjoining doorway.

A rusty streak blisters the surface of the claw-foot tub that rests on four chunks of wood, and there's a distinct whiff of drains. Sitting on the pedestal sink is a sponge so crusty you know it hasn't touched water in decades. That step stool must be for little Laura, pictured in the photos down the hall.

As Toby pulls back into the corridor, music starts up, gypsy violin drenched in melancholy, but when he glances around, he spots a speaker tacked in the corner where he'd hoped to see an old gent in a frayed suit, sawing away.

Hirsch adopted folk music in his compositions, wove old tunes into sophisticated new world caprices and sonatas. The violin crests and hangs in on a long fermata — and that's when Toby hears footsteps climbing the narrow staircase. So far they've been the only visitors to the museum. Leopold Hirsch is a little-known figure on this side of the Atlantic. The steps pause on the landing, and through the sound of music they pick up the gasp of heavy breathing.

A stout man in his sixties pulls himself up the final flight of stairs. He wears a suit of timeless cut with shiny shoes. "Welcome, welcome," he pants, sweat pooling on his brow. "Tell me, fine people, where are you coming from?"

"Toronto," they chorus.

"Excellent." He slips a pad and pencil from his pocket and writes this fact down. Toby notes his badge: THE LEOPOLD HIRSCH SOCIETY.

"You have been born there also?" the man asks.

Eastern European accent, Toby judges. "That's right," he says, watching as this, too, is written on the small pad.

"And you, madam?" Before Lucy can respond, the man begins to cough violently, and the visitors step hastily out of range.

This is how it begins: a propelled spray of saliva, an enclosed space.

"Pardon me, friends," he says when he's recovered. Then he turns to Lucy, pencil poised.

"Born in Calgary," she says.

"And you enjoy our exhibition? Is interesting and provocative, yes?"

"Very," Lucy assures him.

"We have restored this house for the enjoyment of musicians and followers of Dr. Hirsch. Maybe you would like to join our society. The dues are modest." He stares at them in the gloom of the hallway. "Perhaps you have relatives in Poland or some special interest?" When there is no immediate response, he peers at Lucy's badge. "Ah, a guitarist from the competition! Such an honour. I have been waiting for you people to come and visit our modest museum, but you are the first." He flushes with evident pleasure and turns to Toby. "You, sir, are also one of the talented musicians?"

"I hope so."

"Then you must follow me to Special Collections," the volunteer insists. "An area where we allow only certain people, scholars and professional artists." He beckons them toward the stairs, talking excitably. "We will begin with early letters sent back to his father. Perhaps you don't know that Hirsch's father was an eminent psychoanalyst with no less than Dr. Freud as his teacher." He pauses, noting that the pair of musicians isn't following. "So now we descend to the ground floor, to the special library."

"We'll be stuck there for hours," Lucy whispers in Toby's ear, seeing alarm cross his face. He's got to get back to the dorm and practise. Time presses in.

Lucy swings her purse over one shoulder and says crisply, "I'm afraid we must dash back to the university." She touches Toby's arm in a wifely way.

The man seems hurt. "You must be interested in seeing these precious items — letters in his own hand to famous artists, original manuscripts, concert programs ... and many personal articles."

"I'm very sorry," Lucy says.

"Perhaps we can come back," Toby says brightly.

"Yes!" Lucy chimes in. "We'll return once this is all over."

The man's shoulders sink, and when he speaks, it is in a resigned voice. "Yes, when it is over."

Toby feels Lucy's sharp tug on his sleeve. "Time to fly," she says, foot planted on the top stair.

"Go then," the man says, flattening himself against the wall. "A woman must never be kept waiting."

It is the same heavy-handed courtliness that Klaus employs with what he terms "the fair sex." Suddenly, Toby can't get out of there fast enough. He pushes past both of them, hastening down the stairs and out the door to the bustling sidewalk where it is midday and women clip down the busy street in high heels, chattering into their cellphones.

What would Dr. Hirsch make of this new generation of urban sounds? No doubt he would incorporate the ring tones, gypsy violin, even the pneumatic drill upending pavement across the street into some aural tapestry that would first cause laughter from his puzzled audience, then worship.

"Were we very rude?" Lucy asks, joining him on the sidewalk. "I knew he'd suck us into an archival tunnel, make us examine every shoelace and grocery list."

"Imagine reading his letters ..." Toby says.

She looks at him sharply. "You read German?"

He doesn't. Klaus tried to implant the language in his sons' minds, but they resisted, scorning his marzipan rewards for the correct conjugations of verbs. All that remains are a few common words and a handful of nursery rhymes.

They glance up as a shadow passes: a blimp coasts across the sky, trailing a banner that advertises a common analgesic tablet. At the same time a taxi blares its horn, mimicking the opening of Beethoven's Fifth while a kid strides past, earphones leaking hip-hop beats.

Lucy squints at him, using her hand as a visor. "Toby Hausner," she says, "you've fallen for that piffle about the Receptive Cone."

The dorm foyer buzzes with a fresh batch of conventioneers. The army cadets have disappeared, replaced by members of an international human rights organization. Delegates in jeans, saris, and suits line up before the gowned table to receive their registration kits. With jet-lagged ardour they pump hands and clap one another on the back while Lucy threads through the crowd, muttering apologies.

When she reaches the elevator that will whisk her up into the women's wing, she calls back to Toby, "Come by at six for cocktails."

He lifts an arm to protest. Cocktails! He must work until the sun sets and until his hands plead for mercy.

Moments later he slips into his cell. The guitar case lies across the cot, lid propped open. Somewhere far below the Metro rumbles.

Toby begins playing the trio with his fretting hand planted in seventh position, when of course he should have begun back in second, allowing for the cathedral-bell chime and a smooth transition. He worked this out months ago. Seventh position, he quickly discovers, leads to instant crisis and an open string thunking — so much for the cathedral chime.

He scrambles in his suitcase to find sheet music he hasn't looked at in weeks; mistakes pop up at surprising times, when memory is most confident.

Never play a mistake twice, for it will burn new neural channels. Play it correctly five or six times before pressing on. That's how you compose new memory, the one you want to live with.

The bully boys have won, and it's a dark day for the institute.

President Luke lets out his belt a notch and can't stop himself from smirking. He has the nerve, once the board meeting is over, to walk Jasper to the door, slip that hairless arm around his waist, and say, "We're counting on you, as ever."

That Jasper will hand in his official resignation by Monday.

Just twenty minutes earlier Jasper presented an itemized list of Luke's activities to the executive while they stared fixedly at their agenda sheets.

"The office can't continue to function like this," he explained. "I'm afraid it's Luke or me. You must decide."

And so they decided.

And still they won't look at him, for Jasper has become contaminated, like those poor souls in D Wing across the street, breathing through thrice-filtered air.

TWENTY-ONE

LUCY, DRESSED IN A WRAPAROUND SKIRT MADE FROM SOME gauzy Indian cotton, peers at Toby's right hand, while he stares down at the crown of her head. She flips the hand over and examines his palm, making small noises of discovery. "I've seen this before," she says, and he catches the perturbation in her voice. She looks up at him, steady gaze. "Have you been told what it means?"

"That I'm part ape," he cracks. He knows he has a weird right palm — two deep lines instead of the usual heart, head, and life.

She doesn't smile, and suddenly he's on edge. Last thing he needs is Lucy deciding to predict his future. It's an old fear, people looking at him with concerned eyes, seeing something scary he doesn't see himself.

They perch on her bed in a dorm room like his, yellow spread crumpled beneath.

"Where's the drink you promised?" he asks.

With reluctance she drops his hand and pads off barefoot to the kitchen. He hears the crack of ice cubes and soon she returns holding two tumblers of Scotch. Taking one, he settles against the pillows at the head of the bed as she heaves herself beside him. There's nowhere else to sit in the cluttered room, the solo chair being piled with clothes and sheet music. Someone across the hall is strumming chords that sound jazz-inflected and improvisatory.

"Trace doesn't exactly practise," Lucy says. "She doesn't want her program to get stale."

They exchange smiles. No one is so good that she can leap from one recital to the next without practising a great deal. Some of the tension leaves Toby's body — one less competitor to worry about. Slugging back the Scotch, he gasps as it attacks the back of his throat.

"Of course, the moment I leave the pod, she's hard at it," Lucy adds.

The bed is unmade, which shocks Toby slightly — so like his mother's distracted housekeeping and unlike Jasper who plucks micro-fluffs off the carpet and tut-tuts over wall smudges. The window ledge is littered with cosmetics and a toothbrush, inadequately rinsed.

You are in this woman's bedroom, Toby.

The warning is noted, a pesky voice that some might call conscience.

"Give me your palm again," she says.

Amber liquid fires up his mouth and throat and chest. It's not just an instrument that creates sound; it's the entire realm of sympathetic vibrations, the edgeless world.

Lucy reaches out, and his hand slides like a fish onto hers. She touches the flesh firmly. "Your palm is nearly square," she says, tracing its edges. "And the fingers are surprisingly short for a guitarist. A classic fire hand."

"Meaning?"

"Meaning, my dear —" she arches her eyebrows "— that you are excitable and highly creative." She holds his palm to eye level and examines it for several seconds before saying, "Most unusual."

"Why?" He can't disguise his curiosity.

"Twinned with the simian line ..."

"The what?"

"You see it in primates, these two deep creases." She strokes skin around the contours of flesh and bone. "I would guess that you live intensely, perhaps with an undercurrent of fear."

He starts to pull away again, but she grips firmly.

"You have enormous gifts, but of course you know that." She frowns. "Such gifts are often wedded with shadows."

The room feels tiny, a shoebox to set a pet mouse in.

"I don't mean to frighten you," she says.

"Just tell me if I'm going to win."

"I'm no soothsayer." She hesitates. "But I'd put my money on you."

He inhales sharply.

"When you play, it feels dangerous, and I want nothing less from music."

He drains his glass, feels his insides burn. Her hand curls over his and lifts it to her cheek. He feels her excitement. She wants to be part of the ride.

Across the hall, Trace switches on the hourly news in French. Spatter of gunfire and sirens — the rest of the world screams from inside a radio no bigger than a slice of bread.

Lucy tilts her head so he won't notice the beginnings of a double chin. Women try to protect him from signs of age; they don't want to frighten him or incite pity. Women like Lucy run through fire to rescue their boys. His own mother disappeared when the saucepan erupted with flames, and Felix found her huddled in a corner of the yard, pointing a fire extinguisher toward the compost.

She touches her lips to his fingers, then slips one into her mouth and bites down gently. "You've been eating potato chips," she observes.

"What are you doing?" He jolts upright in the bed.

"Don't worry." She reaches to turn off the lamp, and the room snaps into sepia. She is aware of light and shadow and he is the camera.

"What are you doing?" he repeats.

She ignores the question.

In the museum's nursery she lifted the child's mirror and stared at herself. Each glance offered an opportunity for self-improvement.

Without danger there is no beauty — isn't that what she meant? Without danger there is only the earnest plucking of amateurs — and he has never been an amateur.

"I can't do this," he says, beginning to swing his legs over the side of the bed.

"You have all of tomorrow to prepare for the final."

"There's still a couple of spots I'm not sure about." He knows this sounds lame.

She looks at him with arched eyebrows.

"I messed up the Villa-Lobos this afternoon," he says, which is true. "Something I played perfectly for a month." He lifts his arms dramatically. "Vanished."

"You've worn the thing down to a nub."

It's possible to play a piece so much that it stops making sense. He slips into his sneakers, discreetly wiping his finger on the sheet. "I have to get it right before the day is over."

She smiles. "Of course you do."

He's wasting precious time. That section, played immaculately a hundred times, capsized for no known reason. Don't over-think what the body knows so well.

Lucy hears the door of the pod open and pictures Toby waiting impatiently for the elevator. She can still taste him on her tongue, salty sweet, remnant of barbecue chips. The radio is silenced, and she hears Trace leave her room and make her way to the kitchen.

She reaches for a comb that she drags through her hair. A glance in the mirror shows a flushed face and smeared mascara. Hard to believe that mere days ago she was preparing bagged lunches each morning, composing nutritionally rich sandwiches that the twins would let fester at the bottom of their rucksacks, and doing her best to wedge practice time between catering jobs and phone calls from ticked-off vice-principals.

That life, her so-called real life, feels like a dream.

By the time Lucy reaches the kitchen, Trace is pouring boiling water into the teapot.

"I read his palm," Lucy says.

"Whatever."

The girl is embarrassed, maybe even disapproving.

Lucy begins scooping crumbs off the counter into her cupped hand; someone around here has to attend to domestic chores. "What do you make of me competing against people half my age?"

Trace looks up and says, "I think you're brave."

"Really?" This is just what Lucy needs to hear.

TWENTY-TWO

POTASSIUM SLOWS HEARTBEAT. EAT ONE BANANA IN THE MORNing, then another an hour before walking onstage.

Beta blockers? Your heart will still thrum, but your hands can't shake. The drug increases concentration, but it's a fuzzy focus at the core, a sort of tunnel vision.

One more thing: never look directly at the judges. This is hard, because they will be looking intently at you, noting the way you move — points for presentation and artistic impression.

The four finalists have been invisible all day, confined to quarters. Tomorrow they will stride onstage for the last time, but now they have gathered for supper with their colleagues.

"Last year I was one hundred percent convinced I would win," Javier says in elegantly accented English. "But taxi crashes into an autobus on the way to the performance, so I was late and in extreme rush. No good." He shakes his head in sad remembrance.

You could draw a map of Argentina on his starched shirt cuffs. In Buenos Aires a maid takes care of laundry. Her name — he would be surprised by the question — is Adelita.

"So we all play Villa-Lobos?" Trace asks with an elaborate yawn. "Reckon I should glance at the music." She hauls herself out of the chair while the espresso machine roars. "Anyone got a copy?"

Someone does and hands it to the girl who chews on a string of licorice as she reads through the score. Toby watches this performance. He isn't fooled for a minute. She knows the piece backward and forward. They all do.

Lucy sits at the other end of the lounge engaged in ardent conversation with the other dismissed contestants. This is how the room has divided itself tonight. The ones left behind huddle in one corner, chatting, while in the other corner the select few who will head into the final heat stare at the floor and speak in nervous bursts. They are different breeds, though everyone tries to pretend that this is not so. It comes down to the rhythm of heartbeat, that elemental.

Only Marcus roams around the suite, a beer can tucked in his pocket and his hair sticking straight up.

Toby flexes his hands, fire hands that will burn through tomorrow's program. Practising has gone well today; the vapourized section of Villa-Lobos returned just in time.

Someone has ordered in Chinese, and it arrives in cardboard cartons with tiny pillows of soy sauce. Trace snaps open a pair of wooden chopsticks, then another, and passes them around. For a moment the room falls silent as aluminum lids are pried off the containers, paper napkins unfolded.

Jasper would be horrified by the lurid General Tao's chicken balls, slick with grease and sugar, but Toby dives in, sitting crosslegged on the floor, his back to the wall.

Trace drops beside him, her plate loaded with rice and vegetables and bony fish.

"No Chinese restaurants on my island," she says. Her heart-shaped face slides into scalp, no boundary of hair, and the vein at her temple pulses with each chew. "No Chinese people, period, except the brothers who own the marina." She peers at a frill of brown fungus before popping it in her mouth. "Back home one of my best friends is a quad. You heard of Guillain-Barré syndrome?"

Toby has not.

"Quite the horror. Now her arms and legs don't work, so sometimes I feed her. One day she goes, 'Trace, how come you're avoiding the tomatoes?' And it hit me that I was feeding her like I feed myself."

Her small ears nestle close to her head, lobes implanted with tiny silver stars. "It's not as easy as you think to feed someone," she says, then plucks a piece of glistening chicken off his plate. "Let's try."

Toby pulls back, half laughing. "I don't think so."

Briskly, like a mother with a small child, she aims the chopsticks toward his mouth. All that's missing is airplane noise.

He protests, "I'm not at that stage yet."

Klaus fed Karen every day at the home. She'd sit at the table in her wheelchair, bib tucked under her chin while he'd cajole, "One more bite, *liebchen*," tipping a spoon to her mouth.

"It's an experiment in giving up control," Trace says.

"I don't want to give up control."

"That's just the point. Nobody wants to."

He lets the wooden sticks slither between his lips, just this once. She watches as he chews, and after he's swallowed, she prongs a flowerlet of broccoli and tips it into his mouth. When a kernel of rice lodges on his cheek, she brushes it off before he can get to it. This is what a mother does — no, this is what a lover does.

Suddenly, Toby can't wait to get onstage. Momentum surges, a mighty storm brewing. Whatever he's eating is ammo, is blood juice. He's tasting himself.

"Enough?" Trace says, lowering the chopsticks. Her eyes are wide open.

"Listen up you buggers on the smart side of the room!" It's Marcus, who stands on a chair holding a can of beer aloft. "We want you geniuses to know that it's a hell of a lot more fun at our end. Seriously, we drink to your good fortune, but remember —" he tilts the can to his mouth and says "— you're playing for all of us."

There's a distinct pong of "boy" in Marcus's dorm room — so reminiscent of the twins' lair at home. Lucy crouches on the carpet and tucks her legs into a half-lotus, a position she proudly manifests due to rigorous yoga training in the past six

months. Half a dozen competition dropouts have made their
way here after supper, and it was Marcus who poked her in the
ribs and urged, "Join us in the lads' clubhouse."

She smiles now, a bit too cheerily, and chastises herself, for
she has as much right to be here as any of them. More right, if
you take into account the fact she made it to the semis, a sore
point with some of these guys, but their fragile egos will repair.

The Bosnian guitarist whose name she never remembers
cranks open the window and blows cigarette smoke into the
courtyard. He's wearing a fringed buckskin vest picked up at
one of the souvenir shops downtown. Eyeing Lucy, he offers a
meaningful nod, which she mirrors, though she has no idea what
they're communicating. Armand, of all people, lights up a monster joint and passes it around. Tex draws in, coughs, and passes
it to Lucy, who inhales and instantly feels a jolt in her head. It's
been a while. Because of the twins, she and Mark stay clear of the
stuff, allegedly to set a good example, not that it's done a bit of
good. The sense of disembodiment that follows the toke is pleas-
ant, and she wonders how many of life's pleasures she and Mark
deny themselves because of the boys. Noisy sex for one.

She's the only woman in the room — what else is new? Why
don't more females play classical guitar? One of life's great mys-
teries. Tilting her head backward until it taps the wall, Lucy
bathes in the familiar testosterone bath.

Tex, sitting on the crowded bed, tunes his instrument. No
one pays attention when he starts playing. Instead they keep
yammering in varied accents about the finalists and judges
("Javier, he holds back until the finals ..." "Portia, I play for her in
Aspen. She loves dramatic phrasing ..."). But one by one voices
drop off as Tex launches into the simple "Pavana" by Luis de
Milán, the Renaissance composer. He plays with fluid accuracy,
each chord hovering before dipping into the next. Any musician
in the room could play this piece in his sleep, but for them the
race is over and finally they can listen without fear or dismay.

As Tex crunches the final chord, Marcus reaches for his own instrument and points to his backup parked in the corner. "She's yours," he tells Lucy.

Her mind scrambles as she unhitches the case and flips open the lid — what might she play? The Bosnian eyes her and performs another of his enigmatic nods. After a quick tune-up, she rolls into good old "Malagueña" — soulful and redolent of Andalusian cafés, not that she'd know, having never visited Spain. Mark keeps saying they'll go, and last year she even booked a flight, then Mike was sent home for tagging the cafeteria wall and they decided it was unwise to leave the boys on their own for a week, even with Mark's mother in charge.

This backup guitar has a fatter fretboard than she's used to and the entire instrument feels boomy, aching to sprint ahead. Lucy plays while sitting cross-legged on the floor, not the most brilliant position as the instrument rocks on her lap, but something lovely and unexpected happens as she enters the middle section. Tex joins in, improvising a harmonic line, then Marcus adds bass, padding out the sound. Competition nerves melt away as they sprawl on bed and floor. This is why they come to international events — to play together when the day is done and nothing is at stake. This is where joyous music happens, not on the stage where they are pierced by light and judges' stares.

Someone passes around a bowl of chips, and nimble hands dive in. Lucy feels the music rise inside her, untethered and sentimental, almost lustful. She half shuts her eyes and slows down the phrase, feeling the other musicians follow.

Tex passes his guitar to Armand who, without missing a note, continues the harmony, but with a sharper tone. They could be gypsies hunched around a roaring fire, caravans looming in the shadows. The joint comes around again, and the baby-face Quebecker slips it between Lucy's lips.

If the twins could see her now, as she is, really is, not their mama.

It's past midnight when Lucy reaches the women's pod. She coasts down the hallway, slightly stoned, a sensation that makes her feel detached from her body. Is this how the twins feel when they smoke up? Small wonder they sneer at her warnings to quit.

Despite the late hour, Trace's light is on and she's going over the same phrase again and again, a tortured renegotiation of every detail. It must have hit her that she has to appear onstage tomorrow, the world's eyes bearing down.

Such a relief to be free from that stress, Lucy decides. Yet a tiny voice nips at the edge of her mind: *If only it was me stepping out there, audience filling the hushed auditorium ...*

She pauses outside the girl's room, and the music stops. There is a light clank of instrument being propped against the chair, then the door opens and Trace stands before her, wearing boxer shorts and a man's undershirt, showing thin, bare limbs.

"You should be sleeping," Lucy says, aware of a thickness in her voice.

"I can't." Trace grips her own elbows, collarbone shooting forward under the loose top. "Every time I lie down I start to freak out."

"You're bound to be on edge."

"What if mess up tomorrow? Everyone will say I'm too young, that I shouldn't have made it this far. Do you think I'm too young?" Without waiting for an answer, Trace keeps chattering. "So I got thinking that I've been playing the rondo all wrong, putting in those sforzandos because I thought they were cool, but they're not cool. They're stupid, and it interferes with the rhythm, which is what my teacher told me, but I thought I'd be all dramatic and everything —"

Lucy steps forward and wraps her arms around the girl. She feels the brittle cushion of her body, that shaved head tentatively pressing into her shoulder. So different from the twins who dive into her arms like Spitfires — and that's when they're feeling friendly.

"I'm fucking scared," the girl says. Her breathing is off kilter, too shallow and fast.

Lucy rubs the girl's prickly head. The boys, as newborns, chirped like fuzzy chicks, the thumb-sized depression of fontanel pulsing in their soft skulls. You kiss the most vulnerable part; it beckons, needing your most tender care.

TWENTY-THREE

MIRANDA AND JILL FROM UPSTAIRS SHOULD DEAL WITH THIS pyramid of dog shit. Jasper scoops the feces into a plastic bag and ties a knot, then notices the rat, or what's left of it, that their yappy pooch, Polly, attacked a day earlier. That makes two rodents spotted in twenty-four hours. He hopes this doesn't signal an infestation. The corpse lies prone, nearly hidden in the crabgrass in front of the row house. Crouching over its remains, Jasper prods delicately with the trowel. Its skull is intact, eyes opaque, teeth bared. The abdomen is torn open, and a trace of entrails lies like a dried umbilical cord. Brownish fur, underside a light colour. The Norway rat will creep through any space bigger than half an inch — smaller than the width of your baby finger. Cellars here are porous, as crumbling masonry competes with the shifting sands of lake soil. He glares at the clinic's rear door where graffiti blazes despite earnest removal attempts. Their dumpster is shut, as per regulations, but rodents have advanced olfactory skills. Jasper suspects a scary birth rate, lured by medical waste. He pushes the tip of his fedora back, remembering not to touch his eyes.

Abruptly, the back door of the clinic springs open and three men and one woman step into the sun. Working their cellphones, they hasten toward a red SUV parked illegally in the laneway.

"An obvious gap in screening protocol," one of the men says in a self-important tone that Jasper immediately recognizes.

Luke.

Pull the cap over brow, but not in time.

"Jasper!" The man stops in his tracks and sings out the name: long lost friend.

Jasper must look like a retiree, yard work in the middle of the day, and he uses the trowel to hoist himself up out of a crouch. These khaki shorts aren't exactly flattering, nor is the Bacardi Rum souvenir T-shirt.

Luke gives him the once-over. "I didn't know you lived here," he says, natty in chinos and fitted jacket.

The rest of the crew hangs back and smiles in that way people do when they aren't sure if they're going to be introduced.

"We were just —" Luke sweeps a hand toward the clinic.

"Checking screening protocols," Jasper finishes.

"Part of a schematic overview of all neighbourhood health units in the downtown core."

"I know," Jasper says. His initiative, the result of many meetings with the ministry. He organized the approach, created the checklist, and contacted administrators to book time slots. These people waiting in the wings are from the Ministry Task Force.

"So this is where you reside," Luke says, scanning the row of attached houses.

Reside — a Luke word.

Jasper reaches for the small of his back, which seizes up at such moments. An ad for his position at the institute appeared in today's newspaper. It now requires a master's degree and competence in computer programs he's barely heard of.

"I didn't realize this lane existed," Luke says. He's positioned himself on the edge of the yard, respecting Jasper's property line, an unexpected courtesy. "Very tucked away, aren't you?"

"That's how we like it."

Luke nods with emphatic agreement while his colleagues cast impatient glances at their phones.

Jasper booked the clinic visits back to back, no time for dithering. He slaps the trowel against his thigh now, miming a casualness he doesn't feel.

"Luke!" the woman from the task force calls. "We need to be across town in fifteen minutes."

Luke waves at her while his gaze remains intent on Jasper. "I'm so sorry it came to this. Things were ticking along well. I thought we had a good rapport." He hesitates, shifting weight, and asks almost plaintively, "What happened?"

"What happened?" Jasper echoes. Where to begin the litany of betrayals and miscues?

"We all had such faith in you," Luke continues. "Your depth of experience, your strategic skills." He stops, noting Jasper's look of astonishment. "You turned on me," he says, lifting his palms, "and I still don't know why."

In twelve minutes he'll be meeting with the intake supervisor at East End Rehab to go over the revised action plan. For this task he needs copies of the guidelines and the supplement, available only on the password-protected TGI site.

Someone toots a horn. Luke turns away, stepping carefully over the litter of weeds and debris. He hasn't seen the mutilated rat. That's a mercy.

When the oversized vehicle reverses down the laneway, warm tears stream down Jasper's cheeks. For a moment the ground beneath him seems to drop away — could it be that he got the whole situation wrong? Did he gang up on Luke when the poor man was only trying to do his best?

Unthinkable, he assures himself.

"I smell victory," Toby says, making a bugle sound through the phone that just about annihilates Jasper's eardrum. "One judge says that even if I don't win, he'll book me for a recital at his college."

"That's great, Tobes." Keep the boy on the line.

"So it's all happening, my pet."

The endearment, uttered so carelessly, strokes Jasper, such tenderness being rare in the boy.

"It's like I can't fail," the voice insists.

Impossible to get through to Toby when he's on a tear. You see someone racing toward the edge of a cliff, you don't wait for the cliff to grow a fence — you act.

They hang up, and Jasper scrutinizes the living room. This is where he laid his gardening gloves an hour ago, drooping over the back of a chair. Here's the magazine splayed across the table, one corner stuck in the butter dish. How odd to return home and find everything exactly as he left it, no changes to interpret, no signs of another's existence. This would be the texture of a solitary life.

Fold clothing and drop it into the pack: wallet, hairbrush, toiletries. Something to read on the short flight to Montreal.

TWENTY-FOUR

PAPERY SKIN AND SORE BONES DON'T FRIGHTEN US. IT'S WHEN the insides start to leak that we jump in with mops and diapers and oversized bibs. Lakeview Terrace isn't where Jasper aims to end up. Here the chairs are covered in washable vinyl and the library displays large-print *Reader's Digest*s and a selection of audiobooks. The advertised terrace? A concrete ledge jutting out of the second floor where, if you squint through the maples and if the prescription of your glasses is up-to-date and you've been taking your glaucoma meds, you might catch a glimpse of lake water.

Klaus chooses to live here, rather than stay in his home, a mystery to them all.

Mrs. Smiley gets right to the point. Jasper has told her, twice, that he's in a hurry and he indicates his backpack.

"Your father-in-law has been carrying on an affair with one of our nurse's aides," she says crisply.

Father-in-law: it was Jasper who insisted on this term, yet it still sounds odd.

"I beg your pardon?" he asks.

They sit in her office, a corner room decorated with framed photographs of residents engaged in activities such as swing choir and gentle calisthenics. He's shoved the pack between his knees, letting it touch the antiseptic floor. To get inside the building he had his temperature taken, then completed a checklist of questions about recent travel and any new or unusual symptoms. Don't they know that once a patient's temperature rises, he's been shedding virus for days? They should be checking for red patches behind the knees, the precursor.

Mrs. Smiley, director of Lakeview, is frazzled. Any day someone in her institution will exhibit positive symptoms, then what? Shut the place down? Quarantine staff and residents?

She repeats the sentence.

"You're kidding," Jasper says.

"I am not." Mrs. Smiley doesn't smile and she certainly doesn't kid. "We had to let Ramona go."

"Ramona?"

"The aide in question."

"Right." Must be rules about consorting with residents.

"Do you know if Mr. Hausner's son is aware of the relationship?" she asks.

"I'm sure he's not."

"Because it's been going on for quite some time." She taps her pen on the desktop. "Quite some time."

The phrase lingers while Jasper calculates. "Klaus just moved in six months ago."

Mrs. Smiley, an attractive woman in her mid-forties, leans back on her swivel chair. "Evidently the affair preceded his residency here."

"Preceded?"

"By some years."

This floors Jasper. "I'm sorry, but I'm having trouble believing a word of this."

She nods, anticipating his reaction. "Frankly, we've all had a start. Ramona has been with us for well over two decades." Then she reaches for a manila envelope and spills its contents over the desk: greeting cards, the old-fashioned kind illustrated with flowers; others with religious images — a haloed Jesus tucking a dappled faun under his arm, nativity scenes; and one card embossed with a big number seventy, the kind you give people for important birthdays.

"From Ramona," Mrs. Smiley says. "Written to Mr. Hausner over a period of a dozen years."

"A dozen years," Jasper repeats.

Mrs. Smiley shakes the envelope so that a tiny photo falls out, the sort taken in a railway station booth. She slips this across the desk so that Jasper can examine it closely. He palms it like a communion wafer and stares at the image of Klaus wearing an open-necked shirt. The man is smiling with what Jasper can only describe as joy, an expression he's never seen liven Klaus's features. He looks startlingly like Toby, minus hair, same smooth cheeks and those small, even teeth. Perched on his lap is a little girl who must have moved as the shutter snapped, blurring her features. She is dark-skinned with pigtails.

"Who is this?" Jasper asks.

"Ramona's daughter."

So Ramona is black. Of course, most of the nurses' aides around here are. Black or Filipino. His mind ticks: Klaus hooked up with a woman of colour, a term Klaus would never use. Everything Jasper knows about the man explodes into dust. The feeling is both a shock and exhilarating. Jasper hears himself approach Toby with the news: "You'll never guess in a million years ..."

Mrs. Smiley lets her steady gaze linger, then finally Jasper gets it.

"Are you suggesting ..." he begins.

"The girl's name is Celia."

He is speechless.

"It seems that all those years while your father-in-law was visiting his wife at Lakeview he was also visiting Ramona."

They stare at each other, facing facts.

"So he visited his wife to get near Ramona," Jasper says.

"I don't like to speculate on his intentions."

"What does Klaus say?"

"Mr. Hausner is not being co-operative. He insists that if Ramona has been let go, then he must leave right away. Our management team here agrees. You can imagine how rumours fly in a place like this."

"I bet."

"Can you take him home by tomorrow at the latest?"

"Home?" Jasper lets out a squeak of dismay. "Not possible. His house was sold months ago."

Mrs. Smiley laces her fingers together. "I understand, but we can't hold a resident here against his will. Mr. Hausner is a man in full possession of his faculties."

"I'm en route to Montreal," Jasper pleads.

"I understand," she repeats in that soothing way that makes his skin crawl, "but Mr. Hausner will have to find other lodgings as of tomorrow, 5:00 p.m."

With Toby conveniently out of town, guess who is in charge? Will Klaus even agree to come to their flat? This is what we do for the ones we love — take in their ejected relatives. Jasper already feels the stirring of martyrdom.

"We'll figure out something," he says.

"Excellent."

While Mrs. Smiley looks at him, he fingers a greeting card, realizing it's one of the set of Amazonian scenes Toby gave to his old man last Father's Day. This one contains Klaus's careful handwriting:

> R: I hailed you in the corridor, but you were pushing Mrs. Vail in a wheelchair to her bath. Why do you ignore me since I moved in? What have I done to offend you? K.

Mrs. Smiley rises to her feet. "Thank you for your prompt attention in this matter," she says, relief inflecting her voice.

Klaus darts out of room 313, sliding his plaid suitcase across the floor into the hallway. This obstacle forces residents to squeeze around it as they pass, using wall rails as support. Jasper raises a hand to greet his father-in-law, but Klaus pays no attention.

Jasper's presence is still an embarrassment, though Klaus has come a long way since the early days when he wouldn't look his son's lover in the face. He scurries back into his room and reappears carrying a stack of magazines, *Scientific American*, judging by their bulk, which he sets on top of the suitcase. Not a trace of stiffness now in his trim body. He kicks off the ridiculous sneakers and steps into his leather oxfords.

"Klaus!" Jasper declares in a voice pitched an octave lower than usual. He strides forward with a rolling gait, arms raised to help with luggage.

"All set to go here," Klaus says.

Two old ladies in jogging suits peer around a doorway. "Pride cometh before a fall," one says.

"What on earth have you been up to, Klaus?" Jasper asks, glancing at his watch. The flight leaves in two hours.

"Don't speak to me as if I were a halfwit," Klaus snaps. "This geriatric institution has pulled rank."

"You can't just walk out without a plan."

"I can and will do exactly as I please. Where is she?"

Blush of panic. "She?"

"The third-floor monitor. She should be preparing my medications." Klaus straightens and tugs the sleeves of his blazer. "Once we settle that bit of business we can exit this building."

Jasper won't let him bully him as he bullies his son. "Where to, Klaus?"

"To Mrs. Bradshaw's apartment, and get that silly look off your face." He names a street in the north end of the city noted for its subsidized housing and drive-by shootings.

"Ramona?" Jasper manages to ask.

"Mrs. Ramona Bradshaw, yes, that is precisely to whom I am referring."

"Does she know you're coming?"

"I certainly hope so." Klaus attempts to look confident, but there is a tightening in his expression.

"Mr. Hausner, your medications." This is Teresa, hall monitor, a young nurse holding a bag of pill bottles. She is not smiling. Lakeview Terrace's perfect gentleman has worn out his welcome. The staff feels betrayed by this small, neat man, the devoted husband, so caring of his sick wife, so lost without her that he chose to come here before his time.

"Thank you very much," Klaus says, making a point of meeting Teresa's chilly stare. He pockets the bulky package.

Toby should be here: this is his father.

"We'll get Paul to carry your bag down," Teresa says, her tone relenting just a little.

Paul's the jack of all trades at Lakeview, a Newfoundlander who taught Klaus how to play dominoes. Suddenly, the doorways are full of residents leaning on walkers and canes, watching the dramatic leave-taking.

The old boy's a bit of a hero, Jasper realizes.

"So you're leaving us, mate," Paul says, heaving the suitcase effortlessly over one shoulder. He sticks his toe out to hold the door of the elevator while Klaus and Jasper step in. The smell of lunch is trapped in the cubicle as they chug downward, cream of something soup and toast.

Jasper's mind works fast: drop the old man in a cab and send him to Ramona's. When Toby and he return from Montreal, they'll tackle the problem, if indeed there is a problem.

Does he have cash for the long cab ride? Jasper hates to ask, for Klaus is a proud man.

"I've plenty of money," Klaus says, reading his mind.

Image of Klaus stirring a pot of ox-tail stew in a high-rise kitchen while a child plays underfoot. His own modest house sold for less than expected, due to an infestation of termites introduced by a rustic wooden cross placed on the mantel two years ago. Must have been a present from Ramona. They always wondered where the sudden yearning for Christian symbolism came from.

Klaus hesitates before working his limbs into the taxi. Suddenly, he's looking unsteady, even frail, in the light of day.

"I can't go with you," Jasper tells him. "My flight leaves soon."

"What flight?"

"I'm going to watch Toby play in the finals." Klaus just stares, so Jasper adds, "Of the guitar competition."

Klaus leans his forearm on the open door of the cab. "You shouldn't have let him go."

TWENTY-FIVE

MONTREAL BLISTERS OPEN WITH A RAT-A-TAT-TAT OF DRILLS carving through concrete.

Check messages while the cab rolls down a side street. Jasper squints to see the tiny screen: "Urgent from Luke: sandwiches from Oct 4 meeting issued from contaminated carrier."

That was the final executive meeting: three tomato-and-cheese panini; three smoked meat with pickles ordered from the deli downstairs.

Jasper sampled both items before the meeting began. He's watching his blood sugar these days and doesn't like to go more than a couple of hours without chow.

"Home quarantine," the message continues, "14 days. Forward info to other contacts."

"Crazy people!" the cabbie cries, braking hard.

"People" being a man driving a graffiti-covered truck that pulled in front without signalling.

So Jasper's finally been caught on the spokes of the epidemic. It comes down to a bite of sandwich, a prep cook who may or may not have sneezed into the mayo.

Horns blare, someone shouts a flurry of curses in French, all involving the Roman Catholic church.

Fourteen days: Jasper knows the drill. Two weeks trapped inside with daily tracking of symptoms: dry mouth, unusual fatigue, sudden decrease in blood pressure, sore throat and joints, the dreaded rash.

Names of contacts.

His mind splashes names, places, tiny interactions, every keypad tapped, supermarket melons squeezed for ripeness, seatmates in the flight that brought him here, cab driver who is now pulling into the curb.

Klaus.

Mrs. Smiley.

Did he cough onto his open palm before touching the airport ticketing machine? A surreptitious nose pick before shaking Mrs. Smiley's hand? Not to mention pulling open a series of doors at Lakeview, its frail residents riding the last vestiges of their immune systems.

He's a stain soaking in all directions, bleeding invisible ink.

"Deli worker is PUI," writes Luke.

That's person under investigation, by no means a sure thing. Probable case, but not following the usual definition as the virus mutates and adapts. A self-respecting virus is always a step ahead of its pursuers.

"Ten minutes. *Dix minutes*," a voice calls from the other side of the green room door. "Auditorium is packed," the volunteer adds in a tone of awe.

Toby has no intention of being infected by the nerves of a keyed-up kid in a Guitar Congress T-shirt. He hears excited chatter as another might listen to mice frolic in the walls.

Hiro is finishing up his recital on the auditorium stage, which is why Toby keeps the door to the room firmly closed. Nerves are just another aspect of technique, to be funnelled into heat and light. This is elation, not fear, that shoots through his body. He lifts his hands and stares at his palms — steady and ready for battle.

Jasper's cab pulls in behind the building, which is more modern than he envisioned, a late 1970s concrete block with an interior courtyard. A bilingual banner with a stylized drawing of a guitar tells him he's in the right place.

The backstage corridor hums with volunteers issuing muted orders. No one pays the least attention to him as he enters with his overnight pack. The walls are made of poured concrete, and half the overhead lights seem shot or turned off to conserve electricity. To one side a room is marked with a sign, VOLUNTAIRES, and he glimpses a crew of young people folding slices of pizza into their mouths.

A virus is thousands of times smaller than a bacterium, which is in turn many times smaller than a human cell. One cough might contain a sea of particulate matter; a dirty fingernail becomes the size of a football stadium.

Until now Montreal has been clear.

A youth in a headset mouths, "Performer off," and this must be the Japanese boy Toby speaks of, Hiro, a warrior's name, now striding down the hallway with guitar clutched to his side, his shirt transparent with sweat. He's berating himself in Japanese, and upon seeing Jasper, switches to English.

"I fuck up gavotte," he wails. "Wrong notes and vibrato has terrible control."

The look on his face is frightening, as if he met his own death on the lighted stage.

———————————

Inside the green room Toby hikes up his trouser legs and crouches into a headstand. Such a relief to feel blood spill into his cranium, a splendid warmth that flushes brain and ears. He sees the underside of the practice chair, mounds of chewing gum stuck there by rattled performers. Teeter sideways, right himself while the vein in his forehead throbs.

"Nine minutes, Mister Hausner," a voice warns from the corridor.

His spine stretches, feet tap together.

He will play with all his heart: that simple. Everything else is imagination.

The building has seen better days, Jasper observes as he jogs down the hallway, following the hand-drawn arrows. In some spots the concrete has begun to shed, exposing a pebbly surface. The ceilings are low, built for optimal heat conservation: Montreal's winters are cruel. He feels a whip of excitement, imagining the scene to come. Hard to keep a silly grin from exploding off his face. The boy will be in the green room, racing through scales, jittery as hell.

Toby swings to his feet, enjoying the rush of dizziness as vestibular liquid adjusts. He tucks in his shirt and, as for his stringy hair, nothing to do but sweep it behind his ears: a musician shouldn't look like a banker.

Onstage, Javier is tricked out in his Latin lover ensemble — cream shirt a gazillion threads per inch.

Toby sips just enough water to moisten his lips and throat. He sure as hell doesn't want to have to take a whiz out there. Pulse elevated but not scary. He won't pick up the guitar until he's ready to leave the room; music builds inside this cone of silence. He stands, willing himself to be still before the walk down the short corridor. Only his hands pump once or twice at his sides. He stares at a point on the wall just below the clock.

Breathe.

Focus.

Breathe.

A polite knock on the door and a dishevelled Hiro pokes his head in.

"I anticipate personal surprise for you," he says.

"Not now," Toby cautions.

Hiro hovers in the doorway, dressed in his Beatles suit, skinny pants and ankle boots. He beams. "Is boyfriend, I think."

"Jasper?" Toby says, thrown. How could his lover calibrate the exact moment before he begins his march to the stage? Breathing begins to stack up in his chest, tight and nasty.

Has he been following him all along? Suddenly, this seems plausible — Jasper darting behind lampposts and doorways, notebook in hand, watching for signs of trouble and stress. Jasper his healer, his keeper, his lover, his —

He stares at his hands, shaking now.

"*Quatre minutes.*" The volunteer pops four fingers above Hiro's head.

This must be the green room, Jasper thinks, sliding past the two young men blocking the door. In his mind it was all much more glamorous. Instead, tatty broadloom smells like stale cigarettes and beer.

Toby stands in the middle of the performers' room, looking handsome and lost. When he spots Jasper, his face freezes. The kid is surprised, maybe even shocked by this sudden appearance. For a tiny moment he seems not to recognize Jasper.

"I couldn't stay away," Jasper says.

Toby nods. "You mean well."

What a peculiar thing to say. This is where they should fall into each other's arms, but instead a formal feeling enters the cramped room. Toby's eyes twitch, the only sign of inner commotion, but there is no hint of a smile. The anticipated roar of greeting doesn't materialize. Instead there is this awkward silence. It's Jasper who finally steps forward and seizes the boy's hands — such a relief to feel solid flesh — but these hands are icy cold when they should be pink and warm, the fingers juiced with blood, ready to dance.

The volunteer clears his throat and rasps, "Nearly time, sir."

Since when did Toby become a "sir"?

"You don't have to do this," says Jasper.

Toby breathes audibly. "I know."

Jasper understands that he may be too late. The lad is boxed in. Toby's hands pull away, leaving behind only the chill. He says something that Jasper doesn't hear, then leans over to lift the guitar out of its velvet-lined coffin and starts to meticulously rub the soundboard with his sleeve. A spotlight will pick up every smudge.

Look at the animal eyes that glance around the room. He's about to stride down that hallway with its pocked concrete walls, and Jasper knows in his bones that he'll come back a damaged creature.

"Better grab a good seat," Toby says, nodding toward the hallway. His voice sounds reedy, and he heads for the door himself. Jasper reaches to pluck a stray hair from the boy's shoulder as he squeezes past, parody of the dutiful spouse.

Toby's face sets into a mask of concentration, no doubt envisioning the walk to centre stage through the glare of light, followed by the adjustment of stool, then the tune-up. Jasper feels the ritual unfold in his own body. Judges will be sitting in a row near the front, watching for slip-ups, hearing every glitch in the performance.

From some distant place flutters applause. Javier has finished his program. They didn't hear a note back here, for the guitar is a stealth instrument.

"*Deux minutes!*" the volunteer announces, holding two fingers aloft.

Toby enters the hallway; he is almost gone.

"It's about Klaus," Jasper says urgently.

Toby stops in his tracks. "What about Klaus?"

"Mrs. Smiley called."

"Yes?" Hurry up, his eyes say.

"To report a disturbing situation." Jasper feels giddy with his news.

"Is he all right?"

"Depends what you mean by all right."

Toby steps back into the room and reaches for the water glass.

"*Une minute,*" the volunteer chirps.

Both men stare at him with bewilderment, for he is of another world.

"Your old man caused an uproar at Lakeview," Jasper says.

"Tell me later."

"You need to hear this now, Toby." The audience and judges can wait. He is in the best of hands.

Toby gives in, resting the base of his guitar on his shoe while the doorway teems with volunteers.

"Javier is off!" someone cries.

The muted sound of clapping dies down, and the auditorium is quiet, expectant. It's a soft, buttery evening, every surface slick with humidity, Indian summer's last hurrah.

"Turns out Klaus has been carrying on with one of the nurse's aides," Jasper says, speaking quickly. "That wide-hipped Caribbean woman who's been there since forever — Ramona Bradshaw. Think of it, Toby, your father with his old world prejudices." He hears himself laugh. "All those years we thought he was racing up to Lakeview just to feed your mother pureed vegetables."

Toby's jaw clenches, and he pretends to study the mounted photographs of musicians on the far wall. Klaus kept his mother alive. This is something they all know. He'd drive up to Lakeview every day, first in the Buick and later in the Honda, and spoon-feed his wife because if he didn't she refused to swallow.

"They found letters, plus a snapshot of her daughter who looks half-white. Toby, do you suppose —"

"Ramona?" he interrupts. "She used to send us Easter cards." He forgot to warm his hands in the sink of hot water — too late now. The discarded banana skin splayed on the window ledge grows browner with each passing minute, the fruit's potassium already absorbed into his bloodstream. He remembers to stare into the bulb of overhead light, an old performers' trick. You accustom your eyes to the spotlight so you won't be blinded when you walk onstage.

"I'm going," Toby says, lifting his instrument again.

Please stop me is what he means.

"Klaus has left Lakeview," Jasper says, waiting for the look of surprise, even alarm.

Toby's face is bleached white.

The main theme rises in minor thirds, bend that upper note, so sweet — nothing could be clearer. The rest of life swims by, so many hungry fish.

"Close your eyes, my delicious angel," Jasper says, placing his hands on Toby's shoulders. They've been through so much together. He's lost his job, but he won't lose Toby.

Open your mouth and shut your eyes.

It's a heated kiss, tongue working inside the familiar chamber.

I'll give you something to make you wise.

The volunteer draws back from the doorway, and there is a burst of tittering in the hall. Jasper doesn't care, but Toby breaks away, wiping his mouth and smoothing the front of his shirt. He smells feral, a wild creature that has been trapped.

Watch that angular body march down the corridor toward the stage, guitar tucked under his arm, no sign of hesitation, as if he could trick himself into confidence.

Jasper's mouth feels jazzed up, alive. Toby would never manage on his own, the worry of Jasper being stowed away in quarantine, bills to pay, food to buy, long solo days and nights. They'll be in it together now, daytime TV their ally and confidant. The virus passes through liquid and membrane, man's best friend.

Toby disappears between layers of curtain at stage left, while Jasper climbs the carpeted stairs in the dark, finding a choice position in the middle of the auditorium's balcony, second row. A woman shifts her purse to make room, and when Jasper whispers an apology, she replies in French. He smiles in that anxious way Anglos do when they don't understand what has been said and know that they should. These guitar aficionados filling the hall have left dinner early, forsaken a second glass of wine to watch Toby and his colleagues compete. There is the heady fun of comparing performances and guessing who might pull off a career-altering win. A gladiator sport, Jasper decides. His neighbour scratches notes on her program, awarding points to the departed Javier for tone, technique, presentation, and overall artistry. Soon she will do the same for Toby.

Prickling sweat: Jasper's. Elevated heartbeat: ditto.

Rustle of curtain, then Toby enters the stage area, hesitating a beat before striding toward the padded bench. After all these years, he is back and wants to savour the moment. Light breaks icicles in his eyes, and the hall swells like a single breathing mammal.

Reaching the bench, he bows deeply, acknowledging applause that Jasper hears as strident, even menacing. He twists the knob so that the bench rises to its full height while hundreds watch, noting his lank hair and mottled complexion.

So far away, a pebble dropping into a deep well. Jasper's neighbour makes a gasp of surprise, then scribbles on her program. He glances over but can't make out the words in the dark. Had she been in Paris, witness to the historic breakdown?

Beginning to tune, Toby crooks his head to stare at the ceiling while listening to sound reverberate in the packed hall. He makes small adjustments, then closes his fist, opens it, a way of dispelling extra energy. This feels like a different auditorium from two days ago, much of its brightness dampened, the seats now thick with flesh and clothing. He will need to use more nail to ensure clarity.

He lifts his right hand over the sound hole, wrist flat, fingers curled — now or never.

Jasper picks up the program and fans himself. They shut off the overhead ventilation so its noise wouldn't distract. No one else seems to notice the dead air. They sit in rapt concentration, eyes fixed on the faraway figure hunched over his instrument.

The prelude unfolds with a slow, thoughtful beauty, and Toby draws out the line, making a grimace with each peak of phrasing. The final bars slide into a ritardando measured with increasing slowness yet keeping tempo intact. That's the trick of it, not to fall into timelessness.

After the final chord, he waits before lowering his hands for all fragments of sound to decay. His eyes remain closed, as if playing for himself.

Jasper feels invisible — balcony, row B, seat 11. Look up, dear boy. But those blue eyes lift and stare blindly into the spotlight.

The gavotte goes well, tricky finger stretches nailed, soon to be followed by the manic gigue. But first a pause to adjust tuning, and Toby's swallowing hard, trying to moisten his mouth and throat. Tug at the collar as heat presses in.

The gigue is, to Jasper's ears, rhythmically spotty. Toby stares at the fretboard, watching his own fingers jump, hypnotized by the action. Tension creeps into the phrasing, causing awkward jerks and clipped transitions.

Jasper's neighbour waits until the end of the piece before making notes, then she leans over to whisper to her husband, a portly man with a beard. She's one of those women who take up an instrument in later life, Jasper decides, inspired by articles that describe the brain's plasticity.

––––––––––––––––––––

Next up is the two-movement piece by the Catalan composer Toby is so fond of. Lots of jangly bits, syncopated and showy, meant to sound like the performer is flying by the seat of his pants, though of course he must maintain complete control. He begins with a flourish, series of rolling chords, followed by *thwaps* on the soundboard with the wrist, then his palm. The audience sits up. They love this already. What they don't see is the stiffening of his spine as the thing Toby most fears begins to happen: alien thoughts nip at his concentration.

Not that round-faced woman who wears a nurse's smock and running shoes? "Mr. Hausner" is what she calls Klaus, though doesn't he call her Ramona?

He's overplaying; the buzzes and tiny mistakes mount up.

All those drives in midwinter, careening through blizzards to arrive at Lakeview and push spoonfuls of tapioca pudding into his wife's mouth to keep her alive.

Actual wrong notes pop up, and audience members raise their eyebrows. Someone whispers in the row behind, and Jasper whirls around to land a glare. Between movements Toby pulls a handkerchief from his pocket and wipes the fretboard dry.

Opening snap of the allegro is loud enough to wake the dead, but Toby is beyond caring. What he feels now is the concrete wall, another word for his treacherous mind. He has no idea where he is, and the auditorium retreats to a tiny aperture, a pink asshole that slowly shuts.

Quarantine means pizza delivered through a half-opened door and a television that blares around the clock. It would be like living above the Arctic Circle, no night, no day. They won't get sick, Jasper decides, but two weeks in precautionary isolation is the law.

He'll have Toby to himself — isn't this what he wants?

Then one morning it will be over, no fevers or rashes, but the boy will have grown mute and unapproachable, blaming Jasper for the possible viral kiss. The concert experience, now a hazy dream, will have left him shell-shocked. Re-entry into public life equals Jasper arranging therapists' visits; Toby has pawed through months in an anxiolytic haze before. Every time Jasper sets out of the house he'll be afraid of what might happen in his absence, and when he returns home, he'll be wary of what he might find there. They'll give him a neural MRI. Jasper will insist on it, for who knows what lurks in the folds of the cerebellum. When the boy stares woefully at his flaccid genitals, Jasper will explain about pharmaceutical side effects.

There was a time when all of this would tempt, watching the mutilated flower unfold its petals and bloom under his care. Yet as he sits in the auditorium balcony peering down at his flailing lover, Jasper knows he can't possibly do it again. The very thought causes a shudder of despair, and he lets go of the breath he's been holding since the beginning of recorded time.

Left hand zigzags up the fretboard, right fingers roll. Bit of a march thing happening. Glimpse of the judges' lights clamped to their seats, and for a moment Toby forgets the program order. Black ice. Regain footing. Cresting the opening movement of the bolero, jack it up a notch. No one plays this piece so fast and lives. Remember to breathe: a man can go five days without water, thirty-two days without food, but you need the basic exchange of gases.

The guitar he had in the old days was a honey of an instrument, juicy tone loaded with butterfat, left on the subway when Toby decided it was a mad dog.

Klaus buzzes apartment 1204 on the intercom, not realizing the gizmo's broken, and when no one answers, he slips through the front doors of the complex, tagging along with a group of residents.

Well-dressed retired white fellow, they think as he squeezes into the crowded elevator, planting his suitcase between his legs. He stares at the numbers as they light up, feeling a flare of almost unbearable excitement: she will greet him with her large hands, then cackle with pleasure. It has taken them far too long, practically an eternity, to get to this point. Never in his life did he imagine such delight would come to him. By the time he reaches the twelfth floor, he is alone in the elevator and no one witnesses his giddy smile.

He walks down the carpeted hallway, tugging the suitcase behind him. The building is worn at the edges, and he hears squalling kids behind the row of locked doors. It feels like home, a far cry from the institution he entered to be near this woman. Ramona, a name with three vowels; this is where she lives and these are her people.

And because of her he has become the man who can stride up to apartment 1204 and knock firmly on the door.

He waits, hearing a clattering of dishes within followed by heavy footsteps. She's a robust woman, his Ramona. In a moment she will swing open the door and he will see that broad face, that welcoming smile.

Ramona peers through the spy hole. "What are you doing here, old man?"

The smells in the broadloomed corridor tantalize: curried goat and fried bread and spices he's never heard of. He sold his house for her, got rid of everything except this suitcase and a few photographs.

He points to his chest and calls out, "It's me, Klaus."

A single brown eye blinks from behind the dab of glass. After a hesitation the door pops open and she stands before him, a full-figured woman with her hair wrapped in a towel, as if she's just stepped out of the shower.

"I've come," he says, choosing a simple phrase.

But she's wagging her head. "Why do you keep pursuing me, chasing after me like some kind of crazy stalker man?"

He steps backward, nearly tripping over his suitcase.

She's not finished. "I try to be polite all these times and tell you nicely, but I guess I got to spell it out. I'm not your girlfriend and never have been." She's pointing now, finger stabbing the air. "I saw what was going on all those years, you sniffing around. Those cards I sent weren't enough for you. Don't you understand I had a job to hold on to? Past tense. What awful thing did you tell them to get me canned?" Her voice rises a notch with every sentence, and her speech tumbles out as if she's been holding it in for days, months, maybe years. She tugs the towel off her head, revealing the springy hair he knows so well. "You leave me and my daughter alone!"

He's stepped into a raging ocean. Any minute the wave will roll back leaving ripples of gleaming sand.

"You take advantage of my friendship, make me feel bad," she says, shaking the towel in front of him.

"I don't want to make you feel bad," he stammers. "I love you."

She wags her head again, and that kind face has transformed into a mask of anger. "I'm calling the cops if you don't haul your sorry ass out of this building. You got me sacked. You're no friend of mine!"

She gives him one last look, exasperated, as if she's talking to a child who won't mind, then shuts the door and pushes the deadbolt across.

Klaus is breathless, chest squeezing tight. Inside, she's moving around, talking to someone — maybe the TV. He drops onto the edge of his luggage, suddenly exhausted, sapped of will and desire. His brain isn't working right. Something in there has splintered.

"What's wrong, grandpa?" A boy of maybe sixteen stands in front of him, baggy jeans falling off his backside. "You're looking woozy, if you don't mind me saying."

"I'm perfectly all right," Klaus tries to answer, but the words catch in his throat.

The boy pulls out a cellphone. "Someone I can call to bail you out?"

Klaus staggers to his feet. "I made a mistake." Hearing himself speak, he gains a whisper of confidence and tucks his fingers under the handle of the suitcase. "Where might I find the elevator going down?"

"Only one way to go," the boy says, pointing down the hallway. "You be on the top floor here."

He should have phoned first — that's what a gentleman would do, not just turn up on her doorstep like a refugee. He'll try again in a day or two, bring flowers and chocolate. He'll think of something. Klaus caught a glimpse of the front of her apartment, family photographs lined up just so on the wall, a small piano, and patterned curtains blanking out the sunlight. Wasn't that an upholstered chair in the corner? He could set his feet on the stool while they discuss the upcoming provincial election. She will be happy for his company, a man to cook for.

Almost convinced, Klaus heads toward the elevator, suitcase wheels tracking the carpet in his wake.

Trace knows what will happen if she wins: her dad will quit his job on the boats and drive her to concerts while her mum will keep teaching at the island school. A person can make good money playing solo gigs — ten grand a year. Maybe twenty. She'll stay at hotels, eat at restaurants, maybe even teach a bit.

Sometimes she gets nervous and has to pretend not to be. Don't smile, she warns herself, or you'll look like a cretin. Manuel Juerta gives her an actual wink as she sets up, adjusting footstool, et cetera. He remembers how she played in his room, and she holds that private concert in her hands now, a moment of perfection waiting to be re-entered. Before hitting the stage she made herself puke: better to play with an empty gut. They love the way she looks up here, so young, not exactly girl, not exactly boy. They watch her lithe body as she gets ready to play, that cropped scalp smooth and perfect, like an egg, an extra-terrestrial egg.

Where she lives, the rocks are covered with moss and lichen as they tumble into the sea. She goes barefoot, even at school, where they let her, because of her gift.

Silence bundles the auditorium, and she lifts her hands and begins to play.

TWENTY-SIX

"How long do they take?" Trace moans. She crouches by the wall of the lobby where she can watch people file out of the hall. Somewhere five judges are starting to confer, and the very idea makes her feel sick. "How long?" she repeats.

Armand hovers like her personal bodyguard. "Sometimes twenty minutes," he tells her. "Other times they argue behind closed doors and an hour goes by. One year, in Seville, they took two hours."

She tilts her head back and moans again.

This is what she wanted, right? To get off the island and take her music into the larger world. The moment she stepped onstage she felt the hall pulse like a new planet waiting to be born, then it began, the performance of her life. But it went by so fast, too fast to be spun into memory.

Audience members aim smiles her way before dashing to the snack table, tucking in to cheese and crackers like a shipwrecked crew.

Trace hasn't eaten for eighteen hours. She's a heron, very still and alert.

"You played beautifully, my dear," a frizzy-haired lady says, palming a Triscuit and cheddar.

Trace thinks, I've forgotten how to smile like a normal person.

"Very impressive," a man in a jean jacket tells her as he squeezes past en route to the bar. She can barely nod. Armand reaches out and slaps her on the shoulder. He's finding her nervousness funny. She's not even going to try to fake being casual, not like Javier and Hiro, who stand surrounded by their fans,

probably saying just the right thing, being charming and handsome. Meanwhile the judges are comparing notes in some closed
room, deciding their future.

"Where is our friend and colleague, Toby?" Armand wonders
aloud. He hails Marcus and Salvatore, who dart past, gulping beer
from plastic cups. "Have you seen Mr. Hausner?"

"Haven't set eyes on him, mate," Marcus says. "What did you
think of his performance — train wreck or total bloody genius?"

Salvatore's eyes focus first on Trace, then Armand. "Toby
Hausner is scary," he says in a soft but clear voice.

"Music should be scary," Marcus insists. "Who wants to
listen to some pussy strumming? When that man plays, you
don't nod off, though there's no way he'll win this thing, not a
fucking chance."

Trace feels a rocket of excitement. so Toby is out of the game.
Marcus would know. He may be lurching around now, wasted,
but he's a big deal back in England and still can't believe he didn't
make the cut, a massive calamity.

Javier breaks into the gathering and captures Trace's hand,
then lets go with a sharp squeeze. "I predict a fine career for you,"
he says before disappearing back into the crowd, the vents of his
jacket flapping. Ten out of ten for presentation.

Trace is decked out in wraparound pants from Tibet,
black shirt with sparkles, and lots of mascara. It was Lucy who
painted on the dark lashes and brows to give her face "definition from afar."

Armand's voice rumbles in her ear. "The Argentine musician
is spooked by you, but of course he cannot show it." Armand
likes knowing things; it's all the power he's got left. "Your life can
change in a heartbreak," he adds, snapping his fingers.

Heartbeat, he means. Maybe she likes her life the way it
is, kayaking between islands at dusk, jamming with Bo in his
cabin and playing concerts at the community centre. She can
smell the old wooden building now, wet timber and coffee

brewing as the audience files in, each face known to her since she was born.

Manuel Juerta stretches his arms over his head and yawns. At the same moment something in his neck cracks and he lets out a gasp of pain — not the old problem again. He was forced to take a year off performing a decade ago.

"We have reached an impasse," Jean-Paul says, tossing his pen onto the table.

The judges have taken over the volunteers' lounge, eating leftover pizza and drinking warm cola.

"She's so young," Jon Smyth says. "None of us has heard her — or of her — before this week. We don't know what she's capable of."

Manuel massages his neck. "I only know what I hear with my ears and see with my eyes. Unfortunately, I do not have the gift of forecasting the future."

The other judges cast their eyes toward the ceiling at this recital of Manuel's favourite theme. He's right, of course, but he is also wrong. They *are* in the business of creating futures.

Portia leans forward, skirt tugging her knees. "There's not one competitor we can dismiss out of hand."

Sober nods greet this statement. It is what they have been arguing for the past forty-five minutes.

"Yet we must not be tempted to invoke a tie," Portia adds.

"I am not so sure," Visnya says. "Perhaps it is a suitable compromise."

"No," Portia insists. "Our constitution forbids it." She glances at Jean-Paul, who is supposed to know these things.

He lifts an official-looking file folder but doesn't venture to peek inside.

"A tie means no one wins," Portia says, then reaches for the pitcher and pours herself a tumbler of water. "Proof that we haven't executed our duty."

When Jean-Paul fails to agree, she jumps in again. "So we run with the safe choice? Because we know he won't shame us — or himself?"

"There are two safe choices," Visnya points out.

"Or go with the girl, the exciting unknown?" Manuel says, ignoring his colleague, the Bosnian musician.

He has the grace to blush when Portia glances his way, though he might easily remind her that they're all compromised: Jean-Paul taught Javier at summer school; Visnya has taught Hiro and Javier at a European conference; Portia thinks she tutored Toby Hausner in a master class many years ago. It is why they are so nervous about this girl from a western island; they don't understand how talent may flourish so far away from their tender care.

"She gets better each round," Manuel reminds them.

No one can argue with this fact.

"We still have four choices," Jean-Paul tells them in a world-weary tone. "Until we agree that at least one must go." His eyes flutter shut for a moment.

Manuel thinks, That stepdaughter is giving him grief.

"And of Mr. Hausner, what do we decree?" Jon Smyth inserts. He skids his palms back and forth across his bony knees.

There is a short silence, then everyone starts speaking at once, a clamour that only dies when Jean-Paul raps the table with his cup. "We understand that this young man is the most important talent but —"

He needn't say more. They all heard how Toby Hausner played like a virtuoso but disastrously lost focus — and pulled off a brilliant recovery at the end.

"So we return to the process of elimination," Jean-Paul says.

Portia clears her throat. "If I may be allowed to suggest a useful mechanism." She looks around, making sure they're all attentive. "We write on a secret ballot a list of our top three contenders."

"That always produces a compromise winner," Jean-Paul objects. "Everyone's second choice wins. Is this what we want?"

"What we want is to finish up here," Manuel says. He is thinking of the poster taped to the wall of his office at the *conservatorio*, the great Spanish painter's sombre vision of the ancient guitarist, a man who forgets to eat, whose skin and instrument are tinged blue with discarded dreams.

"Speak of the devil," Larry whispers to his cabal of defeated musicians, and they freeze as Hiro, the Japanese finalist who just played a superb but perhaps too-measured program, shoulders through the lobby crowd. The slightly built man stands in front of them now, nodding and smiling, pretending he hasn't noticed how conversation collapsed with his arrival.

Hiro escapes as soon as he can, and the group, made up entirely of musicians who didn't make it past the first cull, returns to its impassioned critique.

"He was holding back," a French guitarist says.

"A respectable performance," disagrees a Uruguayan. "No major mistakes."

"If you don't count missing an entire bar in the gavotte."

The lobby bell rings. It is time.

At this moment Manuel is crouching outside the auditorium building, buried to his calves in autumn leaves gathered by the janitor in preparation for disposal. He presses the phone to his ear, but Lucia's voice keeps cutting out.

"... back at the hotel," she says faintly.

"Eric is back working at the hotel?"

"... particular care ..."

"What particular care?" Manuel squeezes the phone, as if to pump it into action. But she disappears in his hand, an evaporation of voice. "Eric is released from prison?" he shouts.

A dim "yes" greets this question, followed by a crackle of speech, impenetrable.

Then suddenly, clear as day: "Manuel, take a pen and paper."

"Pen and paper," he repeats, searching in his conference bag. "Yes, I have this," he cries, retrieving the recital program and a pencil stub.

Nearby, two young guys are toking up and whispering in French. He saw them inside earlier with their scruffy leather jackets. They're students of Jean-Paul.

Lucia bellows instructions. He must compose a shopping list: fine-point marker pens, age-defying emollient oil, tampons, pantyhose in assorted sizes, the usual hygienic tubes and jars.

He scratches the names of these items on the margins of the program, adding more as she rattles them off, feeling not irritation but relief. So he is to be welcomed home, after all. The virtual conservatory floats away, cut free. The job in California recedes. It never existed. His real life is always back on the island.

"Manicure scissors, not the cheap ones. Manuel, do you hear …?"

Javier has lost his studied air and chatters non-stop to Hiro in the corner of the lounge. Whatever happens, they are brothers, are they not? He has just parsed every second of his own performance and waits for Hiro to do the same, but Hiro hardly listens. His smooth face rests in the country of waiting. Javier yammers on about how Asians have special powers of concentration while Hiro's eyes squeeze shut — until finally they hear it, the amplified chime.

Javier stops mid-sentence. The waiting is over.

Toby huddles outside the exit door, smoking. As ash drops onto his lapel, his mind is spinning: what happened in there? He played the living crap out of the program. His hands still sting and he'd let in the whole damn army: Jasper, Klaus, some woman called Ramona.

A bell rings from within. It is time.

He drops the cigarette, grinds it with the toe of his shoe, and enters the lobby.

Jean-Paul takes the stage and taps the microphone. Where has their Cuban friend taken off to at this crucial moment? A hiss of feedback greets the audience members as they hasten back to their seats for the long-awaited announcement. Jean-Paul feels their excitement, the burr of anticipation.

Manuel arrives, nick of time, short legs trotting up the stage stairs, waving both arms above his head. Boisterous applause greets the tardy entrance. His colleagues — Portia, Jon, Visnya, and Jean-Paul — stand under the competition banner at centre stage, trying not to look irritated by his display.

Manuel approaches the microphone, pink and wheezing from his dash. Pulling a handkerchief from his pocket, he makes a show of wiping his brow: the Maestro sweats, the Maestro is human.

Portia beams. They love him out there. With Manuel pinned to her virtual conservatory, she'll coast into the presidency of the federation. Sticking out of her bag are three hundred flyers she got Jean-Paul's secretary to print up — her proposal laid out on official letterhead.

"The envelope please," Manuel booms.

It is a joke. There is no envelope.

"We choose a winner because we must," Manuel continues, a hand pressed to his chest as his breathing settles. "You could say music is not a contest and you are right." His colleagues nod agreement. "But we find this year such an exceptional performance that we — I — have no hesitation in making this proclamation."

Javier and Hiro take seats to the side of the auditorium. Javier buttons his jacket and tugs his cuffs so that they show just the right amount below the sleeves. Pat down hair, sniff his own cologne — suddenly Javier finds himself praying for the first time since his sister lay in a hospital bed near death. Hiro sits with erect posture, palms pressed to knees. Destroy mindless hope in its tracks. If he wins, then he will float up to the stage and accept the prize, offer a formal Japanese bow. And if not, nothing has changed. He is the same man, winner or loser. He stares straight ahead, unaware that he is barely breathing.

Trace remains standing at the back of the hall in a sort of trance as Manuel Juerta's words bombard the auditorium. In twenty-four hours she'll be paddling her kayak out to the point and this will all have disappeared.

Armand, who is seated, turns around to smile and offer a goofy wave.

"She plays with such intensity," Manuel continues, "displaying a deep but understated spiritual dimension, coupled with a high degree of technical expertise." He is reading off an index card.

Wait a sec — *she?*

Her skull seems to crack open. Everyone turns around to look; there's only one "she" left in the game. Trace's knees begin to crumple. Thank God for the wall — and what a din. They're clapping like maniacs, stomping feet, yips of approval.

Oh, my God, she mouths, and for a moment she wants to run straight across the continent to the cabin her parents built with their own hands, unsheltered from wind and rain, because they believe in braving the elements. But instead she straightens and inhales, feeling air swoop into her lungs, a welcome puff of buoyancy, and she's smiling her head off, Tibetan pants flapping against her calves as she races up to the stage.

Lucy is the first to jump to her feet, applauding furiously, cheeks high with colour. "Brava!" she cries, greeting the next generation with fervour. Tears stream down her face, and she doesn't bother to wipe them away.

Armand seizes Trace's wrist as she passes, and for a moment she can't tear loose. His grip leaves bite marks in her skin.

Skip up the stairs to the stage where Manuel presses a clammy arm around her shoulders and guides her to the microphone, and she is facing an audience again. Her whole body quivers, legs bending like grass in the wind. "Speech!" someone yells from the back of the hall — must be Armand. What can she say? Not the usual crap about being surprised and shocked and undeserving, because the truth is, the moment her final chord died in the upper reaches of the auditorium, she knew she'd nailed the performance of her life.

A stranger marches to centre stage from the wings, young guy dressed in a collarless jacket, hair shellacked.

"Last year's winner, flown in from Rochester, New York — Terence Church — will present the award," announces Manuel, stepping aside.

The applause jacks up another notch.

This Terrence person drops a check for twenty grand in Trace's moist, open hand, then he gives her something else, a note that unpuckers in her palm. Neat handwriting advises: "Don't spend the money on real estate. I got shafted due to subprime rates, and now I'm homeless."

"Trace, stand here, will you?" someone cries, pushing her to the centre of the huddled group.

She stands, pocketing the strange message, and stares into the shooting stars, a hundred cameras zapping, and feels practically epileptic. Her folks will be at Billy's house down the road. He's got Internet. They'll be sitting around his kitchen table drinking elderberry wine, her dad in his flannel shirt, her mum in overalls. She waves to them, to everyone.

"Isn't she fabulous?" someone asks.

Lucy agrees, of course. The girl is being swarmed in the lobby. Cameras are raised high for optimal views while Trace stands almost still in the middle of the fuss, except for one hand running over her velvety skull. The young men bunched in the corner are semifinalists, girding themselves to congratulate this teenager who blew them away.

"Must be her mother." A man grabs the sleeve of a friend, and they pull back, making room for Lucy who is pressing through the crowd, a wide and slightly chaotic smile on her face. When she reaches the girl, she leans over to brush her lips against the smooth forehead. At the same moment Trace reaches to seize Lucy's wrist, holding on for dear life.

That's when Lucy allows herself to imagine what it would be like to hear her own name called, to be the one to trot onstage, skirt swishing. She feels the stairs cant under her feet, the sudden lash of light as she reaches centre stage. The scene erupts in her mind: how the twins pick up the phone and yell, "Yeah, Mum!" Then Mark's voice enters: "When will we see you?" Judges pump her hand, and a rigorous schedule of recitals is being discussed.

Trace lets go, washed into the sea of well-wishers, her small head bobbing like a cork.

Give me just another minute, Lucy pleads, but it's too late, for reality sneaks in and with it a distinct sensation of relief.

Or this is what she tells herself.

Toby stands in the corridor, arms splayed against the wall, lower vertebrae pressed against concrete. It's always the back and shoulders that cramp after performance.

So the girl from the western island wins. She's younger than he was in Paris, but she held it together. Something he didn't manage to do, not then, not now.

In both cases he played who he was at that moment. It was messy, but you could also say it was true.

Volunteers hustle down the corridor for final cleanup, looking frazzled this late in the day. They offer twitchy smiles, as if Toby might suddenly bark at them or start singing hymns — but one thing he is not is crazy. Dropping his arms, he leaves from the rear door of the hall, pushing past a group of students lounging on the steps, wreathed in cigarette smoke. They fall silent as he passes. He's someone to watch, all right.

That could only be one man perched on the ledge next to the tree, spine erect, as if to slouch were to court death. Jasper balances a cardboard tray on his lap while lifting a gravy-smeared fry to his mouth. Jasper — who thrice-washes spinach leaves, slices minute amounts of fat off his pork chop, and winces if he spots Toby downing a Smartie — is devouring an order of the deadly poutine.

Glancing up, Jasper says in a measured voice, "We need to talk." He shifts to make room on the ledge.

"Later," Toby answers skittishly. He gets the feeling that if he sits down next to Jasper he'll never leave.

The instrument is right where Toby left it by the window in the green room, his name printed on a tag, a volunteer standing guard outside. The room is neutral now, nerveless. He plucks the guitar out of its case, tunes, then jumps right into the piece that fell apart onstage. Here comes the section where focus temporarily vanished and the Ramona story muscled in. He feels the tightness in his gut return. Klaus with a girlfriend all these years? Beyond impossible. And why did Jasper choose such a moment to spill the news, right before he needed to walk out onstage? Hands falter for a bar or two, but his mind clamps down. There will always be life going on at the margins. You must incorporate the jet buzzing overhead or your lover's intent at sabotage. Music is not an orchid under glass.

He finishes playing, wipes his palms on his pants, and looks up, alert to a rustle at the doorway.

"Brilliant, my friend," says Jon Smyth, poking his head in. "I was going past and heard you. Hope you don't mind."

"Of course not," says Toby. He feels calm now, like a man who's just loaded up on carbohydrates.

"Come visit us in Texas. We'll get you a concert and a class to teach."

Toby rises to his feet. "I'd like that."

"Put on your dancing shoes. Manuel's booked some Brazilian band for the after-party. Lots of girls decked out in feathers." Jon offers a salute before disappearing.

Outside the building, Jasper has pitched his tray of chips and is checking his phone for messages. Toby stops a short distance away and stands, watching. Jasper's closely trimmed hair is showing grey, and his skin glows as if buffed by a chamois. How seldom does Toby stare like this. It's always the other way around, Jasper watching Toby.

He steps into Jasper's field of vision, and the man glances up and starts talking. "You played reasonably well, not that I'm an expert. Here and there some stumbling, but —"

"There's a party," Toby interrupts, and Jasper tips his head back, a frown settling on his face. "Brazilian music," Toby continues. "Lots of dancing and carrying on."

"You know I can't bear noisy nightclubs. And as I've said, we need to talk." Jasper pats the space beside him.

"Later," Toby promises for the second time, hiking the strap of his guitar case over one shoulder.

Jasper starts to rise, then stops, nodding vigorously, as if it were his idea to put off the conversation.

"Sure you don't want to tag along?" Toby asks.

"Quite sure."

The two men hover, not quite ready to part.

Toby notes something strange in Jasper's expression — not love or fear, and not the familiar furrow of concern. This is something remote and cold.

The unsettling moment is interrupted by peals of laughter, and Toby looks up to see Lucy grip the winner's hand as the pair dashes toward a waiting taxi where Portia waits.

"I should go," Toby says, nodding at the women. Now Jasper will say, "Come home with me."

But Jasper says nothing, so Toby trots toward the cab, guitar case tucked to his side. He feels his lover's gaze drill into his back; who will he be without this fretful stare?

A buffet table, picked over by the ravenous musicians, is set near a raised podium where the singer and band make a deafening racket. The over-amped bass guitar pulses to the edges of the make-do club that's taken over a floor of a warehouse in St. Henri. Scattered helium balloons bob near the ceiling. Is that a fog machine belching smoke? The singer sports purple ostrich feathers fluting above her bustier as she leads the band in samba beats. Spotting the newcomers, she beckons them in with a baton that rains confetti.

Someone is shouting: Armand, shirt untucked, leaps around the middle of the crowded dance floor, his face a grimace of joy or maybe pain. Who are all these people? Students and federation members and half of the concert audience jam the club, mixed with others who look as if they wandered in from another party.

Toby hates crowds, doesn't he? Yet after a short hesitation, he presses through the mash of dancers, led by Portia, who pressed next to him in the taxi and now keeps a vise grip on his forearm while shouting something about a virtual conservatory. "We will enter each other's studios with the click of a mouse!" she informs his assaulted ear. Finally, she lets go and launches into solo dervish spinning, both arms extended over her head, chin tilted high. She starts slowly, then works up speed, a long chiffon scarf fluttering in her wake.

Jasper would hate this din, would insist that "deafness lurks," not understanding that ears need to be tested, to be crammed with noise after days of delicate guitar plucking. And what *was* that expression cast into his face a moment ago? Something new, something frozen and unforgiving.

Toby unbuttons his collar and finds the beat in his hips and shoulders, while Trace climbs onstage and fits a tan-tan drum between her knees. Manuel Juerta hangs nearby, arms folded, looking pleased with himself. When the singer tosses a fistful of candies into the crowd, everyone lunges. That's Hiro in his muscle shirt, reaching for a chocolate kiss. Javier, minus his jacket, shimmies across the floor, eyes shut in some sort of trance. That must be Lucy sidling up to the stage, wearing her baseball cap with visor spun to the side.

Portia glides past, scarf unfurling, and as it trails across Toby's face it clings like film, and for a moment he can't see or breathe. Pawing clear, he rips into a dance, fists pumping.

It's as if they've all been released from prison.